About the Author

Marisa Silver is the author of the novel *Mary Coin*, a *New York Times* bestseller and winner of the Southern California Independent Bookseller's Award. She is also the author of *The God of War*, *No Direction Home*, and two story collections, *Alone with You* and *Babe in Paradise*. Silver's short fiction has won the O. Henry Award and been included in *The Best American Short Stories*, *The O. Henry Prize Stories*, and other anthologies. She lives in Los Angeles.

Praise for *Little Nothing*

A *Huffington Post* Book Club Suggestion
An *O: The Oprah Magazine* Fall Pick
One of *The Millions* Most Anticipated Books of the Year
A *LitHub* Book You Should Read

'Marisa Silver's fantastically inventive new novel counters expectations at every turn…The novel's open ending lingers unsettlingly in the mind….Silver manages to transform the fairy tale without losing its power.'

Washington Post

'…parable and a full-fledged, richly told story, with clearly drawn characters who beckon us to come along with them on their journeys…Silver shows us her capacity for fleet-footed writing.'

Huffington Post

'A beautifully told, heart-rending, can't-put-it-down read…her language is simply stunning.'

Minneapolis Star-Tribune

'Wild, witty and mesmerizing…Marisa Silver writes beautiful, seductive prose that always manages to be both wise and fleet; her inventive, romantic novel is compassionate and moving in wonderfully surprising ways.'

Dana Spiotta, author of *Innocents and Others*

'Silver has created a gorgeously rendered, imaginative, magical yarn.'

Booklist

'*Little Nothing* is a magnificent something, an inventive, unexpected story…I can't imagine what else anyone would want from a work of art.'

Cynthia D'Aprix Sweeney, author of *The Nest*

'By turns haunting, fanciful, and poignant, *Little Nothing* is the latest example of why Marisa Silver is one of our finest, most protean storytellers.'

Boris Fishman, author of *A Replacement Life*

'*Little Nothing* is the key to its own box, which opens and opens, transcending the limits of the very tale one thought one was reading. There is no limit. There is only the vaporous wonder of transformation, and the kernel of a spirit of a thing that can go on, and does. This book is a beautifully realized riddle.'

Rachel Kushner, author of *The Flamethrowers*

'Star-crossed lovers…Pavla serves to remind readers of the moral of the story, that a good soul can find transcendence in the face of unbearable odds. And in Danilo readers will recognize their own longing for transcendence and meaning as he transforms himself through pain and sorrow into a man of courage and ingenuity.'

Publishers Weekly

'In *Little Nothing*, Marisa Silver doesn't waver…she delivers a tale as mysterious as anything the Grimm Brothers might have collected…*Little Nothing* celebrates not only the unruly and lost parts of all our lives but also the possibility of their reordering and comprehension.'

Los Angeles Times

'Silver's storytelling skills are finely matched to her themes…meditative passages bloom with life.'

New York Times Book Review

'A dark fairy tale that pulses with life and anger, *Little Nothing* is a remarkable piece of fiction – fantastically written and beautifully crafted.'

Bookbag

'Unflinching, brutal, and yet exquisitely beautiful…unlike anything I've ever read before.'

Christina Baker Kline, author of *Orphan Train*

'Following one woman's transformation, *Little Nothing* reimagines the boundaries between mother and child, human and non-human, possible and impossible. Lyrical, raw, and urgent, this exquisite novel will take you to the outermost edges of heart and mind.'

Amity Gaige, author of *Shroder*

'A beautifully told, heart-rending, can't-put-it-down read…Silver masterfully balances a riveting plot with deep meaning – exploring love and its inadequacies, the persistent and unequal power of sexuality, the cost of being an outcast in a fearfully conforming society.'

Star Tribune

'Silver turns the oral tradition into fine literature with *Little Nothing*, a masterful work of fairy tale and folklore.'

Shelf Awareness

'Marisa Silver's fourth novel, *Little Nothing*, is a marvelous book…[it] is steeped in strangeness, but it's driven by a basic question that frees the best novels and their heroes when the time comes to explore their worlds: What if there's something else out there?'

Barnes and Noble

'*Little Nothing* is a siren call to self-acceptance, yet tells its story with a fantastical bent that will engage the reader. It's a wild ride, one that combines literary skill and wages an emotional battle like no other.'

BookReporter

'Bestselling and award-winning author Silver (*Mary Coin*; *The God of War*) has created a haunting tale of magic realism, both fabulist and earthy.'

Library Journal

'Pavla, born strangely disfigured, is the "little nothing" of the title; Danilo is the young local who loves her. All very conventional – and the only conventional things in this strange, glorious tale of transfiguration and wild nature. Trust me: you'll have to read it to understand, but you'll be transfixed. Silver, once a movie director, uses her trained eye to talk about the remarkable thing that is the female body – and how Western society misunderstands it.'

Aleteia

LITTLE NOTHING

MARISA SILVER

ONEWORLD

A Oneworld Book

First published in Great Britain and Australia by Oneworld Publications, 2017
This paperback edition published 2017

ISBN 978-1-78607-236-8
ISBN 978-1-78607-128-6 (eBook)

Illustrations by Jason Booher
Printed and bound in Great Britain by Clays Ltd, St Ives plc

This is a work of fiction. While, as in all fiction, the literary perceptions and
insights are based on experience, all names, characters, places, and incidents
either are products of the author's imagination or are used fictitiously.

Oneworld Publications
10 Bloomsbury Street
London WC1B 3SR
United Kingdom

MIX
Paper from
responsible sources
FSC® C018072

For Henry Dunow

LITTLE NOTHING

Před*stavte si květinu!" the midwife yells,* her voice reaching the baby as warped and concave sounds. "Pictuuure a flowaahhherrr."

Next, another voice, closer this time, the sound so near that if the baby could stretch its arm it might touch it. "You bitch!" the voice howls. "You monster! Get out of me now!" Agáta Janáček is enraged that this should be happening to her even though she has wished for it and prayed for it, consulted the gypsy witch Zlata, and buried amulets of animal bones wrapped in the hair of a virgin for it. But old as she is—and tough threads of gray streak her hair and sprout from the colorless mole on her chin and thinly veil her pubis where there was once a dark, luxurious thatch—the old stories of childhood hold sway. Her mother warned her about this moment. It was a cautionary bedtime story chanted night after night: little Agáta, the prettiest girl in the village, lives in a magical paradise filled with delicious honey-scented medovnik and talking bunny rabbits. Then one day, a terrible monster comes and whispers in her ear words sweeter than any jam, sweeter even than her favorite candies that hang from the Christmas tree each year and which she is forbidden to pull off until Christmas Day, even though this means surrendering the low-hanging chocolate treasures to the mice and rats who skitter across the floorboards at night and gorge themselves, their nocturnal pleasures mapped by a trail of black pellets. But little Agáta cannot resist the tantalizing whispers of the monster and she allows him to touch her face and stroke her body and climb on top of her and shove his hard sausage between her soft thighs. *Unh . . . unh,* her mother would grunt, her voice a striking imitation of the guttural efforts Agáta heard most nights coming from behind the thin lace curtain that separated her parents' bed from the one she shared with her five brothers and sisters. And then, what next? Her mother would continue: Pretty Agáta grows fat as a pig, fat as a cow. Her little tzitzis, once tender and delicate as meringue, become achy and so swollen they have to be held up by a harness of cloth that winds round her back and halters at the nape of her neck. Months go by, and the beautiful, smooth skin of her belly becomes striped like a zebra's as her flesh stretches and pulls. And then finally, after backache and fat fingers and a burning in her gut so fierce she will think a match has been struck inside her, Agáta's body will split in two.

First the body and then the heart. Good night. Sleep tight. The bedbugs will surely bite.

But her mother is long dead and is not here to sigh and shake her head with false sympathy for her daughter's pain.

"A *flowwerrrr openingggg*," the midwife calmly insists.

"You bitch, you whore, you fucking fuck!" Agáta rages, her voice becoming clearer to the baby as it begins to swim through the dark tunnel, its head pushing against something hard, then something soft, then something hard again, as if it were a flimsy boat, banging up against rocks then drifting into a calm eddy only to be drawn back helplessly into the propelling current once more. "You ugly whore who no man will fuck even with his eyes closed!"

The midwife laughs. She has heard far worse. "A rose opening," she persists, "the petals pushing out . . . out . . . *Ano. Ano.*"

The baby twists down and up a U valve, which is something it will get to know very well when Václav Janáček, the father, (who, by the way, is nowhere to be heard, who is hiding in the chicken coop that smells like hell, having been neglected by his wife these past twenty-seven hours of her hair-raising labor) will set his child to crawling around the crude plumbing of the first sinks and toilets in the village.

And the midwife shouts: "It's blooooming, blooming, I can see the bud . . ."

"A whore with so much hair growing on your face a man thinks he is making love to a mirror—"

"It reaches for the sunlight, up and up and up and—"

Agáta lets loose with a wretched sound that is so loud in the baby's narrow ear canal that the dawning light is occluded by the sheer thickness of the roar.

"Yes! Yes! A rose! A beautiful pink . . . a beautiful. . . a—"

———

AND NOW, Václav hears nothing coming from the house, not the curses of his wife, nor the scream of an infant, nor the triumphant exclamations of the midwife who can add one more to her tally of live births, only the infernal squawking of the hens. In his panic he picks up a cackling rooster and stuffs its head under his armpit, an action he will regret when he has to buy a replacement for the suffocated bird.

The silence is so dense that it is just as hard on the baby's eardrums as any sound. It is the silence that will become a refrain, when a stranger falls speechless in the child's presence, or when a villager pushes her children behind her skirts as she passes in the narrow market lanes to protect them from what might be catching. The child will learn to hear the complicated messages that fill these silences just the way, years later, imprisoned, it will stand in an unlit cell and study the darkness until all the hues that make it up have been accounted for and named, a painstaking ritual that proves that out of nothing comes everything.

Just as now, out of that hush comes a sound at first so soft that it could be a whisper traveling from the farthest star, from the outer reaches of the universe where all time goes, where all history, all wars, all arguments between husbands and wives, all the unanswered wishes of mothers for their children to be perfect and to live long and happy lives gather and mingle, making small talk about the deluded humans who thought that the past was something that could be put away and forgotten, who believed that the future was a story they could make their own. The small sound begins to stretch and expand until it finally ruptures:

"Ayeeeee!" Agáta howls in fright. "What is this thing?"

THIS THING, of course, is a baby. Forty centimeters of baby to be precise, although no one bothers to measure. No one thinks to enact the rituals of inspection that normally attend a birth—the delicate washing, the finger and toe counting, the near-scholarly examination of genitalia for signs of future procreative success. No one offers that the child looks like the father (eyes like the downward smile of nail parings) or that it has a mouth shaped like a perfect raspberry-colored bow that Agáta will finally but not now, not yet, claim as her legacy even though she is so old that her lips are no longer supported by a full set of teeth and have nearly collapsed inside her mouth. No one mentions that the baby has hair the color of dead grandmother Ljuba, whose flaxen locks were her pride, for to make these comparisons is to lay claim, to stamp the child as family so that when the cord is cut and the baby is finally free of Agáta's body, everyone will know to whom it belongs. For Václav and Agáta to assert ownership would be to admit that they are cursed, that this child they have prayed for, waited for, that comes to them after neighbors have joked about Václav still being able to stand at attention and about Agáta's womb being filled with cobwebs has turned out to be this *thing*, this foreshortened object, this disproportionate dollhouse version of an infant. It is as though, coming so late to the feast, the plumber and his wife have been given only leftovers, the hardened heels of bread and the tough ends of beef, that others have passed over.

"A GIRL," Václav says, still smelling of feathers and dead rooster. He hasn't yet touched the child, only ordered the midwife to unwrap the swaddling to reveal the naked declaration of its worth. He speaks with a little hitch of satisfaction as if the sex somehow proves that the fault is not his. Agáta, who has not yet looked at her daughter since that first, alarming view, lies on the bloodstained bed with her back turned away from the onion basket that serves as a cradle, staring at the varicose cracks in the wall, praying either to sleep herself to death or to wake from what must surely be a nightmare. All the while she murmurs: *Is it real? It isn't real. Is it?* Even when the baby mews from hunger, Agáta does not reach for her. What use are her false comforts?— her milk has not yet begun to flow. The midwife shows Václav how to settle the baby with sugar water, collects her money, then leaves the house in a hurry, not eager to prolong her association with this blighted birth and damage her reputation.

A day later, Agáta's milk has still not come in, but she is not surprised that it is unwilling to spend itself on such a lost cause. Exhausted by the birth, she sleeps and wakes and then, remembering what she has brought into the world, sleeps again, leaving her husband to administer the sugar water. Perhaps she hopes that if she pays the baby no mind, the child will simply disappear, return to the land of wishes it came from, and that she will wake up with only a memory of a vague but unnameable disappointment that will be forgotten in the daily skirmish of cleaning and cooking and arguing vegetable prices with market cheats. But her crotch will not let her forget. A thing so small ripping her from front to back so that she has to bite down on the handle of a wooden spoon when she pees. Returning to her bed, she glances at the baby girl, who is so tiny, so nearly not there. Her head is too large for her torso, her arms and legs too short. She looks like a rag doll sewn together from cast-off parts. Each time Agáta wakes, it seems possible that the baby's existence is just a magician's trick, and that if Agáta were to look in the basket, she would find only newly pulled scallions.

"MY LITTLE MOUSE," Judita, the village wet nurse sings as she rocks the baby against her bosoms that are long and heavy as giant zucchinis. Her brown nipples are so thick that the infant girl gags each time Judita pushes her small face into her curd-smelling skin. "Every one of my little mice grows big and strong and so will you," she commands, shaking the baby in order to get her to suck.

Judita's house, a dirt-floored room with walls blackened from a haphazardly swept chimney, smells sweetly of infant puke. Here, along with three other newborns, the plumber's daughter is rotated from the left breast to the right, then into the hands of

Judita's eldest, Vanda, whose job it is to strip and wipe. The sixteen-year-old's expression seesaws between the crinkle of disgust she feels for these shitting machines that are her daily burden and the hard fury of hatred she bears toward her mother, whose body and its uses signal her own utilitarian future. Vanda's task complete, she hands the baby off to her younger sister, Sophia, who diapers the child in sun-starched, wind-smelling cloth that has just been taken down from the line. It is Tomáš, Judita's idiot son, who is in charge of washing the dirty diapers in a barrel whose water is not changed often enough, a job he has been given because he performs his mucky task without complaint. After the baby is cleaned and freshly attired in diapers that are much too large for her tiny body, she is placed in a hay-filled crate, where she dozes and wakes and waits for her turn on the line once again. It is as efficient a system as any being implemented in the new factories in the faraway city where, the villagers have heard, men in white smocks hold stopwatches and notebooks and workers are occasionally sucked up into the machines so that who knows what accounts for the brilliant red of a bolt of cloth? Still, after weeks, when it becomes evident that even Judita's rich milk, responsible for so many of the village's pudgy, no-necked boys and girls, will not work miracles on this tiny, misshapen body, she grows frustrated. By the second month, her little mouse becomes her little rat; by the third, her little cockroach, a freakish, thumb-sized enemy determined to bring down shame on the wet nurse and ruin her business.

"Enough!" she declares one day. She carries the baby from her house down the main street, stomping past the corn chandler and the harness maker and the town gossips with her recalcitrant package held out in front of her as if she were returning bad meat to the butcher and making sure that everyone in the village can smell the proof. She crosses the rickety bridge spanning the river that splits the town in two then marches to the plumber's cottage. There, she finds Agáta on her knees in the garden yanking a clutch of knobby, dirt covered beets from the ground. Agáta's eyes grow fearful at the unexpected sight of her child, who she had hoped not to see for at least another month or perhaps ever again. She stands and backs up a few steps, her pickings shielding her useless breasts. But Judita is adamant, and the final payment for services is rendered: root vegetables for baby.

"But what am I supposed to do with her?" Agáta says, cradling the infant awkwardly so that the child's head flops over her forearm like a heavy bulb.

"First," Judita says, "you could try giving her a name."

BRONISLAVA MEANS WEAPON OF GLORY, Rosta, seizer of glory, Ceslav, honor and glory, and Miroslav, great glory. But these names that Agáta chose for each seed Václav planted inside her over the decades of their attempts were the ones she buried along with the residue of every miscarriage. The couple's imagination is dulled by thwarted hope and, unable to project any glorious future for the stubby child they have managed to bring to life, this dwarf child who mocks their years of effort, they can only conjure the prosaic. They call the baby Pavla, which means exactly what she is, which is little. She is narrow of body and short of limbs. Her eyes are round and watchful, her gaze both passive and disarmingly intrusive. Although it is impossible, her parents cannot help but feel she can see inside their minds and that she knows their private and sometimes horrible thoughts. She is an uncomplaining baby, as if she senses any kindness turned her way is provisional and that she ought not to draw more attention to herself than is necessary. She remains as quiet as any item in the cottage, as still as the portrait of dead Teta Ivana who picked a rose, pricked her finger, and died of infection, as still as the cuckoo clock that is never wound because Agáta and Václav have no need for timepieces. They feel the passage of the day in their bones, know instinctively when it is the hour to rise, to eat, to work, to sleep, when to commence the weekly argument when Agáta tells Václav that he is courting a terrible fate by refusing to go to Mass, and Václav tells Agáta that he will not believe that God intends for Father Matyáš, who as a boy did questionable things with the back end of a sheep (As did you! Agáta always reminds him. But I grew up to be a plumber! Václav replies) to be the conveyer of His word.

Left mostly to her own devices, which, at four months, are considerably few, Pavla lies in the wooden crib Václav bartered from one of his neighbors in exchange for a cracked commode. The slats create the frame through which Pavla watches Agáta excavate the dark eyes of potatoes with a bent-knuckled knife, yank stringy, gray tendons from chicken legs, wring out newly washed laundry, throttling wet sheets and Václav's undershirts in her muscular hands, and make the soap that she sells at the market. Agáta heats the rendered cooking fat then mixes it with lye that she makes using ashes from the hearth. The blue glass bottle in which she stores the poison catches the sunlight and Pavla's attention so that the very first object she attempts to grasp is this ephemeral cobalt sparkle. Then Agáta stirs and stirs and stirs, stripping off her sweater, then her apron, then her shirt, then her skirt, until she is down to her underclothes. Her skin drips with sweat, her arms and breasts and stomach shake with her exertions. Of course, Pavla knows nothing of rendered fat or lye or the laborious process of making soap, or that her mother drops chamomile flowers or rose petals into her molds because with this small, inexpensive effort, her soaps can fetch a few more coins at the market. But what she does understand is that her mother is a digger, yanker, wringer, twister, and an aggressive and sometimes angry stirrer, and so is somewhat relieved to be left alone. Pavla also observes her mother in the rare moments when the potatoes are boiling and the laundry is hung and there is no fault in the world of her home that she must immediately attack and remedy. Then Agáta will stand next to the open window without moving, barely breathing, as if the wind that charges her hours and days has unexpectedly died down and she has been left stranded in the incomprehensible sea of her life, suddenly aware that she has no purpose except to avoid the one that is staring at her though the bars of the crib. To counter her creeping terror, Agáta tells stories. She speaks not to her audience but to herself, the sound and memory of the old fairy tales as soothing as the bit of worn, soft chamois cloth she carried in her pocket when she was a girl and that she rubbed between her thumb and forefinger when her mother first told her these same stories, the bit of cloth she kept hidden for so many years in a small wooden box, intending to pass down the comfort to her own child. But now, this sentiment seems foolish. Maybe it is even the cause of her heartbreak, because everyone knows it is bad luck to second-guess fate.

In the Land of Pranksters there reigned a king . . . There once lived a poor, penniless man, truly a pauper . . . A good many years back it must be since the goblin used to dwell on Crow Mountain . . . and the story she tells again and again, the one that little Pavla, even though she cannot yet understand it, will remember all her life:

Once there was an old grandfather who went to work in his field. When he got there, he saw that an enormous turnip was growing there. He pulled and pulled, but he could not yank the turnip out of the ground, so he called his old wife. The man held onto the turnip and his wife held onto him and they pulled and pulled, but still, they could not pull the turnip from the ground. So they called their little granddaughter. The grandpa held onto the turnip and the grandma held onto the grandpa and the granddaughter held onto the grandma and they pulled, but still no luck. And so they called their dog. And the dog held onto the granddaughter and the granddaughter held onto the grandmother and the grandmother held onto the grandfather, who pulled the turnip, but still nothing. And so they called their kitty, who got in the back of the line and pulled the dog, but the turnip wouldn't budge. Suddenly, they heard a little voice coming from a hole in the ground. It was the voice of a mouse. The grandfather said, "Oh, little mouse, you do not have the strength to help us," but the grandmother said, "Let her help us if she wants to." So the grandfather held onto the turnip and the grandmother held onto the grandfather and the granddaughter held onto the grandmother and the dog held onto the granddaughter and the kitty held onto the dog and the mouse held onto the kitty and they pulled and pulled and pulled and . . . the turnip came out of the ground! And the grandmother said to the grandfather, "Sometimes the littlest one can be the biggest help."

Each time Agáta reaches the end of the story, she dismisses the stupidity of the moral. "What a ridiculous bunch," she might mutter, or, "Anyway, everyone knows that a giant turnip would be as tough as an old shoe."

As the hours pass and the light in the room softens and the corners recede into shadows, and as she listens to the low drone of her mother's recitation, Pavla sees both less and more, for Agáta in shadow is somehow the purer distillation of her character: dark, wary, certain that this world she lives in is not as real as the one she visits in her tales where mountain kings and speaking rams are more comprehensible to her than the day's weather or the queer human she has made.

"OH HO, MY WIFE!"

It is evening and twilight gives up its fight, and the night sky settles over the village. Agáta shakes herself out of her reverie and becomes all energy and spin, engaging importantly with whatever is at arm's length—a sock that needs darning, a soup that requires spicing, even, because she can no longer ignore the sweet stink of baby shit, her daughter. The door of the cottage opens and a dark shape fills it: Pavla's father is home. The tools of his trade hang off Václav's thick leather belt and he jangles when he moves. This inadvertent music provokes his daughter, who waggles her little arms. When Václav notices this reaction, he shakes his hips again, and to his surprise, his daughter's eyes grow wide and her mouth forms its first, wobbly smile. This is the opening conversation of Pavla's life and she does not want it to end so she manifests a noise that sounds like the bleating of a goat.

"Don't upset her," Agáta warns, not wanting to have her maternal skills put to the test.

"She's not upset. She's laughing!" Václav says, taking off his tool belt and dangling it over the crib. Pavla makes her sound again and watches as her father's astonishment turns to pleasure, his smile unmasking a mouthful of brown and rotted teeth that emerge from his swollen gums at odd angles like the worn picket fence that surrounds Agáta's garden and fails to keep out the scavenger deer. Pavla will do anything to keep seeing these teeth and so she laughs and waves her arms and feels, for the first time in her life, but not the last, the exquisite pain of love. In a few years, she will put Václav's screwdrivers and wrenches and bolts of all different sizes to use, dressing the long tools in bits of cloth to make faceless dolls, and stringing washers on twine to fashion necklaces for her mother. For now, she follows the symphony of her father as he crosses the room and sits on a hard chair and waits for his wife to pull off his high boots whose soles are impacted with sludge. It is Agáta's great shame that the handsome farrier she married so long ago, the boy who rode the horses he shod back and forth along the main street supposedly to try out his work but really to show off his powerful thighs to the village maidens, saw advantage in turning his skill with iron and his eye for chance to, of all things, indoor plumbing. "Horses will soon be a thing of the past," he explained to Agáta, the girl who was most impressed by those powerful flanks, as he lay on top of her in their marriage bed, pushing her knees closer to her face to improve his angle of entry. "But everyone shits once a day. Sometimes twice, if they're lucky."

The work was slow at first. The villagers were used to chamber pots and being able to study their bodies' expulsions for signs of good or ill health, and the notion of what was once inside them disappearing before their eyes made them suspicious. Even Agáta refused the improvement, not fully believing that it was possible for a body to eliminate its waste anywhere but in a boiling-in-summer, freezing-in-winter, always pungent outhouse. Time and again, people would fold their arms and narrow their gazes and ask Václav, "But where does it go, really?" His answer did not satisfy them because even though they talked a good game about heaven and hell to keep their children in line and satisfy that idiot, Father Matyáš, these were realistic people who had a pretty good idea of where they would end up for the rest of time, and who did not fancy the notion of sharing eternity with piles of their neighbor's crap. But eventually the idea caught on. Now, years later, Agáta is the wife of a man who makes a decent living unclogging the drains and pipes of villagers who have finally stopped squatting in the fields or pouring their slops out of windows to fertilize their flowers but who have yet to learn the idiosyncrasies of modern waste disposal. They are forever putting all manner of objects down their toilets as if to bury their secrets. Love letters from mistresses or the bill for a frivolous hat purchase, fistfuls of hair cut off to approximate some newfangled style advertised in a gazette brought from the city by a peddler, the gazette itself—all these things and more create odiferous backups that warp floorboards and stain rugs. His clients regard plumbing as a sin-exonerating miracle, a daily confession, which is reasonable given the narrow confines of the indoor WCs that are built into the corners of rooms or fashioned from standing wardrobes, and owing to the contemplative and sometimes prayerful minutes spent therein. The villagers have no interest in Václav's explanations about the curved and narrow pipes that render their efforts at obfuscation useless. More than useless, as it turns out, for all it takes for a marriage to crumble is for a husband to be present when the plumber exhumes a clot of bloody towels flushed away because a mother of six has decided a seventh will be the death of her. In fact, Václav turns out to be the opposite of what people assume. He is not a man devoted to the eradication of unmentionable things but one whose very presence brings them to light. When he enters a house, the owners will not look him in the eye, as if he were judge and jury and taxman all at once. He has taken to demanding his fee up front because no man pays another to witnesses his humiliation. But Agáta cannot complain. Her husband provides a living for her and now, she supposes, for the unfortunate issue of her aged womb.

During the first half year of Pavla's life, except at mealtimes, when she is fed warm goat's milk and vegetables macerated to a soupy pulp, or during diaper changes, she has little contact with her mother who doesn't know what to make of her fractional child. Every seven days, she lifts her baby from the crib, removes whatever oversized garments have been left on the doorstep by pitying neighbors, and washes Pavla in a basin. When her daughter is naked, Agáta will sometimes let her eyes wander over her child, but just as she feels her tears begin to collect, she sets to scrubbing, using not a perfumed soap but one that is as harsh on the skin as gravel. Let silly women spend money on fancy toiletries they think will keep their husbands close. A body needs to be scoured like the inside of a pot. Holding up one arm, then the other in order to get into the creases of bunched-up baby fat, she reduces her daughter to parts and eradicates the implications of the deformed whole. If Václav is home, he might do his

hip-shaking, tool-jiggling dance to entertain Pavla and distract her from her mother's ministrations, but more often than
not, he stands next to the basin and tilts his head to the side,
studying his baby as if she were another plumbing problem in
need of a fix.

BUT LIKE A RAT or icy wind, love creeps in. When winter comes,
and there are no vegetables to pull, and the life of the village
turns hushed and isolated, Agáta comes to Pavla's crib more
often and lifts her up, even when she has been cleaned and fed
and still smells of—yes, lately, she cannot resist—roses.

"Who are you?" Agáta says, holding Pavla so that they are
face-to-face. She is finally curious about this strange being
who she has brought into the world and whose musical sounds,
those triplet thirds that move up and down the scale, and
whose beginning words, despite their rubbery incoherence,
quicken her heart. If the child could speak she would say, "I
am Pavla," for that is all she knows about herself at this point
having not been subject to the fantasies of a besotted mother
spinning her baby's extravagant future of whirlwind romance,
loyal children, and wealth. During the next months, as the
cast-iron lid of sky hovers over the land, and as villagers are
less eager to go outside to throw chicken bones where they
belong, when the logic of "If I ate this piece of paper/bit of
twine/pig's knuckle, it would come out the other end anyway"
holds sway against the ice that seeps through the soles of boots

and the bitter air that slices cracks into the lips and hands on a journey to the compost heap, Václav's plumbing business picks up. As soon as he leaves the house each morning, Agáta opens the standing wardrobe, pulls up a chair, and with her daughter on her lap, gazes into the mirror that hangs inside the door. The reflective glass has browned and crackled around the edges so that only in its center does it allow for a true, if fuzzy, reflection. The two study each other. What Pavla sees: a woman whose occasional smile sneaks out only to be snatched back, as if Agáta recognizes her error.

And what does Agáta see?

She tells a story:

"A mother had her baby stolen from his cradle by a wolf, and in his place lay a changeling, a little monster with a great thick head and staring eyes who did nothing but eat and drink. In distress she went to a neighbor and asked her advice. The neighbor told her to take the changeling into the kitchen, lay him on the hearth, and make a fire. Then she should take two eggshells and boil some water in them. That would make the changeling laugh, and as soon as he laughed, it would be all up with him. The woman did everything just as the neighbor said. And when she put the eggshells on the fire to boil, the blockhead sang out: *I'm as old as the Westerwald but I've never seen anyone try to boil water in an eggshell!*" And he roared with laughter. As soon as he did that, a pack of wolves appeared carrying the rightful child. They set him on the hearth and took the changeling away, and the woman never saw them again."

When she finishes, Agáta looks at her daughter in the

mirror. Certainly she must be a replacement for the child Agáta expected. But then again, Pavla was taken away to Judita's milking house, and now has returned to take her rightful place in her crib. Agáta tries to ignore a pall of self-doubt. Holding her daughter against her breast, she feels Pavla's tiny heart pulsing against her wing-like backbones. Her daughter relaxes in her arms and grows heavy with sleep, and Agáta feels the pride all mothers feel when they have successfully ushered their children into the land of gentle dreaming. She holds her girl close and, she can't help it, she sings the song her mother sang to her so very long ago: *Good night, my dear, good night. May God himself watch over you. Good night, sleep well. May you dream sweet dreams!*

Should she be allowed to invoke God? Wasn't it against God that she took the gypsy's remedies? Wasn't it He who paid her back for her pagan infidelity? Would God now, after all this, place within her the feelings that are stirring her heart? She pictures Father Matyáš and cannot help but see him through Václav's eyes: a man too ignorant for the words he delivers, too sullied to touch the wafer that he places on extended, hopeful tongues, too wracked by drunken tremors to hold the cup steady with his long, bony fingers. The same fingers that he uses to pat the heads of his altar boys and smooth the collars of their frocks even when they don't need adjusting. "No!" she says out loud without intending to, startling the baby. A God that makes that sheep fucker His emissary cannot deny her this feeling that fills her withered breasts and makes her nipples tingle. *Dream a little dream, oh dream it.*

She sings in full voice, not caring that she cannot hold a tune or that the neighbors out tending their black pigs might hear. How many years has she had to listen to them laugh at their children, scream at them, chide them, praise them, wish them well and safe as they troop off to school, off to the fields, off to life? *When you wake up, trust the dream, that I love you. That I'm going to give you my heart!*

By the time Pavla is five years old, Agáta has enfolded her little daughter into her daily routine. The girl's tasks: sweep the floor, clean the chicken coop, carry the fresh eggs to the house in the cradle of her skirt, walking slowly so that the warm and delicate ovals do not jostle against one another and crack. Pavla is handy with a knife and she makes quick work of shelling peas or pitting cherries. Her arms and legs remain short relative to her torso, and when she walks or runs, she moves side to side to propel herself forward, her arms pumping double time. Watching her daughter race after an errant chicken or leap up to try and catch a petal-white butterfly, Agáta feels her chest expand to make room for the brew of awe and heartache that she has come to identify as happiness. Václav has fashioned a step stool so that Pavla can reach the basin in order to scrub dishes, scour her teeth, and wash her face, and he has made her a special riser that sits on the seat of a chair so that, at mealtimes, the shining sun of her round, fair head surfaces above the lip of the table. When Agáta takes Pavla to the shops, the children stare and often laugh, while their mothers *tsk tsk* at Agáta's misfortune and their relative good luck. "Leave me home," Pavla begs each time her mother announces the dreaded weekly trip, but Agáta slaps her. "If I have to do it, then you have to do it, too," she says, not clarifying whether she means enduring the humiliation or selling soap.

BECAUSE THE MAJORITY of houses in the village date from the previous century and have not been constructed with plumbing in mind, the work of retrofitting them for underground pipes is a job suited for the small. By the time Pavla is seven years old, Václav, recognizing both his daughter's quick wit and her unique suitability, begins to take her on his rounds. It is the girl's job to crawl into caverns beneath houses that hold eons worth of cold. Once she has studied these spaces and judged where the dirt is soft enough for digging and where rock forms too much of an impediment, she emerges, dusts herself off, then draws maps of the underground geographies. Because of the incessant comparisons she has been subjected to and is the subject of—*but she's half as tall as my Jurek and they share the same year and name day! But look: her hand is just a quarter the size of my darling Katarina's!*—Pavla has an innate grasp of scale, and from her crude yet accurate diagrams, Václav can determine where the pipes should be laid. Once he has done the laborious work of digging trenches, he hitches up his pants, drops to his knees, and wriggles underground. Pavla stands by the mouth of the hole, and when her father calls for the parts he needs, she hands them to him, sometimes using a pulley system that she and Václav devise with a rope and her Easter basket. She quickly learns the vocabulary of his trade—gaskets and bastard neck bolts, couplings and stems—and she is able to predict what her father will need before he asks for it. Václav and Pavla often work for hours without speaking, the only sound passing between them the clank of metal, Václav's muffled grunts, his occasional, frustrated profanities, and her corresponding giggles. Often, a client will comment about what a good man Václav is to keep his poor daughter close and make her feel useful. Although Pavla can see her father's expression harden, he never responds. That his stoicism is read as heroic forbearance helps his business: villagers are eager for a saint to install and sanctify their toilets. When a job is complete, and a client examines his new plumbing, flushing and then watching in astonishment as the water disappears from the toilet bowl, Václav will give Pavla a conspiratorial wink, and she knows they share the secret of her true value.

The crib remains Pavla's sleeping quarters long after other children in the village have moved into proper beds where the sweating or freezing bodies of their four or six or eight brothers and sisters keep them from rolling onto the hard floor. With no siblings and only one proper bed in the house, Pavla would sleep between her beloved parents, but she resists the transition. She is reassured by her crib, whose geometry is so conducive to her size. Confined, she feels that she occupies a comprehensible space relative to her mattress, the house, the village, the world. She teaches herself to add, subtract, and even multiply using the slats, and by the time she turns eight and finally convinces her fearful and protective mother, and her father, who frets the loss of a good assistant, to let her attend school, she is well ahead of the other children. She is sought after as a seatmate on test days and she obliges by angling her tablet to the advantage of her weak-minded neighbor. That lucky student's result is never questioned because the teacher, Mr. Kublov, no student of science or of much else, believes that Pavla's smallness of stature is mirrored by a corresponding puniness of brain, and that she is the one who cheats her way to a perfect score. She is forced to stand in the corner with her back to the classroom, and Mr. Kublov does not bother to admonish the boys who make a game of pitching nuggets of wadded paper at her back. The girls call her Little Nothing as though there were descending versions of nothing-ness. These girls want to assure Pavla that she counts for much less than the next-to-nothings their mothers tell them they are by virtue of their laziness when it comes to household chores, or the big nothings their fathers insinuate they are by only speaking directly to their brothers. During outdoor break time, the boys devise a game of chase where Pavla is the chicken and they are the farmers. The winner is the one who wrestles her to the ground and administers the coup de grâce. Then she must flap her arms and dance like a decapitated bird. The girls, led by their ring-leader Gita Blažek, are no less eager—they place her in the middle of their circle while they hold hands and raise their arms in an arch and chant: *The golden gate was opened, unlocked by a golden key. Whoever is late to enter, will lose their head. Whether it's him or her . . . Whack her with a broom!* They close their arms around her head like a vice, then administer the punishment. Mr. Kublov watches from his post at the top of the schoolhouse stairs where he smokes his cigarettes and steals nips from the flask hidden in his coat pocket, relieved that the children have found a united purpose so that he doesn't have to break up a fight and risk getting punched or scratched in the process.

These humiliations continue until heavy rains swell the river that separates Pavla and her neighbors' homes from the other side of the village, where the school stands. The bridge is demolished. A fallen poplar now stretches from one bank to the other, but the drop is precipitous and the spindly trunk does not fill the children with confidence. One boy tries to cross, but immediately falls off and lands in the muddy bank below. No one wants to make another attempt, but no one wants to return home and be beaten for playing hooky and forced to spend the day mucking out stalls. Pavla runs back to her house as quickly as her short legs will carry her. Agáta is busy stirring lard and lye. The steam from the boiling pot clouds the cottage's window, and she doesn't notice when her daughter slips into Václav's toolshed and gathers a mallet, a rope, and a set of pulleys. Once back at the river, she hammers one of the pulleys to a standing tree and feeds the rope through it. She puts the remaining tools into her school satchel and tightens the strap across her back. Holding the ends of the rope in one hand, she hoists herself onto the fallen tree. A wind created by the high and swift current makes balancing difficult, but her center of gravity is low enough to stabilize her and her small feet find purchase on the narrow trunk. She envisions the makeshift bridge as just another subterranean corridor below the houses where she and her father work, a tight, enclosed space that enfolds her, and her imagination sees her safely to the other side. There, she hammers the second pulley into a firm root, feeds the rope through until it is taut, and ties a knot. Gripping one of the two ropes, the others nervously make their way across the trunk while Pavla slowly pulls on the other and guides them forward.

The games of chase-the-chicken stop, and if Pavla is remanded to the corner by Mr. Kublov, the other students leave her alone. They begin to seek her out not only to help with their schoolwork but also for the more important job of sneaking into the cloakroom in order to put a dead mouse in Kublov's coat pocket or smear glue inside his hat. Once the students begin their geography study, aided by a wildly inaccurate roll-up map suspended from the top of the chalkboard that shows their tiny country, which is routinely tossed back and forth between sovereign empires as a consolation prize for greater losses, to be the continent's largest territory, Pavla's precise and wholly proportional mapmaking skills are discovered. The children enlist her to draw a detailed schematic of the male genitalia on a large sheet of paper. Selflessly, Petr Matejcek offers himself as a model. During the following day's recess, he and Pavla hide behind the outhouse that is still in use because the mayor does not consider the school, or the children, or education in general worthy of the expense of Václav's services. Without ceremony, Petr drops his trousers. She has never seen a penis before. It looks like a pale and very narrow and really quite useless section of pipe.

"It moves if you kiss it," Petr says.

"By itself?"

"Try it."

Pavla leans forward and puts her lips to skin that is as soft as the belly of a newborn pig and smells just as musky and tantalizingly complex. When she leans back, she watches in wonder as Petr's penis reddens and swells. For the first time, she witnesses something she has never thought possible—that a small, runty thing can magically transform.

"I stick it in things," Petr says, touching himself tenderly.

It makes perfect sense to Pavla, who thinks of washers and fittings.

"You better draw it before it shrinks," he says.

The following day, when Kublov yanks the string and unfurls the map, there is Petr, or at least the truly marvelous part of him, drawn with a hand so deft that were this a lesson in anatomy, the children would know exactly the location of the dorsal vein and they would be able to count the folds of the scrotal sac. The ensuing geography lesson is a huge success. Petr is quite pleased, and even though the children agreed to protect his anonymity, he cannot help but boast of his contribution. He is suspended from school for a month. Pavla and the others lean over their desks, pants and stockings lowered and dresses hiked, their naked bottoms pink and proud, Pavla's no less for being lower to the ground, and wait for the stinging crack of Kublov's walking stick.

They still call her Little Nothing, but the name is now a sign of inclusion, no more incendiary than Toes, which is what they call Tabor Svoboda on account of his ability to write with his feet. These nicknames mark them as a group separate from parents and teachers and Father Matyáš, whose aim it is to separate children from their delights. Pavla revels in her name because she knows that if nothing is little, then it must be something indeed.

Dream *a little dream, oh dream it. When you wake up, trust the dream, that I love you, that I'm going to give you my heart."*

Older now, Agáta's voice trembles up and down the scale, barely hanging onto one note before sliding off. Pavla is ten years old and although she is nearly too long for her crib she still does not want to give it up. Her parents stand over her as they do each night, staring at the inexplicable wonder of their clever and delightful and wholly beloved daughter as she sleeps. But now, although her eyes are closed and she breathes evenly, she is awake.

"There is something odd about her," Václav whispers.

"Are you an idiot?" Agáta whispers back. "She's a dwarf."

"No," he muses. "It's something else, something more strange . . ."

Their faces come even closer so that Pavla can feel their hot breath on her cheeks and smell the night's dinner of onions and chicken feet mingled with tooth rot.

"Could it be that . . . could it be . . . ?" Václav says.

"Spit it out, husband!" Agáta says too loudly for the sleeping child were she sleeping.

"Is she . . . pretty?" Václav asks tentatively.

Agáta blows out her cheeks in disbelief. But then she leans back to take in a wider view. "Huh," she says.

WHEN MOST PEOPLE hear of a dwarf, they imagine court jesters or circus clowns—little, disproportionate people whose physical development seems to have been conceived exclusively for entertainment purposes. A torso of scaled-down adult proportion appended to stubby legs and arms that must adapt to the peculiar physics of their job produces a knee-slapping guffaw if you are watching such a clown try to outpace a galloping horse in a circus ring. A monarch might watch a dwarf duo enact a famous drama of doomed love for the same reason he might order his court architect to construct a miniature version of his palace to be displayed in the conservatory. There is something enticing and discomfiting about viewing one's life in perfect miniature. We are, quite literally, brought down to size. A dwarf, in short, is made for human comedy, not beauty. But Václav is right. As the childish plumpness falls away from Pavla's maturing face, an unmistakable loveliness reveals itself. Her eyes are the deep blue-gray of winter dusk, and her pale lashes are as luxuriant as feathers. The planes of her high cheekbones angle sharply and the small dips where those bones give way to eye sockets create secret, dark spaces that shadow a mysterious gaze. Her hair, however, is her true glory. To call it a color is to misname something that is better understood as the absence of color, as a trick of light. The flaxen locks flow like batter from the mixing bowl. Agáta, whose coarse hair is now fully silver and is hidden morning and night under a maroon head scarf, spends hours playing with Pavla's mane, lacing her fingers through its whorls, weaving it into braids or gathering it on top of the girl's head so that fern-like tendrils cascade down the sides of her face and her neck.

"My hair was once as lovely as yours," she tells Pavla as she stares into the wardrobe mirror past the girl's shoulder, past herself, deep into the forward and backward depths of the glass. "There once was a girl with long, golden tresses who lived in a tower," she begins, but she does not continue because she knows that Pavla will not be able to profit from this treasure and that there will be no prince brave enough to climb the ladder of her profuse femininity and rescue her from her fate.

The villagers take note of this new development. When mother and daughter run errands, the women stop to inspect the girl whose sudden beauty agitates them. They cannot make sense of the pitiful body and the enviable face.

"Such hair!" they exclaim.

"Eyes the color of . . . what color would you call that?"

"And the nose. It is so . . . so . . ."

"From the neck up, she looks just like . . . just like . . ."

Pavla is a sentence they cannot finish, an equation they cannot solve, and their desire to figure her out obviates any privacy she might otherwise hope for. Where once she was the local shame, now she is a good luck charm. If she waits outside the butcher's while her mother argues prices with pock-cheeked Orlik, whose apron is a perpetually stained canvas of the day's murders, women gather around. They touch her head, kiss her hand, and exclaim over her small perfection. If her hair is newly washed and combed and particularly fine in its luster, they will grab at it the way they do when they want to test the authenticity of one of the silk scarves that Mischa Bobek brings to town once a month, his cart resplendent with jewel-toned garments he claims come from a village in a hidden valley of a distant mountain range in a country everyone pretends to have heard of. *Is she real?* they shriek when they cannot separate the girl from her magnificent gift.

In the evenings after such a day, Agáta brushes out Pavla's tangles, trying, with each downward stroke, to erase the residue of those groping, avaricious fingers.

"Am I real, Mama?" Pavla asks, her head jerking back with her mother's pitiless yet adoring ministrations.

"What are you talking about?"

"What they say at the market. And at school."

"What do they say at school?"

"They call me Little Nothing."

Agáta lowers her head until her lips tickle Pavla's earlobe. "When you were born, I pictured a flower, and that flower became you. You are everything to me," she whispers. The slosh and steady rhythm of her breath reminds Pavla—of what, she is not sure. But to be reminded does not always have an object, it is simply a suffusion, and she feels happy, away from the villagers, in the home of her parents, where she has always felt, and will forever be, safe.

"There once was a girl," Agáta whispers dreamily one night as she rubs lanolin into her daughter's scalp. Pavla is fourteen now and she has just been displayed for the admiration of the district magistrate who makes an appearance in the village once a year to collect official taxes and unofficial bribes. As if she were a small child, the man bounced Pavla on his knee, although that didn't stop him from squeezing her newly ripening chest. "There once was a girl who—" Agáta stops short because this is the first time she imagines narrating her daughter's future the way she always dreamed she might during the humiliating years when she and Václav could not produce a living child, the way she forbid herself to do once Pavla was born with no future worthy of fantasy. But Pavla's new if not actual stature as the town attraction has made her mother dare to hope. She continues: "There once was a girl named Pavla who was so beautiful that when a prince rode through the village and saw her, he promised to marry her and take her to live in a castle where she would have all that she could ever want or need."

Pavla pulls away. "But I don't want to go anywhere," she says. She cannot imagine her life outside the village, away from her parents. Her schooling is finished, and she is happy that once again she can help Václav with his work.

"Your father and I, we are old," Agáta says.

Pavla can't draw a full breath. For the first time, she realizes that this is true, that her parents' skin is wrinkled and spotted, that their teeth are falling out, that they groan when they sit and when they stand and complain of exhaustion upon waking each morning, and that one day, a day that will come sooner than the one day other children think of when they have these same thoughts, Agáta and Václav will die and she will be alone. She feels like she has been thrown into the air and for the brief moment she is aloft, the earth has turned so that when she comes down, she recognizes nothing.

That night, she lies in her crib listening to the terrible duet of Agáta's climbing hysteria and Václav's low, percussive interjections as they argue outside the cottage door. Agáta says it is no life for a girl to crawl in shit, and Václav argues that if shit is good enough for him, it ought to be good enough for his daughter. *"But who will maaarry her? How will she liiive?"* Agáta wails. And then, there is a silence that is so familiar that Pavla begins to shake. Where has she heard such silence before? And how does she know that it portends great change?

*T**he following morning,* Václav lifts Pavla onto the bench of his wagon as usual, but instead of the two of them heading off to dig through the bowels of another village home, Agáta joins them. She is dressed in her black church dress and she sits as stiffly and silently and, Pavla notices, as contritely as she does after Václav has been particularly blasphemous around the house and she feels she must represent his shame by occupying the first pew at church, in full, supplicating view of Father Matyáš. Václav shakes the reins, the horse snorts, and the wagon makes its way across the new bridge, through the slowly waking town, and then, to Pavla's utter surprise, beyond it.

This is the first time in her life she has left her village. The maps she studied and defiled at school attest to far-off cities and farther-off countries and so-far-off-as-to-be-unbelievable continents where people are, according to her old schoolteacher, black or yellow or red. But the idea of elsewhere has always been a vaporous and not wholly credible notion. Its allure is qualified by the knowledge that although she has become commonplace in her village and is able to carry on with minimal interference and then only from strangers passing through, the wider world offers no such assurances. And what does she need from elsewhere? She has her parents and their aged, grateful love. She has her old classmates, all of whom have left school and begun their lives of work and responsibility. They see one another on market days. They nod and shake hands just as they have seen their parents do, and with these solemn, awkward gestures they assume the mantle of adulthood and their places in the village's predictable cycle of years.

And yet, here they are, she and her parents, somewhere else. The plumber's wagon bounces along roads not dissimilar to the ones she has traveled all her life, only these are vastly different because she doesn't know where they lead and because of what is now frighteningly obvious: that her parents intend to put her out of the wagon, give her a push, and tell her to keep going and not look back.

Is this true? She looks from her mother to her father. Both stare ahead, grim faced, betraying nothing. She checks behind her to see if there is a bundle in the wagon bed, if her mother secretly packed her clothing and some food for this endless journey to who knows where. But there are only a few lengths of pipe that roll and clank against one another as the wagon bumps along.

"Where are we going?" she asks.

Neither parent answers. Neither can bear to form the words

that will make a lie of what they've said all her life: that they love her just the way she is and that she never needs to change.

That first day, they visit Zlata, the witch who gave Agáta the herbs and taught her the chants that enabled her, finally, to conceive a child that survived pregnancy. The woman's skin is the color of cowhide, and she smells of the cheesecloth bladders that hang off the sides of her barrel-shaped caravan, transforming into the domácí tvaroh that she peddles from door to door. Inside the caravan there is barely room for the four of them as Zlata seems to have saved every candle, scrap of cloth, ball of yarn, and jar of herbs she has ever encountered in her seven decades of life. She sits on a three-legged milking stool, punches the bulky material of her tiered skirts between her wide-spread legs, then studies Pavla with a narrowed gaze, sucking in her upper lip so that all that is left in its place is her furry mustache.

Finally, she turns to Agáta. "You did not follow my instructions," she says.

"I did everything!" Agáta says. "I slept with my head at my husband's feet. I bathed in the piss of a newborn piglet."

But Zlata ignores her. She orders Pavla to lie on the floor, which is carpeted with as many differently colored blankets as skirts the woman wears. Leaning forward on her haunches, the gypsy dangles an amulet above the girl, moving it along the vertical axis of her torso, chanting in her strange language. The percussive, spit-flinging menace of it makes her sound like she is having a fierce argument with herself, and Pavla has the urge to apologize, although for what she is not sure. Zlata tells Pavla to open her shirt. Václav turns away while his daughter unbuttons herself, although he can't help peeking, not because he is interested in his daughter's figure, but because he does not trust this woman whose fertility treatment included the instruction that he and Agáta were not to make love once she was impregnated—thus the head-to-foot sleeping arrangement—and that while pregnancy was being attempted, he was not to touch himself, a prescription that left him in the coop on many an afternoon, bringing himself relief from his urges while chickens pecked for food around his fallen trousers. The gypsy licks her finger and dips it into a small copper pot. When she withdraws it, it is covered with a deep yellow powder.

"Do you bleed yet?" she asks.

"No," Pavla says.

"Are you frightened of men?"

"No."

"You should be." Zlata places her stained finger on Pavla's belly, just above the triangle of pale hair that has recently sprouted, and makes a small cross sign on her skin. "Men are disgusting, but you cannot be a child forever," she says.

After the treatment and after money has changed hands, Zlata gives Agáta a pouch of herbs. "Boil these twice a day and make her drink a cupful while facing north," she says. "This time, do what I tell you," she adds, looking pointedly at Václav's crotch, and although it has been fifteen years, he has the feeling that she is standing outside the chicken coop, listening as he achieves his release.

While Zlata and her incantations may have been responsible for Pavla's birth, they do nothing for her height, although the following month, her bleeding begins. Agáta slaps her across the cheek, then hugs her, then tells her about the monster and the big sausage. Afterward, her face falls and she grows quiet. "But you will not have to worry about that," she says.

A few weeks later, the family sets out again, this time to visit Dr. Andrasko, who lives two villages to the east. He is a tall man who wears a suit, a detail that seems to convince Agáta of his professionalism, although the exorbitant cost of his cure leaves Václav, who believes in a fair price for a fair job, enraged. Andrasko prescribes a draught that tastes of equal parts tree bark and snot to be imbibed three times a day. A month later, when this remedy shows no sign of working, the family travels farther afield to consult Dr. Bosak, who suggests that Pavla hang by her hands from a tree branch for a full half hour on Mondays, Wednesdays, and Fridays, and by her knees on Tuesdays, Thursdays, and Saturdays. Sundays she is instructed to lie prone for the entire day so that her blood and organs can sort themselves out. Dr. Krasny, a half-day's journey away, is horrified that Agáta and Václav would submit their child to that well-known scoundrel, Bosak, and suggests that they rearrange the house so that the girl is forced to reach for such necessities as food and water. In this way, he explains, "The body becomes trained to adapt to a tall world, the way a dog learns to beg for food."

"She's a pretty little thing," Dr. Matusek says (yes, Agáta and Václav are making their way alphabetically through the regional directory). His nostrils flare like an animal that has picked up a scent as he examines Pavla on his table. "She seems limber enough," he says, scissoring her legs into a wide V. "If you leave her with me, I'll see what I can do." Agáta has to put herself between this doctor and her husband's fists as she hurries her family out the door.

DR. IGNÁC SMETANKA wears a white lab coat, works in an office with a proper weighing scale and wooden models of various body parts, and has a framed certificate from a famous university on his wall. A sculptural wave of hair crests over his high forehead and he wears armless spectacles that sit importantly, if unevenly, on his authoritative nose. A young man—he might be only a few years older than Pavla—stands deferentially to the side. He is not introduced. He has chestnut hair, a soft, full mouth, and dark, watery eyes framed by luxuriant eyelashes. Pavla is used to boys taking no account of her, but this young man offers her the slightest hint of a conspiratorial smile when the doctor is not looking. As if they are complicit in something exciting. She's confused by the swift and unreasonable attachment she feels and embarrassed by the vulnerability of her attraction. Even before Dr. Smetanka instructs her to undress behind a screen and put on the examining gown she will find there, she feels naked. While she disrobes in private, she cannot help but think that the young man knows that now she is taking off her dress, and now she is unrolling her stockings, and now she lifts her slip over her head. It is new, this feeling of being watched not because of her oddity but because she possesses something that a man—perhaps this young man—might desire. Does he know that her nipples have become pink and erect in the cold air? Despite the muslin screen, she covers her chest with her arms, but her impulse to hide differs from the mortification she felt years before when her father took her swimming in the river and all the neighboring children saw her in her bathing costume for the first time, the disproportions of her body no longer obscured by a dress. No, this embarrassment is something else, something better, because it comes hand in hand with another sensation—has she ever once experienced this? Is this vanity? Is this pride? She gently touches her nipples, flicks their hardness with her finger, feels a wire of energy pass from their tips all the way down her body and gather in a knot between her legs.

"Is there a problem?" the doctor calls out.

"No," she says, tying the gown around her. When she emerges and notices the younger man take in how ridiculous she looks, swallowed up by this overlarge garment, her humiliation quickly returns, as though it knew to stay close, that it would be pressed into service again. Her mother was right: Who would want her? The doctor gives an order, and before she realizes what is happening, the young man, who she now understands is the doctor's assistant, gently lifts her onto the examining table. She feels his grip on her waist, feels her skin tingle beneath his hands. He is careful not to look at her, but she can't tell whether he is uncomfortable with the intimacy or whether he feels nothing more than he would were he hoisting a basket of yams.

Dr. Smetanka washes his hands at the small sink and then

stands with them held out and dripping so that the young man, who anxiously anticipates the doctor's moves, can dry them with a frayed cloth. She recognizes his attentiveness. She is just as focused when she listens for the particular ratchet of a screw or the tones of differently sized pipes as they clang against a wrench so that she will be ready with the next tool her father needs even before he asks for it. Somehow this thought calms her. Maybe this doctor is like her father and he will be able to fix her, too. These past months of potions and strange exercise regimens, of having her parents measure her against the doorjamb and then trying to hide their disappointment when there isn't any change, of her growing awareness that, despite what they have always told her, she is a mistake that must be corrected—all these things have left her feeling anxious and ashamed, and angry, too, if she will admit it to herself. Her parents have become like everyone else who sees her as a pity, a blight, or as a convenient way to assure themselves that their lives could be worse. She feels more isolated than she has ever felt in her life. There are her parents, standing against the wall, nervous and craven, and here she is, alone.

She lies back on the table and stares up at a spider scrabbling along the ceiling while Dr. Smetanka opens her gown. How stupid, she thinks, to put on the thing only to have him take it off. How ridiculous to insist on the privacy of the screen when now she lies flayed open like a gutted sheep. The assistant, thankfully, has turned his back and pretends to busy himself with something in a glass cabinet while the doctor stares at her body, not bothering to hide his fascination with her deformity. At his instructions, she breathes in and out, opens her mouth wide, turns her head to the left and right, counts from zero to twenty and back to zero again. When the examination is finished, she dresses and is instructed to leave the room while Agáta and Václav remain for a consultation. The assistant follows her into the waiting area and the two stand together awkwardly.

"My family once owned two pygmy ponies," he says, finally.

"Is that really what you want to tell me?" she says.

When he blushes, two wine stains of red spread unevenly across his cheeks.

"Don't worry," she says. "People never know what to say to me."

He looks down at her, emboldened. "What would you like them to say?"

Before she can answer, the doctor's office door opens and Agáta and Václav, looking pale, motion for Pavla to follow them outside. She turns to look back at the assistant, but his head is bowed as he listens to the doctor. The older man claps three times to put a fine point on whatever he has said and closes the office door.

During the ride home, the sky opens up and rain falls heavily. The horse drags the wagon along the muddy roads. Despite that she is cold and soaked, Agáta is talkative. She chatters on about whether she should use paprika on the meat before or after she braises it and Václav, who cares only that food is enough and easy to chew, becomes uncharacteristically engrossed in her culinary dilemma. When that discussion runs its course, Agáta breaks into the song the villagers sing at the Drowning of Morana festival to herald the end of winter. If Pavla were not thinking about the young man and his lovely, glittering eyes, and if she were not busy trying to remember and interpret his every word and gesture, she would understand the workings of Agáta's mind and know which way things were heading for her. When they arrive home, she is happy to be neither suspended from a tree nor made to drink a foul-tasting tea and she hopes that the doctor has told her parents to just leave her alone. The rain lets up. Václav announces that he is going out, but when Pavla offers to help with whatever plumbing job he has going, he tells her not to trouble herself, that he can take care of things on his own.

"Let me help you, Mother," Pavla says, as Agáta slathers the orange spice over the much-discussed piece of meat.

"No, no, darling. You rest."

"But I'm not tired."

"Of course you're tired after such a long trip."

"You took the same trip."

"But I'm an old woman and you are a young girl who needs her rest."

"That makes no sense."

"We should never have sent you to that school if all you're going to talk about is sense."

"An idiot could tell you it makes no sense."

"Are you calling your mother an idiot?"

But before Pavla can defend herself, she hears a familiar sound of metal sinking into earth. She looks out the window and realizes that her father has not gone off to work at all. Instead, he is in the yard, attacking the ground next to her mother's garden with a shovel, grunting and flinging clots of wet dirt behind him onto the chickens, which squawk and flap their wings. She wonders if the doctor has told her parents that if they finally install an indoor toilet, she will grow.

Luckily, and Pavla will soon discover that this is her single bit of luck, the following morning dawns balmy and gives way to a clear blue sky and clouds so optimistic they might have been drawn by a child. Václav takes Pavla outside and introduces her to the results of his nightlong labor: a hole just over a meter deep and wider than any pipe she has ever seen. Pavla gamely scrambles into the pit. When her feet touch bottom, her head barely clears the ground.

"Will we tunnel from here to the house?" she says, thinking already about how her father might reconfigure the wardrobe into a water closet. "Shall I draw a map?"

He hands her a narrow pipe that is as tall as the pit and into which he has bored four small holes at even intervals. It is as useless a pipe for channeling waste as Pavla can imagine.

"Táta, I don't think this is what we need."

The morning sun glints off the water in his eyes. "I love you, Pavlicka," he says, in a voice so sad that she thinks he is dying and that she is standing in his grave.

"I love you, too, Táta."

"I only want you to have a good life."

"I have a good life. The best life."

Agáta bursts out of the house, running and crying, her hands flailing in front of her face as if she were battling a swarm of bees. "Don't do it," she pleads.

"Go back in the house," Václav says to his wife. "Don't look."

"It's good the way things are," Agáta says.

"But what about when we are gone? What then?"

Pavla is right: someone is dying. She tries to climb out of the hole but her arms are too short to lever her weight. "Táta, give me a hand. Get me out of here."

"I can't," he says. Tears pour from his eyes and course down the deep runnels that score his cheeks.

"Táta, pull me up! Just like the enormous turnip! Mother, grab hold of him and pull!"

"Please take off your clothes, my darling," Václav says.

"What? I don't understand," Pavla says.

"Don't do it," Agáta says, pulling on her husband's arm. "I beg of you."

"Daughter, I'm ordering you to do what I say," he says, trying for an authority that sounds like a pale imitation of the other village patriarchs who yell and berate and hit.

"But why, Táta?" Pavla says. Has she been wrong her whole life? Do her parents wish she had never been born? Are they going to kill her?

"Take off your clothes!"

Too shocked to protest or even cry, she pulls her dress over her head. When her mother takes it from her, Pavla grabs onto her hand and neither will let go of the other until Václav gently pries them apart.

"Don't resist, my darling girl," he says as a shovelful of dirt rains down on her shoulders.

"Táta, please! I'll hide. I won't show myself anymore. I won't bring shame on you and Mama. Please stop. I don't want to die!"

DR. SMETANKA'S PRESCRIPTION, Pavla slowly comes to understand as the dirt reaches her ankles and then her knees and then her chest, is that she and the narrow pipe are to be buried up to her neck. Then, over the hours that she will be so interred, Václav and Agáta will pour hot oil down the pipe. The oil that emerges through the perforations will slowly seep around her body and, in combination with the moist earth, cause her skin to become elastic.

"Like toffee," her father says, his mouth struggling to form itself into a smile. "You love toffee."

The sensation of the warm oil reaching her skin is not unpleasant at first. In fact, it is a relief from the clamminess that seeps into her bones. And the infusion of heat seems to put a stop to the nipping chiggers and crawlies that search her body's every fold and pocket for warmth and nutrition.

"A dumpling, my darling?" Agáta says. She sits on a stool next to the hole. She gives Pavla water when she is thirsty and food when she is hungry. She sings and tells stories and she holds up old schoolbooks so that Pavla can read, turning the page when Pavla indicates she is ready.

"If you don't eat your meal," Agáta says, when Pavla refuses the food, "you can't have dessert." As if they are sitting at supper after an uneventful day. As if mothers all over the village routinely plant their children in the ground to make them grow. But Pavla is too exhausted and confused by what is happening to protest. She wonders if her mother has gone mad and crossed over into the world of her imagination, and whether Pavla has not simply become a character in a story where goblins steal children and grotesque crones turn into beautiful princesses, stories her mother tells herself while she stares out the window of the cottage, no longer certain of the contours of her life.

When the neighbors get wind of what is going on in the Janáček yard, they arrive in numbers. Pavla waits for her old schoolmates to revert to behaviors they exhibited before she won their trust and respect, for the boys to water her with their pee as if she were a garden flower, for the girls to hold hands and sing that infernal rhyme and whack her with a broom. Instead, they stand before the hole silent and humbled, as if they are just now comprehending some essential truth about their lives. Seeing her makes them vulnerable to the real and troubling profundity of the very questions that made them once so merciless, when they thought she was not a person at all but an insect to step on or a chicken to behead. They are all of them nothing more than tubers. They have been planted by their parents, their fathers' seeds in their mothers' bellies, in order that they grow and prove useful, and when their usefulness comes to an end, they will be discarded. They are struck through with that queer feeling they experience as a shiver in the bones on those rare occasions when the moon passes over the sun and day and night switch places, or when they receive an unexpected look of love from a father: they realize how brief and illusory is their happiness.

"Does it hurt?" her old schoolyard nemesis Gita Blažek whispers, unsure if she should venture words in this sacred space of revelation.

"It stings a little," Pavla admits.

"Do you want some chewing gum?" Gita's older brother, Radek, asks.

"Yes, please."

Radek removes the piece he was working. Some of the others reach into their mouths and contribute. Gum is a rare and expensive treat, and Pavla is moved by the sacrifice. As her teeth close down on the rubbery clot, it emits the taste of masticated potatoes and sweet tea, and the faintest trace of dejection.

Hours later, after the sun has lowered and her friends have gone home to do their evening chores or have sneaked behind barns to kiss and touch, or to do more than that, as is the case with Petr of the mapped genitals and Gita, who will end up with a baby before too long, Pavla's skin begins to burn. The next time Václav and Agáta administer a round of treatment, the oil, once as comforting as the infusion of boiled water into a tepid bath, touches raw skin. Pavla shrieks for Agáta, who in turn screams at Václav, who tries to be forceful, telling each of them not to cry. But he is weeping, too. Pavla begs and pleads, and he cries out for her forgiveness, and the three of them compose a trio of wails so furious that the neighborhood dogs yowl in response.

And then suddenly, with no warning, the pain seems to slice right through her bones so that not only is her skin aflame but her insides feel as if they have been struck by lightning. She cannot cry. She cannot speak. She cannot even think beyond the suffering. Her mind recalculates and, determining pain to be its new equilibrium, adjusts itself accordingly, shutting down all her other faculties in order not to disrupt the sensation in any way.

Then something astonishing happens: the pain becomes so total, so obliterating, that anything corporeal and sensate buries itself deeply in her center and she perceives it as virtually nonexistent. She feels like nothing so much as . . . well, her schoolmates were right all along—she feels like nothing.

NIGHT FALLS and with it the temperature. Agáta adjusts a woolen hat on Pavla's head and ties a scarf loosely around her neck. She tries to get her daughter to speak or even hum along to her favorite lullaby, but Pavla can't make a sound. All she can do is stare out into the night sky. Once, she would have said that night was simply black. But now she knows differently about color and pain and delusion. Russet red, indigo blue, brown, ocher. She chants this litany to herself over and over, building up a wall of words that protects her from the sound of her mother's voice, the feel of the chill on the tips of her ears and nose, the smell of chimney smoke carried on the wind. She needs to block out any intrusion that threatens to remind her of her being.

Agáta kisses her daughter and returns to the house. Václav, wrapped in a comforter, settles down to sleep beside the hole. "I'm here, my Pavlicka," he murmurs groggily until his words are replaced by his light snores.

He is here. But where is she?

She is with her mother at the flower stall on market day. Agáta is frustrated with her because she has not chosen which flowers to buy. But the roses look sickly and the edges of the cerise petals are already brown. Agáta takes Pavla by the elbow and attempts to pull her from the stall. Go pick your flowers in a field, she says. In desperation Pavla points to a giant linden tree that, oddly, grows in a pot. She wants that tree, she tells her mother. Agáta says she is being ridiculous. A tree is too expensive and there is no way they can carry it home, and why do they have to spend money on a tree when trees grow everywhere and cost nothing to look at? But the flower seller tells Agáta that she will give her the tree as a gift and that her husband will deliver it. Later, when the man pulls up to the house in his wagon, Pavla sees that the branches of the tree have been cut away so that all that is left is a spindly trunk. Plant it in the sun and in a year it will grow back, the man instructs. But Agáta objects. Why did you cut off the branches of our tree? she demands. Because, the man says, I heard a knocking sound coming from the coffin and I had to cut down the tree in order to find out if your daughter was really dead. And then, irritated, Agáta says to Pavla, Are you dead? Are you really dead? And Pavla cries: I'm not dead but *I'm so lonely!*

IT IS DAWN and Václav is frantic, even praying to a God he doesn't care for as he shovels earth from around her. Agáta is on her knees, clawing the dirt like a dog, crying, "Are you dead, my Pavla? Is she dead?" Václav throws down the shovel and pulls his daughter from the hole then carries her to his wagon. She faints during the ride. When she wakes, she is lying on Dr. Smetanka's examining table, except it isn't the same table she was on before. This table is rough-hewn and the edges are raw. She can already feel splinters sliding underneath her skin. But she doesn't mind the smell, which is sweet like wet leaves or fresh-cut firewood. Also, and this is the strangest thing of all, a crank is affixed to one side. She is so bewildered by everything that has happened and is happening that it takes her a few extra moments to realize that her ankles are pinned down by straps and that the doctor's assistant is in the process of lifting her arms over her head and fitting her wrists into another set of immobilizing leathers. She is naked beneath a sheet, and when the material shifts even the smallest bit, she feels as if her skin is being ripped off.

She gasps. "Mama?" But she doesn't say it because she can't make her voice work.

Once she is secured to the doctor's satisfaction, the assistant comes around to the side of the table. She tries to catch his gaze, to reaffirm their connection, but he will not look at her.

"Begin," the doctor says. The assistant turns the crank, and Pavla feels a space open up underneath her. The table seems to be splitting in two. As she is pulled northward and southward, what begins as a tug becomes a pull, and then the pressure in her armpits and around her hips and groin becomes unbearable. She has to make it stop. She forces a sound out of her, but the noise she makes is nothing like her voice. It is low and raw, more animal than girl. The assistant stops. He looks at her for the first time that day. His beautiful eyes are filled with terror.

"Danilo! Keep going!" the doctor orders.

Danilo. She tries to say the name, to make her appeal, but she can't.

"I don't think—" Danilo says.

"Who is the doctor here?"

As the space between the two halves of the table widens, it feels like her arms and legs are being ripped out of their sockets. And as her body stretches, so, too, her mind undergoes an expansion. Pavla is on the table being pulled in opposite directions while another Pavla stands next to Danilo, watching as he slowly turns the crank. The distance between her two selves feels immeasurable—it could be only a couple of meters or it could be of a scale larger by hundreds. Or perhaps the measurements she uses on her father's maps are insufficient and the distance must be calculated in days or even years. In fact, she is not certain that there is distance, because she is no longer confident that she is in a place with the sort of assurance she normally feels, when she can sense the boundaries of her crib, her home, the walk to town, even the distance between her village and the ones her parents have taken her to in an effort to cure her. There they are, cowering in the corner of the room, horrified by what they are witnessing and yet they do nothing to stop it. She wonders who they are, these people she loves, who she believed would protect her. As the Pavla on the table feels her muscles stretch to their limit, the Pavla standing next to Danilo feels another kind of dislocation, for she is no longer certain who she is. The world has become suddenly enormous. It not only includes the girl on the table but it also includes the girl who is watching the girl on the table, and if this is true, it must also include another girl watching that girl, and on and on.

"Stop it! Stop it!" she hears, although she does not know who is speaking, if it is Danilo, her father, or her mother. Or herself. The words spread out around her, invade her ears, her mouth until it seems as if the sound becomes her. And then the noise is so thick in her ears that she can't even hear it. All that is left is silence.

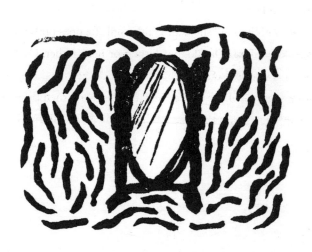

C ome see the Wolf Girl!" Danilo shouts. The day is wet and cold. What few carnival patrons there are wander slowly from one soggy and sagging exhibition tent to another, their shoulders hunched against the steady rain. "The body of a girl, the head of a wolf! Only two koruny!"

Smetanka originally displayed Pavla as the Were-Woman, thinking that the inferred combination of two terrifying beings, a werewolf and a sexually potent female, would make his show irresistible. But one day, when Danilo mistakenly (or not— Smetanka has eyes; he is no fool) announced the attraction as the Wolf Girl, the crowd doubled. It turns out there is nothing remarkable in people's minds about the idea of a grown woman with hair on her face, whereas a young girl trapped in the bloom of her youth by an inescapable hideousness summons up the simultaneous feelings of horror and fascination that are the necessary ingredients of a successful freak attraction. It doesn't hurt that, along with her awful yet stunning transformation, Pavla's body has filled out in the highly appealing manner of a virgin on the cusp. Her bust is of a pleasing roundness, her narrow waist flares gracefully at the hips, and even though her face has lost its former beauty (and Smetanka had noticed what a pretty little dwarf she was when the old couple brought her in) and she now looks out at the world through those eerie, yellow eyes, and though the palest russet down covers her cheeks and the shape of her face is dominated by an elongated nose that could reasonably be likened to a snout, she carries her now tall body with the candid informality of a girl who has not yet been split in two by a man. Smetanka has considered changing this condition on more than one cold and drunken night in the godforsaken caravan where the three of them live like dirty gypsies, but he knows the way an ill-used woman carries her resentment. It hardens her face and thickens her middle and makes her fearful and hesitant and then unpredictably violent, and he has to protect his investment.

Perhaps due to the weather or because the act is not as popular as others on offer—the human skeleton, the three-titted woman, the giant with a penis the size of an elephant's, the great regurgitator—the crowds are sparse. Once the tent is half filled and Smetanka judges the anticipation to be at its peak but not quite beyond it, when he knows that frustrated waiting will erupt into brawls and an unprofitable evening, he pushes Pavla onto the small wooden platform that serves as the stage. She wears a white gown that grabs at her waist and bust, and which she complains, quite correctly, is translucent when she is not covering her body, head, and face with the red cape, as she does at the beginning of every show. Following Smetanka's directions, and they had to rehearse this many times—the girl is no actress—she begins to pantomime the part of a young maiden out for a leisurely stroll. She sashays just as he has told her to, exaggerating the swing of her hips and making sure to part the cape occasionally so that the onlookers can glimpse her figure beneath the gossamer material of her dress. She crouches down to pluck an imaginary rose and then stands and admires it. The crowd begins to grow restless. "We're not here to see Sněhurka and her seven fucking dwarves," a man calls out, demanding his money back. Now it is time for Danilo to take the stage. Wearing stockings and a pair of threadbare breeches and holding a rusty sword by his side, he is the prince. He mimes being surprised then captivated by the young woman with the hidden face. As instructed, Danilo manipulates the sword so that its tip begins to rise. Hoots. Shrill whistles. Off to the side of the stage, Smetanka smiles to himself; the crowd is in his hands.

"Who is this young woman?" Danilo says.

Your mother! Someone invariably shouts. *Your sister!*

"She is the most mysterious lady I have ever seen. I must have her!" Danilo exclaims. "Yon maiden, show me your countenance!"

"I cannot do what you ask, kind sir," she says.

"If you reveal yourself, I will marry you and take you to live with me in my castle and you shall have everything you have ever dreamed of," Danilo says.

Smetanka bobs his head as Danilo makes the sword bounce up and down furiously to the predictable delight of the audience.

"Alas, I am cursed to wander this earth without ever showing my face," Pavla says.

She tells her story: She was born the most beautiful girl in all the land. When rumor of her glory spread, princes the world over offered all their wealth to have her. But at her birth, an old witch put a curse on her saying that if she were ever to expose her beauty, she would lose it.

"You mean to tell me that no man has ever seen your eyes? That no man has ever kissed your lips?" Danilo says.

The men in the audience grow impatient: *Who needs to see the face? Let her show you the lips that count!* But Smetanka is not worried. This small interlude of romance is dedicated to the women who predictably swoon and shush their rude spouses and who, Smetanka knows from months of traveling from one town to the next with this low-rent carnival, will be the ones to insist on a second viewing. These are women who spend their days gutting fish and wiping baby asses and whose only pleasure comes from the belief that all that separates them from their deliverance is a glance from a man of quality.

"If I cannot see you then at least do me the honor of dancing with me," Danilo says.

Smetanka winds up an old, beat-up music box and Pavla and Danilo perform the dance he has choreographed for them—two steps to the left, two to the right, break apart, turn a circle, come together again. As instructed, Danilo's hand slides down her backside. She lets out a low rumble of warning. Danilo takes her noise as an expression of passion and, turning to the audience, winks broadly. And then the climax: Danilo, overcome by love, must gaze upon the object of his obsession. With one swift movement he tears off her cape to reveal not a beauty but a face so unexpected and terrible that he backs up in horror.

The audience gasps. Sometimes, and this is good for business, a woman will faint. Danilo, affecting disgust, flees the stage leaving Pavla alone. In the wings, Smetanka, the exacting maestro, mimes her gestures, as onstage Pavla curtsies like a girl and then growls like a wolf. She watches the expressions before her turn from surprise to nervous hilarity to a reckless abandonment of manners as both men and women shout insults and throw stones and fistfuls of dirt at her. As always happens, someone complains loudly that what they are seeing is not real, that the girl is merely wearing a disguise, and that they have all been tricked. But a man—and this happens every time because Smetanka pays someone in the audience beforehand—steps onto the stage and, putting his hands around Pavla's neck, begins to yank on her head in order to unmask her and reveal the face of a normal girl underneath. Pavla shrieks, sometimes with genuine fright, depending on the force or drunkenness of the shill. Now it is Smetanka's turn to take the stage dressed in a tattered waistcoat and half-stoved-in top hat like the third-rate impresario he is.

"Sir," he shouts over the noise of the audience. "Is she real?"

"She is real!" the man declares.

"There you have it, ladies and gentlemen," Smetanka says. "Behold, the Wolf Girl!"

———

"I'M OFF TO SEE TO SOME BUSINESS," Smetanka announces. The final show of the evening is over. He has tallied the paltry sales, given Pavla and Danilo a few coins each, and left them to clean up the tent. The two are well aware that this "business" has to do with Civan Farkas, the Fattest Man in the World, who brews a putrid but effective trash-can rum, and some cheap and available ladies. When Smetanka finally returns to the caravan, he will either be rageful or weepy or both.

Pavla is exhausted. It is not that her duties are so difficult or that it takes any effort to remember her part. But in five months she has not gotten used to the dangerous energy of the crowd. During her dwarfish childhood when she was pitied and teased, occasionally accused of being the cause of a spate of fever or a poor crop yield, she never felt what she does now each night: that she is one step away from being murdered. She is, after all, the synthesis of two things men have a need to routinely destroy: animals and women.

Pavla and Danilo wander the tent, picking up spent cigarettes and broken bottles.

"It took Smetanka too long to get that man off me," she says, rubbing her neck. Tonight's designated attacker was zealous, and she can hardly turn her head to the right.

It pains Danilo, this charade of violence, the risk to Pavla, and his inability to protect her. Smetanka is surprisingly strong and he prevents Danilo from going back onto the stage to rescue her from whatever brute he's paid. The crowd has to reach a level of frenzy that will ensure future audiences. He picks up an orphaned glove, tosses it onto the pile of collected trash. "We could refuse to do that part," he says, but he knows his words are not backed up by any will. It shames him that it is not Smetanka's strength that holds him back but the threat of being fired. Pavla turns to face him. Although the range of her expressions has diminished since her change, she manages to convey what she means, which is that there is nothing either of them can do to alter the situation.

"I know," Danilo says. He looks away. He is always looking away even though this is exactly the opposite of what he wants to do, which is to stare into her strange and beautiful amber eyes, to trace their outlines, which angle down toward her nose, to study the variegated hues of the hair that dusts her narrow face. The wolfish features are unmistakable and they would be horrible were it not that he can sometimes, when she looks at him a certain way, or cocks her head just so, see the girl he met at Smetanka's office so many months ago, the one whose face was so remarkable that he could think of nothing to say to her other than to compare her to ponies. Her eyes were blue then but no less unnerving, their color unfathomably deep. She was small and oddly formed, and yet her creamy skin, her sumptuous curls, and that gaze which seemed guileless and knowing at the same time—she'd moved him more than any girl he'd ever seen.

But he knows that if he looked at her now the way he dreams of, taking her in fully, letting her see his desire for her, she would be insulted. She is too used to being stared at, to seeing the curious, then leering, then repulsed expressions on the faces of strangers. How could he convey to her that his interest is any different?

And is it? Would he really take her in his arms? Would he lay his cheek next to hers, feel the bristles there, run his hand over her long nose and not be sickened? Would he brush her mouth with his lips?

She picks up a pair of lady's underwear that has, inexplicably, been left on the ground. She twirls it around on her finger and laughs before letting it sail and land on top of the trash. Their cleaning duties done, she wraps herself in a ragged shawl. "You should leave," she says. "Get away from him. I don't know why you don't."

Danilo tries to hide his disappointment. They have had this discussion many times before. Of course she has no option but to stay with Smetanka. Who else would employ her? How would she live? Václav's plumbing business folded once the village learned what he and his wife had done to their daughter. Her parents are living off money from the deal they struck with Smetanka whereby he sends them a percentage of her earnings each month. Her work is all that is keeping them alive. But Danilo is another story.

"I won't leave you alone with him," he says.

"Your guilt doesn't do me any good," she says.

The truth of this stabs him. How could she ever care for him? It was he who built the table, who turned the crank. It was he who didn't have the nerve to stand up to his employer then just as he doesn't now.

He started to work for Smetanka when he was seventeen and his twin brother fell ill with a fever that wouldn't abate. His family did not have the money for the doctor's care and so offered their healthy son as payment. Despite Smetanka's prescriptions, the twin did not survive. After a year of unpaid service to the doctor, Danilo settled the family's debt. But when he returned home, he found that his parents no longer wanted him there. Although the birth of twins had been considered a sign of great luck, the boy's death signaled that the family's good fortune had turned and that they were cursed. Danilo, as the living representation of their failure, made it impossible for his father, a cobbler, to attract new business, and even loyal customers began to take their worn-down shoes elsewhere. Where once every self-respecting family wanted a newborn to wear a pair of Novák soft leather booties at first communion, or a daughter to be shod in a pair of Novák satin wedding slippers on her special day, now to ask the shoemaker to punch an extra hole in a belt to accommodate an expanding waist was to court bad fortune. Danilo was a torture for his grieving mother. When he arrived home from Smetanka's after that first indentured year, she screamed as if she were seeing a ghost, and it was hours before her husband could calm her enough to convince her that Danilo was not her beloved dead son come back to haunt her. But even then, she would not look at him. With no family business for Danilo to inherit, no mother willing to cook for him and give him a bed to sleep in, and no one else in town offering to take him on as an apprentice, all that was left for Danilo was to return to the employ of the doctor at unfavorable terms: in exchange for his work, he would be allowed to sleep in the storage closet and receive one and a half meals a day.

Danilo had little formal learning, but it did not take him

long to realize that the doctor had not much more in the way of medical education. Although there were fat and important-looking texts in the office, they were mostly used to block the cold wind that snaked under the window sash during winter or to crush mice. The storeroom where Danilo spread his blanket each evening was a nightmare bower whose shelves were lined with medical curiosities the doctor had collected over the years from traveling vendors who traded in the macabre. One jar was filled with a baby's foot that had a single toe as long as the sole of the foot itself. In another dangled the translucent hair of an African albino. Suspended in a viscous liquid was, according to Smetanka, a still-beating heart. Although Danilo was reasonably certain a heart could not function outside a body, there were times, late at night, lying awake on his blanket in the airless cubicle, when he could swear that he heard the measured thump of that organ. He would weep, thinking of his brother whose death left him feeling as if he were trapped in a dream of being lost.

Over the next two years, Danilo worked ceaselessly without even a Sunday off to rest. One of his tasks was to formulate the concoctions Smetanka prescribed for his patients' ailments. The doctor would write out specific instructions, and though barely literate, Danilo would follow them as well as he could, using a mortar and pestle to grind various leaves and grasses and twigs along with certain stones the doctor claimed were laced with beneficial minerals. There were relatively few ingredients in Smetanka's home apothecary, and what made each cure specific seemed to be a matter only of proportion and nomenclature. In this way, Danilo produced Essential Carminative for Disorders in the Stomach and Bowels, Famous Patent Ointment for Itch, Much Esteemed Drops for Venereal Complaints, and Sovereign Restorative Infusion for Barrenness. The remedy Smetanka recommended most often was his celebrated Purging Elixir, although one day, Danilo, moved by curiosity, tasted a few of the other treatments and found that nearly all of them produced that explosive outcome.

He felt sorry and vaguely guilty as he watched grateful patients hand over their money for the doctor's bogus cures and he was surprised when these same patients returned to the office a week or two weeks later, carrying presents of fresh baked bread or recently slaughtered ducks, tearfully grateful that their health had been restored. There were, of course, patients, like Danilo's brother, who died despite the doctor's efforts. But somehow Smetanka escaped blame, for the deeply religious people who lived in the town and the surrounding villages knew God's will when they saw it.

Although he was deeply embarrassed to do it, Danilo told Pavla the events surrounding her terrible ordeal while under the doctor's care: As soon as she and her parents left the office after their first visit, Smetanka ordered Danilo to turn away the rest of the day's patients. A miller arrived with his apprentice who was bleeding profusely from the hand, and Danilo had to instruct them to visit the village seamstress, who might just as easily sew on the salvaged thumb as attach a sleeve to a shirt. A woman with a jaw swollen to the size of an orange and as hot as fire to the touch walked away holding her throbbing head in her hands as if she would just as soon take it off and leave it by the side of the road. Danilo chased after her and handed her a vial of Smetanka's Miracle Salve for Toothache even though he knew it was useless and that he would catch hell once the doctor realized he'd given away medicine for free. Finally, at midday, just as Danilo was sitting down to eat his half meal of bread and watery ale, the door of the office opened and Smetanka emerged. His face was flushed and sweaty, and his eyes darted wildly back and forth. In his hand he held a rough sketch that, after sweeping Danilo's meal onto the floor, he lay in front of the boy. The drawing showed a curious table that was split down the middle crosswise. Another drawing showed the table pulled into two.

"Make it work," the doctor said. "You have until tomorrow morning."

It was, Danilo was ashamed to admit to Pavla, an exciting assignment. The challenge of interpreting the doctor's slapdash design and inventing solutions to the problems that arose gave Danilo a remarkable feeling, one he had never experienced before, not when he was a boy learning the shoe trade with his brother under the disapproving gaze of their father, certainly not when he prepared those idiotic potions for the doctor. For the first time in his life, he not only realized he had a brain but that he was putting it to use. The project took him into the night and the early hours of the morning. Mistakes were made. Hours of work had to be dismantled when the trusses on which each half of the table was meant to glide got stuck. But finally, he managed to get all the actions to work in concert: a crank turned, the rope navigated smoothly through the pulleys that he'd mounted on the underside of the table, the split plank opened and closed as smoothly as a jaw. He worked with such concentrated intensity and with such pride in his newly discovered abilities that he did not once stop to wonder what the doctor had in mind for this contraption. Instead, he began to imagine a life for himself where doctors would come from near and far to order medical appliances that only he could make. He would save the reputation of his family. His parents might even allow him to come back home. He would once again taste his mother's eight-hour pork roast. He could feel his tongue swell with the memory of the succulent fat.

The following day, the dwarf girl and her parents returned to the office. Wrapped in a blanket and carried in her father's arms, she whimpered pathetically and seemed nearly dead. Danilo was terrified when, for the briefest moment, he caught her eyes and saw there not a look of misery or fear, but utter vacancy. He could not look at her again. Her loveliness that had so captivated him and everything that had made him unaccountably shy and say stupid things, were gone, not as if these qualities had disappeared but as if they had never existed in the first place and he had dreamed the whole thing up. She was no more inside her body than his brother was when he lay in his coffin and Danilo bent to kiss his forehead. Like him, she was only a container of emptiness. Her beautiful hair was matted. The skin of her neck and face was sallow. Her eyes were as milky and lifeless as the eyes of the blind woman in his village who had memorized the feel of various palms so that she could thank you by name if you were generous enough to give her a few haléřs or a piece of cheese. The petrified father looked at the doctor beseechingly, asking him if they had not understood the prescription correctly, for what the girl had endured the previous night had not made her taller, even by a centimeter. Danilo still did not understand what it was the old couple had done to her, but when the doctor ordered the father to take away the blanket, and before the mother demanded she be covered with a sheet, he saw the terrible burns that covered her naked body and the welts that were newly risen and filled with pus. His vision fogged and he broke out into a sweat. He lifted the girl onto the machine, *his* machine, as his mind, with which he had only recently become acquainted, finally grasped his invention's purpose. Like the parents, though, he was too stunned by incomprehension and fear to question the doctor, and following orders like a dumb mule, he affixed the girl's arms and legs to the straps that he had so carefully made using the leatherwork techniques his father had taught him. When he turned the crank, she made a wretched noise, but he could hardly hear her through the sound of his own scream.

Pavla *did not blame Danilo then* and does not blame him now for what happened. And even though she was angry with her parents for wanting her to change, she does not blame them either. How could they or anyone have known what would happen to her? That she would not only grow as they had hoped, but that with her height would come this other unbidden disfigurement? But just as she learned that love is not always kind and is never simple, she does not allow herself to mistake Danilo's interest in her for anything other than what it is, a blend of guilt and pity and decency. During the long, slow drives following the parade of ramshackle conveyances that carry the fat man and giant man and the three-headed snake and all the other attractions from one town to the next, Smetanka sleeps off the previous night's drunkenness in the back of the caravan while she sits next to Danilo on the wagon bench. Sometimes they trade carnival gossip about the separate romances of the conjoined Chinese twins. All Danilo has to say is "Can you please look the other way?" and he and Pavla fall against each other laughing. But as their bodies meet and then part and then meet again, their laughter becomes self-conscious so that every snort of the horse or crack of stones underneath a hoof feels as embarrassing as if one of them burped. They fall silent, and lulled by the slow rocking of the wagon and the nearness of him, she drifts into daydreams. He will put his hands on her face. He will brush her lips with his. He will— But the fantasy only serves to make her acutely aware of its implausibility. For how does she differ from Ling Ling and Ting Ting, whose names are really Marika and Markéta and who are from a village not far from Pavla's, but who are transformed into Oriental exotics by virtue of white face paint and black kohl? Or from Rosta, who is so thin that you can see every vein and bone in his body through his nearly pellucid skin? Or Juliska, whose folds of belly fat fall down to her knees? Or Leopold, who can swallow a padlock, a colored ball, and a live mouse, chase all of it down with a pint of beer, then regurgitate everything in whatever order the crowd demands? Perhaps, just now, the others are having a laugh at the expense of her hairy cheeks, which Smetanka forbids her to shave, or her ears, which twitch when she is nervous. If it weren't for the clatter and squeal of the wagon wheels she might be able to hear them, for her ears capture sounds she has never heard before. At night, she can hear worms inching up the sides of the caravan. She can hear a blade of grass rub against its neighbor.

How could he want her?

The two leave the tent and walk out into the crisp night. Her stretched muscles have mostly healed but walking is painful. Knowing this, Danilo moves slowly. Anyway, there is no rush to get back to the caravan. As tired as they are, sleep only means that the next night will come that much more quickly and with it more humiliation. They pass the fortune-teller's tent. Inside, her lamp is still burning. A gust of wind, and the wooden board advertising "Fortunate Františka" knocks against its post.

"You don't have money to waste," Pavla says, but she knows Danilo won't be able to resist throwing away his pitiful salary on Františka the Faker, as Pavla refers to the old woman.

"You're the one who said all time exists," Danilo says. "The past exists. The future exists."

It's true. She did say this. And she does somehow believe that what has happened to her and what will happen exist simultaneously, that the story is already written but not yet told. She must be like someone in one of her mother's tales who has existed for centuries of telling and will live on even after her mother is gone. How else to explain her life? As something random?

"You said we just have to look hard and we will see what will happen to us," he continues.

"Františka can't even see her own hand in front of her face," she says, laughing. Her voice is a girl's, but her laugh is a short, scratchy inhuman bark.

"Behold a blind woman who can see the future!" Danilo says dramatically, imitating Františka's husband when he tries to draw people to her tent. The joke around the carnival is that if Františka could have known that the only man on earth who would fuck her was one with a goiter the size of a melon protruding from the side of his neck, she would have foreseen her death and killed herself. There is some rumor that Františka is not blind at all, that the impairment is simply a gimmick thought up by her canny husband. Someone saw her walk clear across the carnival grounds without once stepping in the mule turds that the animals drop as they carry children on laborious circuits around the amusements. Someone else claims to have caught her staring at herself in her mirror.

"Come with me," Danilo says. "Just once."

"I'd prefer to eat," she says, jangling her change purse.

"I'll pay for us both."

She sighs. "You're an idiot," she says fondly, following him.

Inside, the tent is painted blood red, and the flickering lamp casts an eerie glow over everything, including the old, shriveled woman who sits at her velvet-draped table tearing apart a piece of ham with her fingers. "Go away. I'm done for the night," Františka croaks.

"Then why is your lamp still lit?" Pavla says.

"How would I know if it is or not? That rascal who calls himself my husband has not bothered to drag himself home tonight to close up, so here I am, trying to eat my supper and having to fend off the likes of you." She sniffs. "It's that little goat girl, isn't it?"

"Wolf girl," Danilo says.

"It all smells the same to me."

Pavla, like all the resident freaks, is used to talk like this and takes no offense. Anyway, she is too busy trying to suss out whether the woman is a scammer or not. She looks around the tent for clues. A full-length mirror stands against an upended trunk, although a cloth covers the glass. Crude paintings of turbaned mystics and one of an open hand with an eye in the center of the palm hang on the tent poles, but the decorations could just as easily be there to create an air of foreign mystery for the fortune-teller's patrons as for Františka's ocular enjoyment. Certainly the painting of the woman clothed in nothing but a diaphanous scarf that winds its way like a snake between her legs and over one breast must be there for the pleasure of Františka's husband, who is right this moment probably spending his wife's wages on one of the prostitutes who descend like buzzards each time the carnival arrives in a new town.

"We want you to read our fortunes," Danilo says. He puts two coins down on the table to show he means business.

"You have no fortune," the old woman says, devouring the last bite of her ham and sucking her fingers clean.

"Everyone has a fortune," Pavla says.

"No. I'm telling you. You have none. Your fortune is that you have none. Now go away."

"If you are telling us we're poor, we hardly need to pay money to learn that," Danilo says.

The woman shrugs, taking a bite of bread and chewing slowly.

"Take your money back," Pavla says to Danilo.

He reaches for the coins, but the woman is quick and her hand covers them before he gets there.

"You mean we have no luck?" Pavla says.

"So the wolf is the smart one. Smart as a wolf."

"Smart as a fox," Pavla says.

"Fox. Wolf, cat, dog. They are all apparently smarter than that one." She looks directly at Danilo, and for a moment, Pavla is certain the woman can see perfectly.

"I'm smart enough to know it doesn't take a seer to tell us that we're down on our luck," Danilo says.

"I told you, I'm closed for business."

Pavla whispers to Danilo that they should go. She hasn't eaten all day.

"You took my money," Danilo says. "I want my fortune."

"Alright," the woman says. "Here it is: one of you will be brave, one of you will be a coward. One of you will believe. One of you will doubt."

"Which one—" Pavla says, but Danilo interrupts her.

"But what about love?" he asks. "Will I find love?"

"Love!" the woman exclaims. "All anyone wants to know about is love! My God! Is there nothing more important on earth than that? Why don't you ask the necessary questions: Will I have food in my belly? Will I have all my teeth? Will I be able to urinate without pain? But no, it's always love! It's pathetic."

"But what is the answer?" Pavla says quietly. She is not sure she wants to hear. "Will he have love in his life?"

"Yes, he will have love. No, he will not have love. It's all the same to me. Now get out!"

—————

THEY ARE QUIET as they walk the rest of the way home. The giant stands near his caravan taking one of his epic pisses after a night of heavy drinking. He's fallen asleep during the endless evacuation, and Danilo and Pavla watch in awe as he tilts precariously toward his splatter. Just before he topples, he wakes himself with a snort, and they have to run to avoid the wayward geyser. Laughter rings out from the home of Juliska, the Fattest Woman. There is a happy person, Pavla thinks. And it is true. There is never a moment when that woman is not filled with mirth. Her joy seems to reside in the folds of her neck and the jiggle of each buttock, which she can, amazingly, sway in opposite directions. Unlike some of the other performers whose lives of being tormented have made them hard-edged and bitter, Juliska takes as much pleasure in displaying herself as do those who pay to see her. As a result, she never receives the sorts of taunts or the barrage of flying objects that are Pavla's regular due. Pavla once snuck into Juliska's tent and watched her perform. The woman showed off the magnificence of her body as if she were displaying the most mouthwatering desserts. *Here is my giant arm*, she seemed to be saying, allowing a lucky patron to reach out a finger and set the fat into pendulous motion. *Here is my mighty thigh.* The men, for her patrons are mostly men, women not being the least entranced by flab, responded by treating her with enormous care, touching her as though she were something delicate. Because of her welcome and her generous love for them, she had been transposed in their minds into the statue of the virgin they were allowed to carry in the processions when they were boys, bearing her giant wooden body aloft like a miracle. How proud they felt to be given the awesome responsibility to guard that simulacrum of sacred flesh!

Pavla supposes it's different for Juliska and the giant, who have lived with their curious bodies their entire lives and who have never known themselves to be other than the porcine or enormous people they are. Had she remained a dwarf, she believes that she would have been as happy as Juliska. But she has become unfamiliar to herself.

After fainting on the stretching table, she woke up to the sound of saw teeth gnashing against wood. For a moment, she thought she was still in the doctor's office and that something new and even more horrifying was about to happen to her, but then she looked around and saw the slats of her crib on either side of her head. She was home, and everything around her was recognizable if only a bit more snug than she recalled. It was when she looked down . . . and down toward a pair of bafflingly distant feet that she realized the sawing noise was coming from the bottom of the crib, and that her father had, while she was sleeping, removed the slats to make way for her—yes, they belonged to her—very long legs.

Before she could take full stock of her growth, she heard weeping. She sat up and looked over the crib rail (and not simply through the bars anymore) and saw her mother sitting on the chair, her face in her hands.

"Mama, don't cry. Look, I am tall!" Pavla said. But when she reached toward her mother, the pain in her armpits was so searing she fell back against the mattress.

For the first few days, her parents ministered to her with warm compresses and emollients of honey and egg whites to soothe her skin where the hot oil had made it blistered and raw. Once the pulled muscles at her groin had healed and she was strong enough to stand, they helped her adapt to her new height. It was strange to feel her body move through familiar space in such drastically new ways. She felt that she was standing at the edge of a cliff and was always just about to plummet headfirst to her death. Her first steps were stiff and tentative; she did not trust these new limbs to hold her upright. She had to think her way from the sink to the door. *Move your left leg*, she would say to herself, *now the right*. She and her parents even laughed when, reaching for a cup and saucer for her tea, she swung her arm well above the level of the shelf and toppled a bowl of peaches in the process. Her father clapped when she experimented with running from the house to the chicken coop. She no longer needed to lurch from side to side as she once did; her legs carried her smoothly forward. Still, there were moments when she caught both her parents staring at her with frightened expressions on their faces, and her mother wept at night when she thought Pavla was asleep.

"What is wrong?" she asked them the following morning. "I am tall just as you wanted me to be. Why do you look away? Why does Mama cry?"

And it was only then, under duress, that her mother opened

the wardrobe door and beckoned Pavla to stand in front of the mirror they had looked into so often when Pavla was a baby, the one that finally reflected back to Agáta not a terrible mistake but her very own beloved daughter. For the first time since coming home from the doctor's, Pavla saw her face. Slowly, she brought her hand to her furred cheeks, ran her finger down her long nose, stared into the yellowish eyes. She didn't cry. She didn't make a sound. She thought: I am looking into a mirror at a girl who looks nothing like me but who is me. And I am looking at the girl looking at herself in the mirror seeing the person who is nothing like herself but is herself.

"Mama?" she said. "I don't understand. Is this me?"

"You're still beautiful to us," her mother said.

A LIE, OF COURSE, Pavla thinks now, as she walks beside Danilo. But love is filled with lies. *We like you just the way you are. You are still beautiful. We will always be with you.* She believes her parents do not love her less, only that before, she had a child's notion of love that did not include the small treacheries of delusion and fear and shame.

"What do you think she meant by all that?" Danilo says.

"Who?"

"Františka. That I will have love and that I won't have love."

"She meant that you just wasted all your money," Pavla says. "She made a fool of you." She doesn't want to be so harsh.

After all, Danilo is her only friend. But his question to the fortune-teller stung her, paralyzing her hope. "Will *I* find love?" he asked, and made himself clear. If he were interested in her that way he would not have had to ask. She is with him every day of their lives. But he said "I" and in so doing severed himself from her. She is not the future he is hoping to discover by throwing away his money on someone who, whether she is sighted or not, is no more a fortune-teller than Smetanka was ever a doctor.

"You should leave this place," she says for the second time that night. But now, rather than say it to reassure herself of his fidelity, she wants to remind him of his inability to imagine something greater for himself. She decides to despise him for his lack of confidence. It is easier to hate him.

Later that night, Smetanka finally returns to the caravan. His face is covered with blood, and his mouth is two teeth poorer for whatever scrape he got himself into. He is filled with sloppy, borovička-fueled rage about how little money the act brought in.

"You are neither wolf nor girl," he yells at Pavla. "You are nothing."

"I know," Pavla says calmly. "I'm a little nothing. Although I'm a bigger nothing than I used to be."

Smetanka opens his mouth to speak but what emerges is a slurred and inarticulate growl.

"Perhaps you should be the one on stage," she says. Danilo, lying on a clump of clothes that serves as his bed, laughs.

Smetanka lunges for her, but Danilo quickly crawls between them and pushes Smetanka, who is so drunk that he falls easily.

"You owe my parents ten percent, don't forget," Pavla says.

"Ten percent of nothing," Smetanka says. "You're not pulling in the crowds, and anyway I was robbed tonight."

"Ten percent," Pavla says. "That was the agreement."

A month or so after the stretching treatment, Smetanka had shown up at her parents' door. He'd presented his offer as a great opportunity, claiming that some of the world's most important medical advancements were first introduced "on the circuit," and that once the learned men of the academies got wind of what a small provincial doctor (and here, Smetanka smiled with false humility) had discovered, he would be celebrated. His experiment would be written up in important journals. He would be called upon to lecture all over the land. He would take Pavla with him as a living, breathing, and irrefutably tall proof of his genius. She would be celebrated, too. Riches, he said with assurance, would follow. Agáta and Václav were horrified at the thought of selling their daughter, but before they could chase the doctor out of the house (Agáta actually wielded her rolling pin), Pavla intervened. In the month following her startling change, she watched her father's business dry up. When the neighbors got wind of what had happened, they came to the door to slake their curiosity. They barely hid their delight in discovering that although the girl, who was so much more beautiful than any of their daughters, had grown to a normal size, her face had taken an alarming turn for the worse. *Those sickly yellow eyes! That unfortunate facial hair! She looks a bit doggish, don't you think?* Pavla was, once again, her mother's disgrace. She took to concealing herself in the standing wardrobe to avoid their naked stares. And while she crouched among her father and mother's clothing, inhaling what was once the comforting scent of flowered soap that lived in the fibers of her mother's dresses and the sharp odor of grease on her father's shirts, she saw plainly, as if a light were shining in the darkness of the cabinet, that the rest of her life would be spent hiding from the world. She would be trapped in the confines of the small cottage. Her longest journey might be the one from the front door to the garden to pick carrots and beets and back again.

"I want to go with him," she declared, before the doctor had left the house. Václav and Agáta refused, but she prevailed. "There is nothing for me here," she told them.

"We are here," Agáta said weakly.

What more needed to be said? Agáta and Václav knew they had little to offer their daughter. Pavla knew that if she left, her parents' final years might not be filled with hardship. Smetanka might have ruined her, but perversely, his offer was her only chance at life. She made her father agree to the deal.

But now she realizes they have all been tricked.

"I was there," she says to Smetanka. "You shook my father's hand."

"He had a fine handshake. A workingman's handshake. Trustworthy. But I'm afraid the agreement had to do with our work advertising my medical achievement, and, well . . ."

He does not need to finish his thought. The exhibition of "Doctor Smetanka's Miracle Cure for Dwarfs of All Sizes" had been an abject failure. Wherever they went, Danilo would set up the stretching table in the town square. Pavla would lie on it while Smetanka described his "world-famous" procedure to whoever would stop and listen. He peppered his declarations with phrases like "medial compartment of the thigh" or "adductor longus" and "adductor magnus," but no matter how erudite he sounded, no one would believe that the girl on the rack (whose face he covered with a veil to "protect her privacy") was not simply tall to begin with. *Show us the proof!* they said. But even when he made Pavla open her shirt in order to display the stretched skin around her armpits, people were unconvinced. There was no fame. There were no riches. There was only the growing realization that soon they would starve. When they arrived at a town where a carnival had recently raised its tents, Smetanka ordered Danilo to dismantle the table and use the wood to build a stage.

"A handshake agreement stands. Everyone knows that," Pavla says.

"She's right," Danilo adds. "My father paid his debt to you for my brother's care with nothing but a handshake."

"Oh, you backward country children," Smetanka says, peeling off his shirt. Curls of dark hair sprout from the armholes and neckline of his undershirt. "Don't you know that we live in modern times? We live in a world of contracts and courts of law, not I'll-pay-you-tomorrow-for-the-milk-you-sell-me-today. Let me tell you a secret, little girl. Your parents ruined you."

"Whose fault was that?"

"My dear, I did exactly what I promised. Are you not tall? It's really quite remarkable. One day, people will realize what I have accomplished and I will be heralded as the true scientist that I am."

"And this?" She touches her lightly furred cheeks, draws her hands down the odd contours of her face. "Will you be praised for this?"

"Is it my fault that your ignorant parents took the advice of others before they consulted a real doctor? I can't account for the effects of all that gypsy hocus-pocus."

"You are no more doctor than any of them," Danilo says. "I saw what you gave people. I could have spit into a bottle and they would have been no worse off than they were taking your tinctures of whatever-the-hell."

The silence that follows is so taut that Danko, the high-wire acrobat, could slide across it without a hitch.

"If you are not paying for me, then I don't have to be here," Pavla says finally, more to herself than to the others. She finds a tapestry bag and begins to throw her few belongings into it.

"And where will you go?" Smetanka says, peeling off his socks and releasing the mildewed odor of his feet.

"Home."

He lies down. "What makes you so sure they want you back? They may have ruined your life, but you ruined theirs first," he says woozily, and in seconds, he is asleep.

Dispirited, she stops packing.

"Pavla," Danilo says, laying a hand on her shoulder.

She shrugs him off. Listening to Smetanka's mucus-filled snores, inhaling the stale, liquor-soaked air that rises off his skin, she begins to feel like she will suffocate. She steps over him and goes to the door.

"Let me come with you," Danilo says.

"I don't need your pity," she says.

"I don't pity you."

"Really? What do you see when you look at me? Do you see a freak?"

"No!"

"Do you see a girl?"

He hesitates. "I see," he says, stammering. "I see—"

SHE STAYS OUTSIDE all night, pacing restlessly to keep herself warm until she begins to feel like a wolf in every way, her skin and eyes and nose alert to sound and smell, to the wrinkle in the wind that tells of bats in flight. The chirrup of cicadas becomes so loud and insistent she thinks she might go insane. And like a madwoman, she strides across the sleeping village of caravans until she reaches the now darkened tent of the fortune-teller.

"Which one am I?" she says when she enters.

An elephantine lump on the bed moves. "Who is there?" Františka cries out. "We're being robbed! Do something, you idiot!" A thrashing of sheets and limbs, and then the husband stands up. A match strikes and the lamp is lit. His goiter bulges above the neckline of his nightshirt. "It's that she-wolf," Františka says from the bed.

Pavla doesn't care if the woman can see or not. "Who is it?" she demands. "Who is the brave one and who is the coward? Who believes and who doubts?"

"Get out of my house!" the man says, aiming a pistol at her.

"Yes! Kill me. Please. Do it!" Pavla says. She means it. For what is her life now that she knows the contract is a lie? Now that she is sure Danilo hopes for love, but not for her? Now that all she can foresee with or without this fraud's help is her life going on the way it is, one performance, one humiliation after another without end? This is the story that is written for her. She has already stepped into it. She can hear her mother's voice: *There once was a dwarf* . . . "Please," she says quietly. "Put me out of my misery."

"What is she talking about?" the man says. "She's not a dog."

"Put your gun away, you old fool," Františka says.

"Tell me. Please," Pavla says. "Who will he love and who will he not love?"

"Go away," the woman says. "Come back tomorrow and I'll tell you."

"I have to know now," Pavla says. She walks over to the mirror and pulls off the cloth that covers it.

She studies her face. It has changed since she first saw herself in her mother's wardrobe mirror. It is a face that is neither that of a girl nor that of a wolf, but is somehow, and more disturbingly, both. The high cheekbones of her childhood are markedly flared now and are accentuated by how narrow her face below them has become. Her nose, once so precise that a visiting magistrate ordered it to be drawn so that he could have his family portraitist replace his wife's crooked nose with Pavla's for posterity, is now so long that it defines the shape of her face. The hairs that cover her cheeks that at first were disturbing but at least pale now have acquired deep russet undertones. Taken one by one, the strangeness of her features provokes in her a kind of awe, just as her breasts or the new shapeliness of her thighs do. But when she takes in the whole effect, she understands why her audiences shriek. The true horror of her presence is not that she is a hideous girl or that she is a wolf, but that she is a bizarre combination of the two. The fortune-teller comes up behind her. Pavla still cannot tell if the woman sees or not, but it doesn't matter. She seems to know.

"You should have let him shoot me," Pavla says.

"No," the woman says, and for a minute, Pavla sees not Františka, but her mother behind her, staring past her shoulder into the mirror. "You're not going to die," the woman says, patting her back. "Now go away and leave an old couple in peace."

AFTER THAT NIGHT, Pavla's performance changes. When Danilo removes the cape, instead of simpering and pretending to be ashamed and then roaring for effect, she simply stands motionless, looking out at the audience. She waits out the horrified shrieks, the gasps, the catcalls, and stoning until that menacing energy is spent. At that point, the audience, no longer allowed to engage with her as an act, must come to different terms with the fact that she is a living truth, no more fantasy than those who look upon her. Her stillness, her unwillingness to prance and perform, become a different sort of confrontation that makes them feel less superior, vulnerable even, as if their own masks have been violently ripped away and now the truth of their ugliness and their distorted desires are on display for Pavla to see. Each night, as the women drop their hands from their eyes, as the men stop leaning into one another to tell their nasty jokes, Pavla sees in their faces not ghoulish pleasure but confusion. Why is she staring at *them*? What horror does *she* see? She watches as even the most obstreperous of them wither; their shoulders turn inward, their eyes cast about for reassurance. They grab one another's hands. People leave as quietly as they do the confessional. And then they buy a ticket for the next show.

Smetanka is delighted by the turn of events. Word spreads in advance of their arrival in new towns. The carnival's most reliable acts, Margolius, the Combustible Man, who can make smoke come out of his ears and nostrils before flames burst from the top of his head; Evo, the Fish Boy, whose mother has sewn flippers onto his back to go with the fin-like hands he was born with; and three-breasted Magdalena, and even Juliska (and Pavla feels a bit guilty about this), lose patrons to the Wolf Girl. Each night the lines in front of Smetanka's tent are the longest of them all. Pavla stops badgering Danilo about leaving. After all, she has no argument. They are neither of them indentured to the doctor and yet both of them stay.

THE CARNIVAL STOPS are few as the warm months draw to a close and by the time of the first snowfall, nearly all the acts have dispersed. The Chinese twins and the human skeleton travel to southerly countries where the season is longer. The giant returns to his village, where he spends the winter cramped inside a house he shares with his average-sized wife and children. The combustible man has been hired by a circus across the ocean where he will be shot out of a cannon while his hair is on fire. Without a plan, and fretting about money, Smetanka orders Pavla to change the act. Once she has lowered her hood and revealed herself as a wolf to the sparse, cold, and drunken audience, she and Danilo follow a new script:

"You are a wolf!" Danilo says.

"I'm no wolf. I'm a maiden," she says.

"If you are a girl, then you must prove it. Otherwise I will get my gun and shoot you and use your pelt to make a winter coat for my dear mother."

"But I have no pelt. I have skin just like any girl."

"Show me."

And so, little by little, as the stragglers in the audience hoot, Pavla begins to undress. One glove comes off. Danilo demands more proof. She removes the other. Danilo says that for all he knows she is a type of wolf out of Asia that has no hair on its paws. Off comes her boot and so on until she is down to her slip. The exposure of her stretched and scarred body is torture. Danilo falls to his knees before her and claims that hers is the most beautiful female body he has ever seen and that despite her terrible face, he promises to love her forever.

As Danilo speaks, his eyes glisten and his voice trembles. There are evenings when something unmistakable passes between them, and despite her mortification at being unclothed before the shivering onlookers, she feels she never wants the play to end. But she knows he is only acting.

"You don't have to work so hard," she says to him one evening as they clean up the tent. The night's crowd was particularly violent. A man not preselected by Smetanka stormed the stage and grabbed Pavla from behind, grinding himself into her. "You don't have to convince anybody. They just want to see me strip."

"You're making fun of me."

"I'm just trying to save your wasted effort."

"It's no effort. And it's not wasted," he says quietly.

His intensity is unnerving. He starts toward her and for a moment, she forgets who she is. But then her terror overwhelms her, and just when he is close enough that she can smell his breath, she lets out a roar and he backs away.

Danilo does not walk her to the caravan. She supposes he has gone to the tents Smetanka visits to drink and perhaps find a woman he can pay to do what she is too scared to do. Nights are freezing now, and once she is inside the caravan, she lies down, still bundled in her coat. She worries about what will happen to her. The towns are shuttering for winter. Most people will not earn money until planting season, and when even the most debauched and desperate citizens can't afford the price of a ticket, Smetanka will not be able to pay her even the few coins he does now. She can't go home and make her parents' lives more difficult. She has nowhere to go. Maybe she could trade her services as a housekeeper in exchange for a room until the season begins again. She laughs at her preposterous optimism. Who would hire her? She will have to sell herself to the lowest kind of men who would find her an erotic thrill. She has heard women complain about the treatment they receive at the hands of their drunk husbands and lovers. And the carnival whores. Women with bruised faces. Women who cannot walk properly for a week after a rough night. She remembers her mother's stories about the monster and the sausage. She begins to drop off to sleep. With Danilo, it would be sweeter. Such intensity to his gaze, as if he were always on the verge of telling her something she wants to hear. She closes her eyes and lets herself imagine his hands on her face, the face of her girlhood, when she was the pride of the village with her azure eyes and golden hair. His hands pass over her shoulders and her chest. And then they move down. She unbuttons her coat. She pulls up the hem of her dress and finds the warm skin of her belly. Her fingers slide beneath the waistband of her underwear. She lays her hand on the fur that is meant to be there, that all women have. For she is a woman, isn't she? Isn't she? She closes her eyes. The caravan door squeaks open. She hears footsteps, the rustle of cloth. Her Danilo. He's forgone the prostitutes. He's come back. *You will find love*, Františka told him. He must realize that he already has, that she is here, that she has summoned him with her thoughts! His hand is on her arm.

"Dani," she whispers. He moans. She feels the warmth of his fingers on her skin. When he runs his hands over the numbed scars at her armpits and around her groin, she feels nothing. But that insensitivity only makes the feeling of his fingers on the undamaged parts of her all the more exquisite. She feels the weight of him as he moves on top of her, as his leg parts her thighs. He exhales heavily, his breath smells of—

She opens her eyes just as Smetanka grabs her crotch. She screams and tries to push him off her, but he is too heavy. She cries for Danilo, but he does not come. Smetanka spits into his hand and reaches down then pushes himself at her, groping for entry. She opens her mouth to cry out one last time, then just as he is about to enter her, she closes her jaw around his neck and sinks her teeth into his skin. The taste stuns her. It is as if she has been starving and finally had her first bite of meat. She clamps down to secure his neck between her jaws and then shakes her head back and forth to loosen the meat from the bone. And now she can think of nothing but eating more, of filling her belly to steel herself against the oncoming winter. Effortlessly, she throws him off. She mounts his cowering body and attacks his face. She swallows and goes for his stomach, his thighs. She turns him over and bites down on the fleshy mounds of his buttocks. When she has finished, and there is nothing left of him but bone and sinew and hair, she lifts her head and howls.

The *bullet is lodged in her flank.* She twists around and licks the wound, trying to dislodge the nugget of metal, but it is wedged in too deep. She should never have gotten hurt. She should have been nimble and swift and able to run well out of the reach of the mob. But the meat she ate in the caravan was stewed in the same foul brew that drenches the sweat of her pursuers and it has made her slow. Now, as she begins to move again, she feels as if she were pushing her legs through deep mud even though the ground is cold and hard. A day ago, the first snow fell and although it melted quickly in the open fields, here in the forest where, despite a bare canopy, the sun seldom penetrates, it patchworks the ground and gathers in drifts at the bases of trees. The cold feels welcome on her paws, and when gusts of icy wind whip through the branches and seep into the outer layer of her fur, the dullness of her body abates and she feels physically alert. She wants to roll around in the soft snow and numb her flank, to eat mouthfuls of the stuff to moisten her dry tongue. But she hears the snap and splinter of wood, then heavy bodies crashing through thickets. They have been following her trail of blood and now they are close.

She lifts her snout and opens her jaw. The sound begins as a silence in her chest as the bellows of her lungs expand. She tilts her head back to make more space in her throat. The sound needs to travel, she doesn't know how far. For a moment, she hesitates. She is alone and injured. The men are near. Her sound will lead them right to her. But she will not survive on her own. The note vibrates in her gullet and against the roof of her mouth. It starts low, and then her throat constricts so that it rises, up the tree trunks, up to the top of the leafless branches, growing louder as it flies into the frigid, white sky just like the flock of birds that passes overhead. She waits, her ears twitching forward, listening. But she hears only the footfalls of men, and now their voices.

Then a deep sound penetrates the forest. The howl is unbroken and direct. It builds in intensity until it feels as if it is suspended in a long arc from its source to where she stands. Higher cries join in, riding above the first, followed by a percussive flourish of barks. When one call winds down, another layers itself on top so that the pack seems numerous. But she is sure there are only three singing back to her, and that they are not far away. She might reach them before either her leg gives out or the men pull close enough to fire on her again. She moves. The pain explodes and she feels it everywhere—in her leg, her belly, her teeth, the tip of her snout. Her senses close down so it feels as if she were racing blind except for a prick of brightness in the center of her vision. She aims for that light and runs as hard and as fast as she can.

THE THREE WOLVES stand on a snowy rise. Two males are dark brown with black masks, but the third male is entirely white, so white that it is impossible to distinguish its paws from the snow it stands on, so bright that it takes a moment for her eyes to adjust. She slows her pace and moves carefully now. The white wolf snarls at her, baring his teeth. He lunges forward, then backs up, then prances forward again. His tail is poised behind him, level with the ground; his ears lie flat against his head. Unsure, she stops moving. Slowly, the white one advances. The two dark ones follow closely behind his flanks, their growls quiet and tense, their heads held low. As they slowly make their way down the knoll, they keep her in their sights. Once on flat land, they advance. The white wolf's body stiffens as he readies himself to attack. His lips pull back, his ears pitch forward. Then he rushes ahead, snapping his teeth, stopping just short of her. Her leg is on fire and she is weak. She backs up but she doesn't have the energy to run. The white wolf is about to lunge when suddenly, a sharp crack. The white wolf stops moving. The dark ones unleash frantic yips and scatter. Has she been hit again? She waits for the pain to announce itself as it did the last time, first as something precise and almost bearable before it lacerated her, spiraling through her body, knocking her down. She feels nothing but the insistent throbbing of the old wound in her leg. The men have missed their mark and opened up a chance. The white wolf turns and races up and over the crest of the rise. She follows but just as she starts her descent, a man appears. He raises his gun and aims it toward her face. She looks into his dark, liquid eyes. His terror shifts something inside of her and she snarls at him, baring her teeth. The white wolf shrieks as a rock hits his side and he stumbles, sliding the rest of the way down the incline. Three other men are closing in. "What are you waiting for?" shouts one of them.

She doesn't know what those sounds mean. The one with the gun stares at her. His arms tremble, the gun wavers, drawing a wobbly circle around her head. "Pavla?" he whispers.

The others raise their guns just as the white wolf regains his footing. He snarls and charges them. Terrified, they back off and the white one escapes into the woods.

"Shoot the bitch, Danilo!" a man cries as he runs away.

"Is it you?" the man with the gun says. She doesn't understand him, doesn't know why he lowers the weapon, why he reaches out with one hand as if to touch her. She sees the tip of the white wolf's tail disappearing between the trees. What is this man offering her? There is nothing in his hand. No food.

"Pavla?"

She turns and flees into the forest.

DAY AFTER DAY, she trails them as they search for food. They kill a rabbit, a vole, small prey that is hardly enough to satisfy the three of them. Whenever she draws too close, hoping for a left-over bone or a taste of flesh, they turn on her, snarl and bark their warning, and she retreats again, dragging her wounded leg behind her. Snow falls continually now. The cold energizes the pack and they move quickly. She follows them beyond the tree line and across an open field. The wind is so strong that it feels like she is pushing against something solid, and she can't keep up. When she loses sight of them, she follows the scent of their urine.

Finally, when they stop to rest, she gets the chance to catch up. She settles down at a safe distance and they pay her no attention. She watches the two dark wolves tussle. Sometimes one flips the other and takes the bared throat in its jaws. At other times, the game is reversed. Occasionally, the white wolf joins in, but mostly it is the dark ones who vie with each other while the white one looks on, ears up, nose in the air, attentive for the sound or scent of something promising or dangerous. She sleeps only when they sleep, and then she wakes at every noise, fearful that one of them will attack her. When they move on, she trails behind slowly so that at times she can only see the others as shadows through the scrim of snowfall. Sometimes, when she is so weak that her other faculties seem to fail her, she realizes that she is not following them at all but has only directed herself toward the dark shapes of rocks, and she has to find them all over again. After a few days, the bullet settles into her muscle in such a way that, although there is a constant pinch, she can move more quickly. Still, she is starving. The others ignore her, but they do not chase her off, and so she keeps following, watching closely, trying to understand how she might win a place among them so that she can survive.

They walk for days with no food. Then one afternoon, when the snow turns a cast of blue and the forest feels especially still, the white wolf catches a scent and takes off at a fast trot. The others follow behind, their footfalls soundless in the snow. She picks up the odor as well and her body tightens and becomes suffused with a sudden energy so concentrated that she no longer feels her injury or her hunger, only a keen, thoughtless purpose that propels her. Soon enough, she sees the deer. They stand in a clearing, heads up, as still as the trees around them. Then, all at once, they break into a run. The wolves are faster, though, and soon they have caught up and run parallel to the herd. The white wolf leads the others, maintaining a wide margin between himself and the deer. The dark ones follow suit and so does she, running behind the pack. Just as the sun dips below the horizon and it becomes harder to judge the distance to a tree or see where the sky stops and the snow begins, one of the smaller deer slows down and separates from the others. The white wolf narrows the distance between himself and his lone target until he is so close that in one final bound, he falls on the animal and attacks its hips. The deer breaks its stride and stumbles but somehow manages to pull itself up, break free, and keep going. One of the dark wolves lunges at its head, attacking its snout and eyes while the white wolf sinks its teeth into its side, tearing a gash in its hide. The deer falls. The wolves make quick work of opening up the body, exposing the flesh and organs and the still-pulsing heart. The deer pedals its legs, as if it doesn't know that it is finished, that its blood and innards are spilled onto the snow, and that it is being devoured. Soon, it stops moving altogether.

The smell of flesh and blood overwhelms her. Slowly, keeping her body low to the ground and her tail between her legs, she approaches the feasting wolves. One of the dark ones sees her and barks. She stops for a moment, but her hunger is too powerful. When she sees a morsel of flesh lying on the snow, she darts forward and claims it. The white one, its muzzle covered in blood and slick, quivering meat turns on her fiercely. Grabbing hold of the meat that hangs from her jaw, he wrestles it from her, then charges her, forcing her to back off. Defeated, exhausted, she lowers herself onto the snow, taking a small consolation in a bit of flesh that remains lodged in her teeth. She lays her head on her paws.

WHEN SHE WAKES, it is dark. There is no sound. The wind has died down and the cold has absorbed all but a trace of the smell of flesh. She sees the dark outlines of the others who sleep not far from her, and beyond them, the carcass. Slowly, she gets to her feet and, keeping a wide berth, creeps past the wolves, drawing nearer to the carcass by degrees, expecting at any moment that one of the others will attack. When she reaches the eviscerated skeleton, she takes a scrap of hide in her mouth. The first taste sends her into a frenzy and she tears through the remains, crunching down on bones to get at the marrow, swallowing the sinew and tendons the others rejected. She eats until there is nothing left and then she sleeps.

She's woken by a frightened yelp. The two dark ones are fighting. One tosses the other on its back. But instead of allowing the fallen one to get up and resume play, he bares his teeth and clamps down hard on his victim's throat. The downed wolf shrieks. She creeps closer, and then closer still, and then throws herself into the fracas, teasingly pouncing on the aggressor, then falling to the snow. He is still intent on the other wolf, so she stands and swats him playfully with her paw then falls to the snow again and rolls onto her back, exposing her neck. Distracted, he releases the wolf and begins to play with her, nudging her with his muzzle, nipping her ears, grabbing her by the withers, shaking her, letting go. He allows her to stand and mount another playful attack on him before, once again, throwing her to the ground. The other one joins in this mock fight and whatever danger existed between the two wolves is dispelled. The white wolf who has ignored everything up until this point, content to groom himself, stands and heads deeper into the woods. The others leave off playing and fall in with him. She follows, only closer this time. After a while, the white wolf circles back and falls in with her. As she walks beside him, she shifts her stance so that she is lower than he is, her shoulders hunched, her head bent to the ground. He walks next to her for a long time. When he finally pulls ahead to lead the pack, no one chases her away.

*O**f course no one believes him*. He knows it is ridiculous, this idea he keeps trying to convince everyone of: that it was Pavla he and the others—the handler for the dancing rats, the human skeleton, and the man with a prehensile tail—tracked through the forest, that it was she he had in his sights but refused, at that last moment, to shoot. He hardly believes himself that she has inexplicably turned into the very thing she once so convincingly playacted. But he is certain of it. At least he is when he lies down at night and sleep begins to smudge his thoughts, or in those dim, swimming moments just as he wakes, when the line that delineates this harsh, intractable world from the elastic and forgiving one of dreams feels like a porous border he can cross at will, when it still feels possible that his mother has welcomed him back home with kisses and warm food, that his brother is alive, that Pavla has allowed him inside her. This last dream is the most disturbing and thrilling. He is never sure whether he is making love to a dwarf, a monstrous girl, or an animal, or all three at once, and the confusion feels like a ravishment that leaves him spent and delirious, his mind searching the quickly evanescing details of this otherworld that only seconds before felt like everywhere he had ever been and everywhere he needed to go. And then he is fully awake and holding not her dwarfish, girlish, wolfish body but a crushed blanket and a feeling of profound loneliness.

She was right: he is weak. He was too cowardly to declare himself. Even though now he would say she is the most beautiful being he has ever seen, he was too troubled by her long nose, the fine fur on her cheeks, and by his vanity that made him unwilling to admit that he desired the girl that others considered a freak. And even though he would still say that her eyes are the most cryptic and entrancing he's ever encountered, he was terrified by her chilling gaze. Sometimes, he believed she might have hurt him. And yet, she is the only person who has ever been kind to him, the only one to whom—and this, for a youth of nearly twenty, is a sad truth—it mattered that he existed.

WITH SMETANKA DEAD and Pavla gone, Danilo has no work. The possibility that he will be hired by another act, perhaps as a tout for Juliska, who stays to the bitter end of the season because as wives grow hungry and thin during the lean winter months, husbands will pay to ogle the fleshy, bounteous woman, is scuttled by his reputation. No one will hire the coward who failed to kill the marauding wolf that made a meal of his employer, leaving nothing but shredded clothes, a few bones, and a handful of rotten teeth. Danilo sells the caravan for next to nothing but keeps the old mare. He knows wolves can roam vast territories and that he may need to travel far in order to find her.

He rides from village to village looking for work, finding none. When he summons the courage to ask if anyone has encountered a wolf that seems, well, a little bit human, he is met only with laughter or snide jokes about the local Magda or Lenka ("She may call herself a girl but she sure acts like a wolf!"), for every town has its designated ugliest girl who, more than likely, has given herself away on muddy banks or behind haystacks, satisfying the local boys in heat for a smidgen of attention and sloppy affection.

"She'll do you for the price of a nice word if you can summon one!" he's told in one village when a skinny, taciturn girl is produced. "Not brave enough for this beast, eh?" they say when he demurs.

And what if he had been brave? he asks himself as he and his buckle-backed horse ride to the next town so that he can find no work there, too. What if he had declared himself to her? What then?

In the forest, he looked into those yellow eyes and recognized something. A calm resolve behind that gaze, a cool forbearance in the face of such strange and unpredictable fate. He believes, no, he *knows*, that she was not going to hurt him but rather that she was telling him something. He understood what it was he had felt being in her presence from the moment he lifted her onto the doctor's examining table and looked into her eyes: she planted a belief in him that out of the emptiness of his life something might emerge.

"Ach," he says, kicking the mare gently to no effect. "Who do I think I am?"

THE WINTER IS EMPHATIC. One snowstorm follows another with hardly any time for people to recover and grab a moment in the fugitive sunlight to remind themselves that there is a world beyond the walls of their homes. No one is taking on extra hands at the farms. People subsist on cabbage and potatoes and the occasional scrawny hen. There is little money to buy more frivolous items they might allow themselves in the warm months when a new pair of shoes or a length of ribbon seems as much a piece with springtime bounty as new peas, and so there is no work to be found as a shop assistant or delivery boy. Danilo is turned away wherever he goes.

He has more to battle than this annual hibernation of industry and hope. The story of the man-eating wolf and the feckless youth who failed to kill it at point-blank range, combined with the fear and isolation instilled by freezing temperatures and midafternoon darkness turn his story into a curse that follows him wherever he goes. The problem is compounded when word spreads that a wolf pack has been sighted lurking close to a village and its surrounding farms. When a report comes that the animals have breached an enclosure and killed a cow, the looks

Danilo receives when he enters a tavern convince him that even if there were a hundred available jobs that would pay a man enough to last through the grim season he would not be offered a single one of them. Finally, after many weeks, he manages to get work as a servant at an inn. He is paid nothing, but is allowed to sleep on the floor of the kitchen next to the stove.

Toward the end of the winter, another cow is killed and then, in a single night, five goats. A council of five villages is called. A name begins to circulate, first in whispers, then in pronouncements, and then in votes, and a group of men is dispatched to find the famous tracker, Bruno Klima. The way this man's name is spoken in worshipful, if fearful, tones, and the fact that the tracker eschews society and lives a hermit's life in the mountains lead Danilo to expect a pelt-covered giant to come striding into the village, his musket over one shoulder, wolf flesh dangling from his teeth. He is surprised when, a week later, Bruno Klima arrives looking like nothing so much as a government functionary sent to the provinces to conduct some official business. Bespectacled and slight, he wears, yes, a coat with a fox fur collar, but underneath is a fine, worsted three-piece suit. Instead of an arbiter's leather satchel full of important documents, he carries his guns in a polished wooden case. After following the deliberations of the council anxiously, fearful for what might happen to Pavla, Danilo is put at ease by the sight of the man who does not look the least inclined to hunt and kill a wild animal. But the gossip that attends Klima's arrival tells another story: how, pinned to the ground by a bear, he still managed to aim his pistol and shoot the beast between the eyes; how he shot a hawk as it carried off a child, then caught the baby in free fall and returned it safely to its parents; how, during a time of great famine, he single-handedly managed to kill enough deer to keep the villagers from starving. That Klima's meticulous appearance belies these heroics only makes them all the more unlikely and therefore, in the logic of mythology, inarguably true.

While preparing for his new mission, Klima stays at the inn where Danilo works. When the great tracker appears in the dining room for his meals, the innkeeper, whose jacket, washed once a year on the first warm day of spring, serves as a history of the year's menus, is obsequious, as if a dinner service removed too soon or a rabbit cooked to an unpleasant toughness might cause him to be the next target in the tracker's sights. Klima seems accustomed to this kind of deference and, after taking his first bite of each meal, he gives a slight nod to signal that the evening's fare, while not necessarily to his liking, is at least edible, at which point the owner backs away quietly and watches from a safe distance behind the partially closed kitchen door.

One afternoon, while the tracker is out, Danilo enters his bedroom to stoke the fireplace. Klima has laid out all his belongings on the room's small dressing table as neatly as if they were a tradesman's display. Danilo remembers going to the yearly agricultural fair with his father and brother to see the latest instruments for measuring rainfall or wind velocity. His father pretended to understand these newfangled improvements for his sons' benefit although, like all the villagers, he was frightened by the modern. Danilo is particularly captivated by the tracker's toiletries, his ivory comb and brush set, his ornately filigreed nail scissors. Like everyone he has ever known, Danilo uses his teeth to get the job done, saving the thickest thumbnail to serve double duty as a toothpick. He uncorks a small vial and sniffs the lavender-scented water inside, runs his finger along the sharpened edge of a gleaming razor. He knows he ought to leave the room before he is caught snooping but he can't before examining two rifles that lie on the bed side by side like newlyweds. These are gorgeous instruments, their barrels polished to a sleek shine, the handles inlaid with red and green gemstones. They are a far cry from the splintered shotgun Danilo was given to kill Pavla with. Although he was terrified to hold that weapon, he cannot help but run his hands along these gamine instruments with a kind of respectful tenderness. Metal and wooden fixtures lie piled next to them, the works of yet a third shotgun whose body has been broken down to its smallest components. Each is freshly oiled, for the tracker cares for his guns as meticulously as he does his body. Danilo picks up a slim piece of metal that looks like a trigger guard and before he knows it, he has forgotten to lay the fire and is kneeling on the worn bedside rug, the parts scattered around him, fitting them together, one by one. He has never built a gun before but his hands pick and choose the correct pieces as if he were expert at the job. The intensity of his concentration and the small pleasure he receives when random elements slide into their proper places remind him of nothing so much as the hours he spent building the stretching table and that marvelous feeling he had of finally putting the dormant mechanism of his brain to the uses for which it was clearly intended. Of course, back then, the delight he took in the ingenious workings of the table, and even in Smetanka's approval, was spoiled when he realized how the man intended his invention to be used. Still, as guilty as he feels about his involvement in Pavla's torture, he is reminded now of the sheer joy of inventing something that a man can put to use. He supposes this is what his father must experience as he fits together the pieces of a shoe, arranging the backstay and the quarter, the vamp and the tongue, affixing them to the sole and the heel, and then watching a customer take his first step. Even though he was banished from his family, he finds a bitter comfort in this association.

Once the gun is assembled, he picks it up and holds it to his shoulder, sighting himself in the full-length mirror that stands in the corner of the room.

"There are more effective ways to kill yourself," a voice says.

Danilo spins around, the gun still poised.

"But that would be a very good way to kill me," Klima says. Calmly, he reaches out and puts his hand on the end of the barrel, redirecting Danilo's aim toward the floor.

"Forgive me," Danilo says, handing over the gun. "It's not my place."

"No, it's not," Klima says, turning the weapon, studying it from all sides. "You're handy with a gun, then?"

"I'm a terrible shot."

"I've heard you're no shot at all."

Danilo can't hold the man's gaze. Instead, he fixes on the golden watch chain that stretches across his vest depositing its treasure into a small pocket. Somehow, this invisible elegance seems to sum up Danilo's failure. "I guess if it weren't for me, you wouldn't need to be here," he says quietly.

"Well then, I have you to thank."

Danilo wonders if the man is teasing him, adding a final dollop of shame to the mound piled on him by the community, but when he looks up, Klima's expression is serious.

"You know that if a gun is put together badly, it will more likely kill the person firing it than its intended target. It's a foolproof form of sabotage," Klima says.

"I didn't mean—" Danilo says.

"But," Klima says, studying the gun in his hand. "I watched you. You put it together correctly on the first try. You've built weapons before."

Could he be referring to the stretching table? Can it be that word of this atrocity has followed Danilo from village to village as well? No. It's impossible. Still, the man is shrewd, and Danilo has the feeling he knows everyone's secrets. "Not intentionally, sir."

"Well, I can use a man with a bit of beginner's luck."

"Use me, sir?"

"That is, unless you'd rather chop wood in exchange for sleeping with kitchen rats and eating my leftovers. Nothing escapes my attention," he says when Danilo looks embarrassed to have been so carefully observed. "You'll earn five percent of my take. I get paid by the head. And I never miss."

Her hunger is perpetual now. Even though she ate just a day ago, her belly feels empty. Her leg doesn't trouble her—she's adjusted to its limitations—but her body feels heavy and sluggish and it insists on another rhythm than the other wolves keep. As they cross their territory, she falls behind. The dark wolves often circle back, sometimes coming up behind her to sniff beneath her tail until the white wolf warns them off. The two dark ones are filled with jumpy energy and they fight more often and more fiercely with each other. For her part, all she wants to do is dig.

It began when they attacked the cows. Three nights running, they circled a farm, catching field mice and rabbits and then retreating to the forest where it was safe to sleep. Then one night, the white wolf slowly walked toward the big, dark animals and the rest followed. It wasn't until they began to claw their way underneath the fence that the cows took up their lowing. Lights appeared in windows and, after a few moments, men stormed out of the house, shouting. It had taken the white wolf no time to strike the calf. Just as swiftly, the others tore into the body and before the men could stumble within range, the wolves slipped under the fence and ran toward the trees. She and the two dark ones were quickly absorbed by the night, and the shots missed them. But one flew so close to the white wolf's head that it clipped his ear, taking off the tip. The wolves ran deep into the forest and when they finally stopped, she licked his wound. After this, he began to walk by her side and sleep close to her, lick her muzzle and nose her beneath her jaw. She no longer assumed her low stance when he was close. Often, she lifted her backside, and he would lick underneath her tail. When her blood began to stain the ground, she moved her tail to the side so that he could smell it. And then he was behind her and on top of her at the same time. Over the next days, she insisted that he mount her again and again. And then, one time he tried and she snarled at him. After that, he left her alone.

Now the air is warmer and all the snow has melted away. The earth is soft underneath her paws. The others keep moving, but when she stops and begins to dig, they return to where she has settled, and the pack finally rests.

While she is making the den wide and deep, she feels her insides convulse. She has barely finished the job before she has to lie down on the newly churned dirt. Each time one comes out, she bites off the cord and eats the flesh attached to it. Then she licks the pup until her belly churns again, and the next one emerges. By the time she is done, there are four of them. She is exhausted, but the meat of her insides has given her enough strength to clean the last one. When all four attach themselves to her and begin to suck, she sleeps.

She dreams.

She stands by the edge of a lake. Fish swim just below the reach of her muzzle, their nearly translucent bodies darting here and there. When one rises up, she plunges her face into the water, but it slips away. She waits for the disturbance she's created to calm, and once it does, she peers into the surface. But this time, instead of seeing fish, she sees the reflection of a man whose skin is pale and hairless and whose eyes are the color of night and who lifts a gun, points it at her, and—

She wakes. Blindly, they are sucking on her. All of them but one. Where is he? She shakes the others off. They complain with high, squeaking cries and try to burrow up against her and find her teats, but she snaps at them. She makes a full turn around herself until she finds the fourth. She pushes at him with her paw and her snout, but he doesn't move. His body is cold. She picks him up in her mouth and crawls out of the den. The other pups sense her departure and they are distressed, but she doesn't pay attention to their cries.

The others are sleeping in the sun. She carries the pup over to them. They stir and wake. She shows the pup to the white wolf first and then to the others. After a time, she lays him on the ground. One of the dark ones picks him up with the fleshy part of its mouth and walks here and there while she digs. The dark wolf brings the pup and lays him in the small depression she's made. She turns around and, with her hind legs, kicks dirt over the body. She returns to the den to feed the others.

Do you know, by any chance, how to navigate by the stars?" Klima says. The question is rhetorical. It has been a week since he and Danilo set off from the village into the surrounding forest, and Danilo has worked hard to be useful and earn his five percent. He pitches the tent and builds the fires and cooks the potatoes and onions they carry with them along with whatever game Klima shoots each day. In the evenings, he disassembles, cleans, then rebuilds the rifles in order to keep the works from jamming. At first, he carried the load of food and equipment on his back for hours at a time, a talent that can only be attributed to the fact that, for the last years of his life, he has been treated like nothing so much as an ass, and so he is able to manifest that animal's signature attribute. After the fourth day, he fashioned a sled from the new and malleable branches of an alder, impressing the normally reticent Klima who, upon testing the tensile strength built into the struts and stays, betrayed the barest hint of approval. Sometimes they travel by day, sometimes by night, depending on the weather. As the days grow warmer, the wolves, according to the tracker, will move at later and later hours to take advantage of the cooler air.

"I don't know anything about the stars except that they are there at night and gone in the morning," Danilo answers, glancing briefly at the speckled sky. He knows that Klima will not teach him the map of the stars just as the man did not explicitly tell him that wearing an animal pelt so that the fur lay against his skin and not the other way around would save his feet from rain rot. After they killed their first four rabbits, he watched as Klima carefully skinned the animals so that their hides remained intact, then hung them over the fire to dry. When Danilo woke the following day, only two of the hides were hanging. It took him until the middle of the next afternoon, when he could barely walk for the pain of his toes, to figure out why Klima did not seem to have the same problem. When they finally stopped to camp, Danilo worked as quickly as he could to knead suppleness back into the remaining skins, then wrapped the fur around his waterlogged feet. The long-awaited spring brings nothing more comforting than mud and drip, but Danilo is finally savvy enough to take care of himself.

As they walk through the night, Danilo watches the tracker attentively. He tries to figure from the angle of Klima's upward gaze which stars he is using to chart their course. Danilo is wrong more than he is right. After a few hours, a cluster that he thinks Klima is sighting falls away to their right, and by the time Danilo has figured out which stars the man is actually using to orient them, it is nearly dawn and all he has learned about celestial navigation is how it is not accomplished. But little by little, as the nights pile one on top of the next, and with careful observation, he begins to understand which constellations appear in the north, south, east, and west quadrants of the sky. He learns that somewhere on the opposite side of the earth, at that very moment, there are other stars, ones that he cannot see, and that if he waited long enough for the earth to turn, those constellations would be his guide. Sometimes, he passes the long hours imagining some other tracker and his aide on the other side of the world who, right at that moment, are searching the universe for clues that will tell them where to go next. These ideas are so new they quickly slip away, and what he thinks he comprehends at one moment confounds him the very next. Then suddenly he grabs hold of the tail of the idea once more, reels it close, and understands that everything, even the step he takes over this tree stump and that rock, happens in relation to everything else—the stars, the air, the water, and her.

What he doesn't understand is what is taking them so long. Danilo had not known anything about wolves and their territory. He had thought, like everyone else, that the animals, having been last seen stealing from farms, would linger nearby, waiting for their next chance to trap easy prey from the corrals and pigstys. But Klima has informed him that everything he thinks he knows about wolves is the stuff of tales mothers tell their children to keep them close to home.

"Wolves are not interested in us," he tells Danilo as they walk.

"They're not scared of men? Men with guns?"

"Men are scared of men with guns. And if a man imagines a wolf thinks like he does, a bullet will be the least of his problems."

"How does a wolf think?"

"This is the very curious thing about you, Danilo. Your mind is always lost somewhere to the right or the left of the correct question."

Danilo knows he cannot ask what the right question would be; the tracker would never tell him. But as they stray farther into the wilderness and time passes without the tracker explaining himself, Danilo begins to wonder if there is a question at all. A wolf does not think the way a man thinks. To believe that would be to imagine there is an explanation as to how a mother can reject her only living son, or how a girl can turn into an animal. These things have happened on their own terms, ones that defy the logic of how a gun is built or how to reckon distance by the heavens. A wolf is its own term.

As is Klima. It had fallen to Danilo to provision the journey, and it was not long before every shopkeeper and local gossip knew that, for no apparent reason, the great hunter, charged with the duty of keeping the community safe, had elected to take a young, unskilled, untried, and virtually useless drifter as his second, a man who, if the stories were true, could not even kill a wolf when it was staring into the barrel of his shotgun. Still, after their grumbling and while they were collecting the rope and tenting materials and the pure kava that, to Danilo, used to sipping cheap rye or chicory, seems dangerously luxurious, they told him what they knew about his new boss.

Klima had made his first appearance over a decade or two decades earlier (the time, like so many other details of the man's story, was confused by memory and the exaggerating effects of repeated telling) during what was referred to as—and here the voice lowered as if mentioning a fatal disease—"The Disappearances." During one hot and drought-filled summer, when the farms were so dry that fields spontaneously burst into flame, children began to go missing. First it was eight-year-old Otakar Dymek, a dreamy boy and a wanderer who, much to his father's embarrassment, spent his days in the meadows collecting the few wild snowdrops and primroses that clung to life despite the searing heat. His mother was beside herself when he did not return one day at the clanging of the dinner bell, although his father was not disappointed to eat his dinner without being confronted by the bouquet decorating the table, a gut-clenching reminder of the kind of son he had on his hands. At his wife's hysterical urging, he left the table before his meal was finished. Despite his misgivings about his boy, he became alarmed when, searching the meadow, he found the pea green and decidedly girlish toque his wife had knitted and which the vexing boy insisted upon wearing every day and sometimes even to bed despite the heat. Next it was Vesta Lenart, a thirteen-year-old girl, whose body, in contrast to the local crops, bloomed with such fierce determination that it was sometimes whispered that the drought could be accounted for by the fact that her own luscious development was sucking up all available moisture and nutrients. When a pair of her underwear was found knotted in the brambles along the banks of the dry river, the local boys were questioned. But each of them, although conceding that their daydreams and nighttime fantasies were filled with images of their once stick-thin, no-hipped, but now voluptuous playmate, had to admit that they were somewhat frightened by the implicit threat of all that sudden succulence and that none of them had the nerve to speak to her much less carry her off. It was assumed that she had been abducted and defiled by some itinerant soldier, for it was commonly accepted that soldiers were de facto rapists, and so her parents, although they loved her truly and dearly, didn't want her back. But when Marta and Cyril Zdeněk woke one morning to find that their little Ilona, not yet a year old, who slept snugly between her parents each night like a warm loaf of bread, had gone missing and that there were, strangely, three strands of coarse fur and the unmistakable smell of animal on the sheets, panic spread. The Zdeněk bedsheet, Otakar's cap, and Vesta's underwear were brought to the town's most notorious nose, which belonged to the postman, Michal Vachelsky, whose mighty pro-boscis seemed to lead him down the street as he walked here and there delivering the mail. Vachelsky sniffed the evidence and determined that the common odor among the items was not the smell of unwashed scalp or a young woman's privacy but of a single perpetrator. After a reward for capture was raised, the community, smarting from the failure of crops and the prospect of a lean winter, became fixated on the task of apprehending the terrorist, and no one could speak of anything else. Talk of Kra-konach, the giant from the mountains, caused idle farmers to walk their arid fields searching for oversized footprints. False claims were made and quickly scuttled by local experts who took measuring sticks to swaths of flattened grasses and pronounced that the mark in question was either too large or too small or too much resembled the shape of the backside of the farmer who, in order to claim the reward, had imprinted his land with his own ample rump. It was then generally agreed that the culprit was none other than Jezinka, the wicked wood nymph, whose inability to birth children of her own caused her to steal those of others. Her method had normally been to leave a counterfeit in place of the stolen child. But once each village youngster was accounted for, all birthmarks and other identifying signatures verified, it was determined that there were no changelings among them. Finally, it was decided that the kidnapper was none other than Vikodlak. The proof was so obvious that it could only be due to the grandmothers and great-grandmothers and their stubborn belief in those ridiculous tales of giants and goblins that wiser minds had not earlier come to this most obvious conclusion. Those coarse hairs? That animal stink? The town had been visited by a werewolf.

At that time, Klima was a man known by reputation only. Long ago, and for reasons eagerly debated—a shattered heart? A murdered rival?—he abandoned society and became a mountain man. No one, in fact, knew exactly the location of his home, and a message had to be sent to a foothill hamlet where he was rumored to appear occasionally when he needed provisions or an hour of female companionship. While the villagers awaited word as to whether or not the man would take their case, they devised their own ways of insuring their children's safety. During daylight hours, the little ones were not allowed to venture from their homes without adult supervision. At night, they were roped to their beds. Fires, which everyone knew kept werewolves at bay, were lit day and night despite the intense heat and the dangers of widespread conflagration. Scissors and knives or any other objects made of pure iron were laid in the cribs of newborns. Mothers tied wolfsbane around their children's necks, and the whole village smelled of garlic.

Klima's first entrance into the town is remembered with as much rippling pleasure as when the archduke and his new young wife passed through on their way to their honeymoon retreat. The couple did not alight from their car—a vehicle as unfamiliar as a royal in those parts—or even open their window shades to wave to the villagers who had lined up along the road to greet them. The much-anticipated event passed in a haze of dust and exhaust and was over even before the mayor was able to put on his eyeglasses to read his speech. Danilo knows, from the fanfare attending the tracker's most recent arrival, that the introduction of the beast slayer must have been greeted with a mixture of awe and dread, for in the time it took for the message to get to the man and for him to make his way to the village, and despite the ropes and chains and herbal precautions, two more children had disappeared (well, one—the other having unhappily rolled over in his sleep onto the point of a pair of shears).

The hysteria of the townspeople was as much a tinderbox as the bone-dry fields. Klima surveyed the evidence—the sheet, cap, underwear, and the strands of hair that had been kept in a bell jar at the local apothecary—and set out again without a word. After two weeks, a monster was seen at the edge of town:

the werewolf himself. As he made his way down the street, women screamed and men ran for their shotguns, certain that the tracker had been defeated and that Vikodlak had come for his revenge. But when the beast finally reached the town square, it shed its rank-smelling head and hide and revealed itself to be none other than Klima. In ceremonial fashion, he handed the skin to the mothers of the missing who wept and took turns holding it to their breasts as if to commune with the body that had eaten their children.

"**DID THEY REALLY BELIEVE** it was a werewolf?" Danilo asks one morning as he raises the tent for the day's sleep. According to signs—a pile of fresh scat, a wisp of white fur clinging to the debarked lower portion of a linden that, according to the tracker, serves as a scratching post—they have finally arrived within range of the wolves.

"Of course they did," the man says. He puts a charred piece of black squirrel between his teeth and chews thoughtfully.

Once again, Danilo has asked the wrong question. What he wants to know is whether this man, who seems so scientific in his careful observation of nature, his ability to read the stars, and his unerring sense of direction, believes that a person can change into an animal. He does not know how to ask this without confessing his belief in Pavla's strange transfiguration and proving himself to be the unworldly bumpkin he is. "Old women's tales," he says dismissively.

The man shrugs without commitment.

"You'd think that when you returned wearing the skin, they would have realized the story of the werewolf was a lie," Danilo says.

"It's not a lie if it is believed. You seem to believe it. Otherwise you wouldn't be asking me these questions."

Danilo is embarrassed. "I know there are no such things as werewolves."

"How do you know?"

"Because a man can't turn into an animal?" he says hesitantly, unsure how he hopes the tracker will respond. "Because it makes no sense?"

"Most things in this world make no sense. That a woman dies on her wedding day. That murder will put an end to grief. But these things happen. We see them with our eyes. There is no better proof than that."

Danilo wonders if the man is edging up to a personal revelation, but any question he might ask to get the tracker to divulge his history would be, as Klima would say, to the left or the right of the point. Danilo is beginning to understand that the obvious question is the wrong one, and that to interpret the world by way of its most available and reasonable clues will only lead him further down the narrow path that has, thus far, defined his existence. It is only that he does not yet know what the right questions are. He is not adept enough to see, much less decipher, the opaque and irrational narrative that lies beneath what appears to be the likely story. Or maybe it is only that, as Pavla said, he is a coward.

He and Klima crawl into the tent and prepare to sleep. "I've never seen a werewolf," Danilo says.

"Have you ever *not* seen one?" The tracker turns on his side, adjusting his rucksack underneath his head. "We have a long night ahead of us," he says. Within moments, he's snoring heavily.

But Danilo can't sleep. He is so agitated, so excited, he can barely lie still. He did not see Pavla turn into a wolf. And yet, he did not *not* see it. He did not see her grow after her terrible ordeal with the stretching table, nor did he see her nose elongate and the down on her face appear, and yet . . .

So many nights, as they performed their pantomime, squeezed together on that makeshift stage, their mouths were so near to each other that it would have taken only the slightest movement on his part to close that gap, to press himself into her, to feel what he has felt so palpably in his dreams, the suffusing warmth that spreads from their joined lips throughout his body, the weightless feeling, as if he were back home, a boy again, swimming in the lake with his brother, their legs twining and untwining as they played and fought and played again. Diving down beneath the surface of the water, parting the grasses there with the slow-motion strokes of his arms, reaching down and burying his hands in the soft, delicious slime—

He comes with a groan. He looks over to make sure Klima is still asleep, then lies back, an arm cradling his head. He thinks about all those days and nights he and Pavla spent together putting on the show, cleaning the tent, walking through the camp grounds. He always needed to be near her. He believed that if he were not, he would possibly die. Those days begin to feel like the happiest he will ever be allowed.

People paid money to Smetanka in order to prove the man and his claim wrong. They paid money for a fight. And when Pavla unveiled herself as the monstrosity Smetanka promised, the spectators threw empty bottles and cried foul, and would not calm down until the shill ran up onto the stage and yanked her head so much that she suffered bruises and neck spasms. Then, the doubting audience believed the lie, and so the lie became true. But it was never a lie, was it? It was always—the logic makes his head hurt. He closes his eyes and soon is asleep.

BY THE TIME DANILO WAKES, Klima is already getting ready for the evening's work. He unfolds the felt that holds his toiletries and proceeds to shave his day's growth and comb his hair and douse himself with lavender water as if he were preparing for a party rather than a night of slashing through the woods. Danilo breaks down the camp and packs up. They no longer need the sled; they've used the better part of their supplies and Danilo can carry everything that remains on his back. As usual, once Klima finishes with his ablutions, he strides out of camp without a remark, and as the shapes of the trees begin to dissolve into the gathering darkness, Danilo races to catch up before he loses sight of the tracker and finds himself alone and utterly lost.

They spend the next nights walking more slowly than usual. They are drawing close to the pack, and Klima's movements seem precisely calibrated, as if unnecessary motion will compromise him. The night is starless, the moon a smeared presence that lights their path only when the wind picks up and pushes the clouds aside. Klima seems even more surefooted than ever, as if, entering into the wolves' territory, he has become their equal.

"They are on the hunt," he says on the second night, with uncharacteristic excitement. He holds a handful of mud to Danilo's nose. It is too dark out to see the discoloration, but the smell of urine is unmistakable.

"How do you know it's wolf piss?" Danilo says.

"It's not. They are far too clever to leave us such an obvious message."

"They know we're here?"

"If you knew who your most lethal enemy was, would you not keep him in your sights at all times?"

"But that would put us within their range."

"It works both ways."

"I thought you said wolves don't attack humans."

"I said they attack fear."

"You're scared?"

"You are. You fairly reek of it."

Danilo looks as far as he is able in the darkness. He swears he can feel her devastating gaze on him as if she were just steps away. "Are they close?" he says.

Before he gets his answer, they hear the whipsaw of branches. The tracker crouches, then creeps forward. Danilo tries to imitate the stance and soon his thighs start shaking. His loaded pack slides up his spine and presses against the back of his neck. When the tracker stops abruptly, Danilo barely saves himself from falling on his face. He sees dark shapes moving not even fifteen meters in front of him. A low thunder of growls crescendos into a cacophony of fierce barking followed by strangled, desperate grunts: the wolves are attacking a pack of wild boar. Sound and shadow narrate the story. Some of the boar manage to break free and run, their hoof falls rapid as horses'. The wind pushes away the clouds and the scene is momentarily illuminated. A white wolf leaps up and falls on an unlucky boar. It rips into the side of the animal with such force and accuracy that the boar does not even have time to squeal in protest: it is instantly dead. The wolf devours the animal, then lifts the carcass, shakes it violently, and flings it to the side. Tilting its muzzle to the sky, it lets out a magisterial howl. Then it turns and faces the men as if it has always known they were there and was only waiting to attend to the pressing matter of its hunger before concerning itself with this threat. In a second, it charges, its teeth bared. A shot explodes next to Danilo's ear. Every muscle in his body gives out at once. He falls to his knees and vomits.

IT IS MIDDAY when he wakes. The tracker sleeps inside the tent but he has left Danilo where he fell, his cheek lying in his sick. While he tries to clean himself off, Danilo wonders how Klima will treat him now that he has proven himself so gritless. Maybe he will be left to find his way out of the wilderness alone. Maybe the tracker will simply shoot him.

Klima emerges from the tent, stretching and squinting into the light. He looks at the state Danilo is in. "That was quite an entertainment you put on," he says.

"Where is the wolf?" Danilo says.

"Off doing wolfish things, I suppose."

"But you shot it."

"I gave it a warning, that's all."

"A warning? It was about to kill us!"

"That animal is more useful to us alive than dead."

The tracker sets up his daily toilet and begins scraping the stubble from his cheeks.

"Because it will lead us to the entire pack," Danilo says, finally understanding.

"You're learning," the tracker says. "And five percent of one wolf is not going to see you through a month. But five percent of a pack, well . . . that's another matter entirely."

The two work together for the rest of the afternoon, gathering wood to build a fire, drinking coffee, sucking the liquid between their teeth to filter out the thick sludge.

"How can you tell the difference between the urine of one animal and another?" Danilo asks as he breaks down the campsite.

"I can't. And if someone tells you he can, he is lying."

"But you smelled the mud. You knew the boar were near."

"I didn't smell boar."

"So . . . you smelled—" Danilo stops. A clot of feeling is stuck in his throat. He has a memory so clear it is no memory at all but something happening right here, right now. He is in the doctor's office on that terrible day. He can smell the ammonia of her sweat and something he couldn't identify until now. "You smelled terror."

"I always find it interesting that bravery has no smell," the tracker says.

During the next few days, Klima begins to treat Danilo not simply as a lackey, useful for the strength of his back and his ability to build a fire, but as an apt pupil, testing him, praising him, even flattering him when Danilo shows himself to be a keen observer who, despite Klima's inscrutability, manages to absorb much about the tracker's art. In turn, Danilo grows more confident under the man's approval.

"I cannot take the whole pack on my own," Klima tells him, handing him a gun one day.

"You want me to—"

"You've learned how to track a wolf," Klima says. "Now you're going to learn how to kill one."

DANILO IS NOT a quick study.

"It's impossible," he says, after he has missed ten chances to hit a cross that Klima has marked on a tree trunk. Several other trees block a clear path to the target. "The bullet would have to bend."

"Can you see the target with your eyes?" Klima says.

"Yes. But I can also see the things that are in the way."

"If you can see all those things, you are not looking at your mark."

"I am."

"You're not. You're seeing too much. You see the trees. You see the small green buds on the branches over there. You're thinking about how nice it is that spring is finally here. You're thinking how your toes itch and smell like something dead and how you hope this whole thing will be over soon so you can sleep in a decent bed and eat a decent meal."

Danilo can't deny that all of this is true.

"You should see and think none of those things."

"But you see them!" Danilo says in frustration. "You see everything. Even in the dark. You're telling me about this tree and that rock and, oh, we'll reach a creek in a quarter of an hour."

"When you are tracking, you have to notice everything. You have to see what is in front of you and what is behind you. You have to let your mind create a map out of what you hear and smell and touch so that your vision is wider than your eyes alone can take in. But when you shoot, you erase everything on that map except for your target. You shut down your ears and your nose, even the sensations on your skin. If you can make the world that small," and he holds his thumb and forefinger so close they could reasonably hold a single lentil, "then you will hit your target every time."

Danilo lifts the barrel of the gun once more. He tries to do what the man tells him, to stopper his ears, to make his vision so narrow he might be wearing horse blinders. He inhales, holds his breath, pulls the trigger. "Fuck!" he exclaims, tossing the gun to the ground. The tracker laughs. "Shit!" Danilo says. The words feel stronger than any bullet. "Fucking son of a bitch mother of a whore who sucks off the world for free!" he roars, and all the pent-up humiliation he has suffered in his life and the rage he feels about his ineptitude come pouring out of him. When he runs out of words, he falls silent.

"It might be easier to simply shoot the target," Klima says finally.

"I can't," Danilo says.

"Pick up the gun," the man says. "Try again."

T here they are," **Klima says warmly,** as if he has just caught sight of his beloved children from whom he has been separated for a long time. Three wolves rest peacefully in a clearing. A white one and two whose fur is the deepest brown. Danilo is relieved; she is not among them.

A storm is coming from the west. It is only midafternoon, but the sky darkens quickly. A squall kicks up and shakes the trees. Upwind of the men, the wolves don't pick up their scent. The white wolf stands and shakes its coat, then wanders over to a tree and buries its nose in a cleft between prominent roots. After a moment, one, then two more young wolves squeeze out of the hole. The white one lies down and the pups nuzzle his snout and soon his chest heaves and he passes something from his mouth to theirs. After they have eaten, they play with him for a while then gambol over to one of the dark wolves and try to rouse him with pokes and swipes of their paws. When that proves futile, they begin to wrestle with each other, lunging and baring their teeth, clamping their jaws on necks and legs, letting go. Danilo is transfixed. He and his brother used to play just this way, picking fights for no reason other than to test their strength against each other. He remembers walking up behind his brother once, creeping softly just as he and Klima are doing now, and imagining what it would be like to break his neck. His twin was his closest ally. Having been enwombed together, neither felt whole without the other and they were rarely apart. And yet, he can summon the visceral pleasure that coursed through him as he imagined how he could harm his brother. Is it in him, he wonders? This willingness to kill someone he loves?

Klima holds out his palm. The weather arranges itself at his command, and a drop of rain lands on his skin. Then another and another, until a downpour begins in earnest. He wraps his shotgun in a blanket. Danilo does the same although he considers whether he could unload his gun without the man knowing, or if he should make a noise to alert the pack. Klima waits and watches, as heedless of the weather as the wolves are. Why does he hesitate? Danilo wonders. The wolves are in sight. They don't seem aware that they are in imminent danger. The drumbeat of rain buries all other sound. A few more steps and the tracker would be able to line up a clean shot. But Klima doesn't move, doesn't ready his weapon. His eyes scan from left to right and then back again, taking in the wolves, their surroundings, seeing what direction they might run once the first shot is fired. He's preparing his strategy. Danilo knows this; the man has taught him. The tracker narrows his focus just as he instructed Danilo to do and as Danilo is doing now. The heavy rain makes keeping an eye on the wolves that much more difficult, and so it requires a kind of concentration that obliterates all other thought. He no longer feels the water hitting the top of his head, running down his face, soaking through his trousers. The cold wind doesn't trouble him. His eyesight seems more keen as the surrounding darkness becomes total. His absolute focus makes the forest an unobstructed plain. He has stepped out of time and place.

The tracker pulls the blanket off his shotgun and starts his final advance. He moves slowly, sinuously, with fluid calibrations of muscle. For a moment, Danilo cannot help but appreciate the man's finesse just as he did the perfect works of the table he made, the way the crank turned and the rope glided through the pulleys, the entire action sliding without a hitch. How easy it is to admire evil, to become entranced by its singularity of purpose and its amoral beauty.

"There she is," Klima whispers, crouching behind a tree. He motions for Danilo to tuck himself behind him. "There's mama."

A head appears at the mouth of the den, and then an adult wolf crawls out, stretches luxuriantly, and shakes her coat. Even in the gloom and despite the downpour, she is resplendent. Her russet and gold pelt is thick. She looks healthy and strong. Danilo doesn't even try to fend off the improbable; every part of him knows. He could be watching her from the side of the stage or staring into her smoky blue eyes as he lifted her onto the doctor's examining table. Dwarf, wolf girl, wolf—she is all of these things at once, and she is here.

And she is a mother. One of the pups trots over to her and she nuzzles him with her snout, then gently bats him aside. She sits and bites the inside of her haunch, getting at some itch there.

The white wolf rises up on all fours. His ears twitch forward. Alert to his change in behavior, she leaves off grooming herself. The tracker levels his gun and cocks it slowly.

The white wolf falls even before Danilo hears the shot. And then one of the dark wolves goes down. The tracker picks off the other dark wolf on the run, aiming just ahead of the animal as he taught Danilo to do, so that it runs right into its death. The tracker moves so quickly and with such economy that Danilo does not even see him reload between shots. The pups' confusion makes them easy targets. One goes down, then the next. The third is on the run.

"Pick up your gun, boy. That little one is yours," Klima says, shifting his sights toward the mother, who follows after her pup. Later, Danilo will remember everything happening in the time it took to draw a single breath. In the moment, however, it feels like Klima is in no hurry. The barrel of his shotgun moves slowly as he follows the mother wolf's path.

Danilo's hands shake uncontrollably. He has to steady his nerves so that he doesn't do something foolish.

Klima inhales deeply and holds his breath. His finger curls around the trigger.

The shots occur simultaneously. Klima and the wolf fall at

the same time. Danilo is frozen, still aiming his gun at the place where the man stood only a second before. His focus on his target was so absolute that it takes some time for the rest of the world to return to him and for him to realize that the rain is still falling hard, that his shot was so accurate that the man is not even groaning, that his own body is not shaking in fear and panic but that he feels utterly calm. At the corner of his gaze, he sees movement. The pup disappears into the trees. The mother struggles to her feet. Blood stains the fur on her leg, but she took only a glancing hit and she starts to run. Before Danilo can think to call her name, she is gone.

THE THREE ADULT WOLVES and the two pups are dead. The tracker was viciously accurate with his aim, and there is hardly any blood on the ground around the animals' bodies, as if the bullets managed to stop their hearts without piercing their hides. They look gentle in their endless sleep and they look small, too, smaller even than some of the village dogs Danilo grew up around and petted and played with in the stream on hot summer days. The pups look like stuffed toys.

Danilo's shot was not so elegant. At close range, the bullet tore through Klima's body and ripped him open so that the sausage of his guts is exposed. Like the animals, the man seems insignificant in death, hardly capable of killing five wolves let alone all the other bold acts attributed to him. The blast spun him so that he fell on his side. Now he lies with his legs tucked into his chest. Death seems to have reversed time so that he looks like a sleeping child.

The man is dead. Danilo is holding a gun. Therefore Danilo killed the man. But he doesn't really believe it because he cannot recall anything about what occurred, not lifting his rifle, taking aim, pulling the trigger. He'd been a good student. He'd practiced and practiced so that, when the time came, shooting became second nature, no more remarkable than lifting a finger to point out a star. "Killing is beyond thought, beyond feeling," the man had told him, and it turned out that he'd been right.

By the time the rain lets up, it is nearly dawn. Danilo has not slept. Wrapped in a sopping blanket, he walks past the dead man, past the scattered corpses of the wolves. Using Klima's knife, he cuts down a few saplings. He pulls the tenting material from his pack and slices it into strips, then ties the narrow trunks together so they form a sled. He works efficiently and without much thought, but as soon as he tries to move the sodden body, he loses his composure, overwhelmed by the realization that he has murdered a man. The numbness of the night before is replaced by a feeling so raw it is painful, as if Danilo were the one who was shot and all his organs were lying outside his dead body in a bloody stew. A tremor starts deep in his center and spreads through his body, and as he scoops out a shallow grave in the mud, rolls the man into it, and covers him, he can barely stand. He dismantles his sled and uses the strongest of the struts to make a cross, sinking it into the mud, then hammering it into the harder earth below with the stock of his gun.

It takes him four days to find his way out of the wilderness. By the time he reaches a town, he is delirious with fever. As he wanders down the main street, people clear a path around him. He tries to speak, but no one will stop to listen. Finally, a priest comes out of a church and hears his hoarse confession.

"I killed a man," Danilo says, when he finally stands before a constable. "I killed him to save the girl I love."

HE LIES ON A COT in a cell. A jailer brings him a plate of food. He devours the slice of meat and piece of bread. This is the first food he's had in days. He has not eaten bread for—how long has it been? How long was he in the woods with that man? When was the last time he was inside an actual building? He studies his new habitat and feels immediately grateful for its walls, its bars, and its solid iron lock that protect him from the confusion his life has become.

But his comfort is short-lived. After failing to provide a clear verbal description of where he buried Klima, and unable to pinpoint the place on a map the constable shows him, his hands and feet are chained and he is led outside. With considerable effort, he climbs into a wagon and is ordered by the constable and two other officers riding alongside him to direct them to the body. As they drive, they pass soldiers marching in a line, young men no older than Danilo, most of them haphazardly dressed, some of them armed with shotguns, others carrying spades or pitchforks.

"Where are they going?" he asks.

"To fight," one of the officers says. "Something an able-bodied man such as yourself should be doing. Instead, you've murdered your own countryman."

"Are we at war?" Danilo says.

"You really are daft, aren't you?" the man says. "Where've you been?"

"I've been in the woods."

"Fucking a wolf, is what I hear," he says. "Of all the excuses for murdering, that one is something new, isn't it?"

Remarkably, although he has no memory of how he reached the village, Danilo manages to direct the police to the exact spot where the wolves lie, as if, in his feverish state, he'd somehow memorized every hillock and stand of trees and narrow river he'd passed, noticing the intricate geography of the land just as the tracker taught him to do. The animals are mere carcasses now, having been eviscerated by the carrion birds that wheel overhead. He points out the cross, and the policemen exhume the dead man.

THE STINK of the massacre site, the constable announces at the trial, hoping to claim some extra measure of heroism, was enough to kill off all the enemy forces. This statement raises a welter of patriotic exclamations from the crowd. Some begin to sing the nation's anthem before they are hushed by the judge's gavel. When Danilo takes the stand, he is less coherent. He mumbles and stares into his lap when the prosecutor questions him, and more than once the judge has to remind him to speak up.

"Tell the court why you murdered Mr. Klima," the prosecutor says.

"Because he was going to kill her."

"Who are you referring to? State her name for the court."

"Pavla. Pavla Janáček."

"And this Pavla would be?"

"The girl I love. There was blood on her fur, but it was just a scrape. She escaped."

The spectators begin to whisper and have to be reminded to hold their peace.

"Blood on her skin, you mean?" the prosecutor asks.

"She has a beautiful coat," Danilo says. "More red than blond, although she was a fair girl. Well, I'd say her hair was golden. No, not golden. More like the color of light. Afternoon light, I guess you'd say. She was shot once before. By the human skeleton. I don't think she could have survived another injury."

Laughter breaks out in the courtroom.

"Pavla is a woman?" the prosecutor says.

"Yes!"

"Or is she a wolf?"

"Yes!"

The judge leans over his desk to observe Danilo more closely. "Do you need some water, young man?"

Danilo nods and a clerk brings him a glass. He drinks down the whole thing at once while the court waits in anticipation for whatever clarification might be lying at the bottom of the tumbler.

"Thank you," he says, handing the glass to the prosecutor, who looks unhappy to be taken for a servant.

"Now then," the prosecutor continues, setting the glass aside. "He shot her on the left side—"

"Flank," Danilo says.

"And where is this . . . wolf now?"

"She ran into the woods to find her pup."

"She has a child?"

"She had three. Three!" he repeats, amazed.

"Three children now, is it?" the prosecutor says.

"But he shot two of them," Danilo says.

The spectators erupt. The judge silences them. "Are you accusing the dead man of murdering children?" he asks Danilo.

The prosecutor sighs. "The police found a pack of dead wolves, your honor. There were no children there."

"I'm telling the truth," Danilo says.

The prosecutor takes an elaborate glance at his pocket watch to suggest his impatience. "So you are telling the court that this man, Klima, shot at a woman and killed two children, and that the woman, whose left . . . flank . . . was grazed by a bullet, escaped into the woods."

"Yes! That's it!" Danilo says, rising from his seat excitedly. "Thank you."

"Sit down," the judge cautions.

"We have sent investigators to every town in the vicinity. Search parties have scoured the woods near the murder scene. Yet there is no one who has seen or heard reports of such a woman," the prosecutor tells the judge.

"Wolves can travel forty-five kilometers in a day. My Pavla is very fast. You should see her run. Even after all she's been through."

The crowd erupts again. "Young man, the court is not amused by your antics," the judge calls over the disruption. "You would do yourself a favor to answer the questions frankly and truthfully."

"And you would think," Danilo continues, growing more animated, "that muscles once stretched out on a rack would be ruined, but she is like a dancer. If only you had seen her! I would say"—and here he stands again and begins to reenact the pantomime—"'who is this mysterious young woman with the beautiful form? Yon maiden, show me your face!' And then she would say, 'Alas, I am cursed to wander this earth without ever showing myself.' And then we would dance—" He takes the imaginary girl in his arms and performs the dance Smetanka taught them: "Two steps to the left, two steps to the right, break apart and spin. Come together again. And then I would beg to see her—"

A woman in the courtroom shrieks.

"No! Not yet!" Danilo cries. "The wolf girl has not shown her face!"

Explosions, *as if rocks were being hurled from the sky.* The ground shakes. The blasts move from her paws up through her legs and vibrate through her belly. The bombs have ignited the dry brush, and she uses the fires to guide herself through the night. Not long after she felt the heat of the shot skim her leg, she caught sight of her pup, but she was hobbled and he was fast. And then he was gone. She has been on her own for a long time.

Another explosion. Closer. As she makes her way through the thick smoke, she can hardly see. She lifts her head and howls. The sound floats away. She waits. But nothing comes back to her. The smoke begins to thin, and in the widening aperture of light she sees dark shapes strewn on the ground. A hopeful sign. Food has been hard to come by. Animals who have survived have fled the fires and smoke. When she can, she's been feeding on dead horse and picking through the burned flesh of humans for whatever the buzzards have not yet devoured. But she hasn't eaten for a long time and she's hungry.

One of the shapes moves, rises, and turns itself into the body of a man. He stumbles, rights himself. "Oh, God," he says. "Oh, God."

A sound comes from another of the bodies. A low moan. It starts and stops, then starts again. The standing man crouches and picks up an arm. A hand is attached to it, fingers curled. The man studies it, turning it this way and that. For a moment, he tries to find the body it belongs to, but then gives up and places it carefully on the ground. He picks up something else. She recognizes the weapon, knows what it can do. She is about to run, but he puts down the gun next to the arm. She relaxes. He is not a threat. Slowly, she pads closer, picking her way among the dead bodies, sniffing them and the ground around them. A rock hits her on the side of her head.

"Get this goddamn cur away from me."

She jumps back, raises her tail, growls.

"Jiří? Is that you?"

"Me or my ghost. Take your pick. Shoo, you fucking mutt!"

The standing man lumbers toward her, waving his hands wildly, baring his teeth and roaring. She stands her ground, cocks her head.

"Holy God!" he says. "It's a wolf."

"Well, shoot it before it eats me for dinner," the man on the ground says.

The standing man seems more surprised than scared. He lowers his arms, studies her. "I don't think it has a taste for your stinking meat, my friend. Anyway, wolves don't eat people," he says.

"Says Ivan, the genius."

"Says me." Ivan kneels over the wounded man. "Where did they get you, Jiři?"

"Everywhere. I don't know."

"Where does it hurt?"

"It doesn't hurt at all. Ivan, am I dead? Are we all dead?"

"Your trousers are a bloody mess, man." Ivan takes out a knife and slices open Jiři's pant leg. Slowly he moves the fabric to one side. There is nothing beneath it but pulverized flesh. He heaves and vomits.

"That's the effect I have on all the girls."

Ivan recovers. "Are you sure it doesn't hurt?"

"Help me up. Maybe I can walk."

"No, Jiři."

"Just get me on my feet, Ivan."

"I think it's better if you don't move."

"Help me, you ass!"

Ivan crouches behind Jiři's back and lifts him into a sitting position. The effort exhausts both men. Jiři collapses against Ivan's chest. "I don't feel so good," he says.

She sits down on her haunches, gnaws at her side, licks the blood there.

"Jiři?"

"What."

"Just wanted to make sure you weren't dead."

"Who else is alive? Julius? Emil? The lieutenant?"

There is no answer.

"Jesus, Ivan."

"Who knows, I might be dead, too."

Jiři's laughter causes him pain and he groans.

"You shouldn't laugh."

"I'd rather be killed by a bad joke than a blown-off leg."

"You're not going to die."

"I'm never going to dance again," Jiři says.

"The world will rejoice."

"Fuck you."

"Fuck you, too."

"Where's the wolf?" Jiři says.

"Over there. Lying down. Licking its balls."

"Taking its pleasure."

"Who wouldn't at a time like this?"

"You would. You take it wherever you can get it. I'm surprised your cock hasn't fallen off."

"Who's to say it hasn't? I haven't checked lately."

They are quiet for a while.

"Do you think the whole world is destroyed? That all that's left is just you, me, and that damned ball-licking wolf?" Ivan says.

"What is he doing now?"

"He's watching us."

"Smacking his lips, I suppose. Waiting for us to die so he doesn't have to do the dirty work."

"Listen, Jiři, he could fill himself up ten times over without laying a hand on you and me if that's what he was after."

"Everyone's dead, then?"

"Yes."

"Slava, that big fat fuck? They even got him?"

"Even him."

"He's bleeding."

"Slava?"

"The wolf. Come here, boy. Come here."

"What the fuck are you doing? Are you an idiot?"

Ivan pulls a rucksack off one of the corpses lying nearby and slides it beneath Jiři's head so that he can remain semi-upright. Then Ivan crawls toward the wolf, making kissing sounds.

"Oh my God," Jiři says. "It's not your grandmother's ratter, that mangy excuse for a dog."

She watches curiously as the man approaches her, making his strange noise. When he gets too close, she stands and backs away, waits.

"He's a cowardly fuck," Jiři says.

"He's a she," Ivan says.

"How do you know?"

"Now who's the fool? *C'mere, girl*," the man says, his voice rising and thinning out. "I'm not going to hurt you."

He removes something from one of his pockets. The odor of meat cuts through all the other smells. Her tail wags, her ears prick up. She does not take her eyes off his hand.

"C'mon," the man says. "It's a bit of dried beef. Nasty but surprisingly tasty if you don't mind the mold."

"Fool," Jiři says. "You'd feed that cur and let us starve to death?"

"You hungry?" Ivan asks the wolf.

She cannot stand it any longer. She darts forward, snatches the meat from the man's hand, and retreats.

"Ho!" Ivan says, studying his fingers that are, remarkably, still connected to his hand. "That was incredible! Did you see that, Jiři? She didn't even touch me!"

She swallows the morsel and licks her muzzle. The meat does nothing to satisfy her hunger. She sniffs, paces back and forth.

"Do you think they're coming to get us?" Jiři says.

"Yes. Of course."

"I don't think they're coming to get us."

"They will."

"I wouldn't. Why do they need to risk their lives for two lousy soldiers. One lousy soldier and one legless gimp."

"Not legless. Less one leg."

"Not enough legs to kick you in the ass and still be standing."

Ivan rummages through the rucksacks of the fallen soldiers. "Ah!" he says, pleased. He holds up a package of biscuits. He returns to where she sits, unwraps the food, and holds it out to her. She waits for him to come closer but he stops just beyond her reach. With his free hand, he beckons her. He makes that smacking sound with his lips. Slowly, she gets up and walks toward him but when she is near enough to his outstretched arm to make a grab for the food, he steps back. She advances, he retreats, this time withdrawing the food and bringing it close to his body. He holds out his empty hand. What does he want? The smell is too much. She moves closer until his hand is on her head. He rests it there so lightly she can barely feel it. He brings his other hand close to her snout. She takes the food, but more gently this time.

"That's it," he whispers. "That's a good girl."

"You should have been a lion tamer," Jiři says.

Ivan brings both hands to her face and smooths her fur. He does this again and again. Then he slowly works his way down the length of her back. When he is done, he brings his hands to his face and inhales. "Echh," he says.

"You probably smell worse," Jiři says.

The man touches her again. She sits, then lies down, dropping to one side. She lets him rub her belly, scratch her throat. Her eyes shutter.

"Is it going to snow?" Jiři says.

"It's springtime, fool," Ivan says gently, concentrating on carefully moving his hands over the wolf's body so that he doesn't startle her.

"But it's so cold."

"It's probably thirty degrees out. I'm pouring with—what?" He stands up. He runs over to Jiři. "No," he says. "No, no, no, no." He rushes to gather clothes off the dead. He works frantically, shaking bodies out of jackets, ripping through packs to find blankets. He piles all the clothes on top of his shivering friend. Then he runs a little ways, stops. He circles around himself, as if he dropped his plan in the dirt and has to find it. "Hey!" he calls out. "Help us! We're here! Help!" He hurries back to Jiři, touches his skin. "You're like ice."

"I told you it would snow."

"I've got to get you out of here."

"No," Jiři says. "Let's wait. Someone will come."

"There's no one to wait for. No one knows we're here."

She gets up and walks over to the man on the ground. She leans over his face and sniffs him. She licks his cheeks.

"Go ahead," Jiři says. "Eat me up. You have my permission."

She lies down next to him and presses her body against his.

Meanwhile, Ivan has found his plan and with it, the company cannon, the one that has been his and Jiři's duty, these past months, to haul from one battlefield to another, the few horses reserved for the lazy officers who want to keep their boots clean. Ivan and Jiři, friends since childhood, named the cannon Olga to remind them of their fat neighbor who they caught one day bathing by the river, the sheer expanse of her buttocks so mesmerizing that they developed a reverence for her and rose to her defense when others called her names. Truth be told, Ivan was a bit in love with her. They have spent their days alternately cursing the heavy iron wheels that made the cannon so unwieldy and caring for those same wheels with loving attention, greasing the axel, tightening the bolts, polishing the bore as if it were the girl herself in need of their tender affection.

It takes enormous effort to push the cannon over to where Jiři lies covered in piles of cloth and, Ivan realizes as he comes up next to his friend, warmed by the wolf.

"Good girl," he says, patting the animal's side. He touches his friend's face. Jiři's skin is gray. Despite his woozy protests and then his howls of pain, Ivan drapes Jiři's body over the cannon and secures him there, using the dead soldiers' belts and rifle straps. He goes to the other side, lifts the cart handles, and pulls. He barely manages a few centimeters before he stops, winded, his shoulders already throbbing from the effort. Behind him Jiři whimpers. Ivan gets to his feet and tries again. This time the wheels don't even turn. The impossibility of the situation feels like a physical blow and he falls to his knees. He allows himself to weep until a peaceful resignation overtakes him. There is no reason to move. He can stop trying so hard. He will keep his old friend company until he dies and then, eventually, he will die, too. It will be a matter of days, his death. It will come with thirst and starvation but it will not be a terrible thing. It might even be sweet, like when he was a boy in the moments before sleep. How he loved the delicious smell of his mother's skin as she moved her face toward his, the kiss of her eyelashes on his cheek—

Foul-smelling breath works on him like smelling salts and he is suddenly and fully alert, panicked that he slept through the wake-up call and missed his orders. But why is a wolf's face staring down into his? Why is its cold, wet nose nudging his cheek? He is on his feet, ready to form up, salute, and march. *Yes, Lieutenant! Present, Lieutenant!*

At this outburst, the wolf makes a small yelping noise and jumps back. When the situation finally arranges itself properly in Ivan's mind, he checks on his friend. Jiři's eyes are closed and his body, still draped over the cannon, is motionless.

"No, Jiři," Ivan says, shaking his friend. "Not yet. Please." He puts his ear to Jiři's lips. Nothing, and then the barest trace of an exhalation. "He's not dead," Ivan says to no one. Or maybe he's speaking to the wolf, who watches him expectantly. "Okay, it was a stupid idea," he says to her. "If you've got a better one, speak up. No?" he says when she offers nothing in the way of advice. "Well, you're no help at all."

Ivan unties the straps, pulls Jiři off the cannon, and despite the awful moans and garbled protests, hoists him onto his back. "God Almighty!" Ivan cries, gathering his energy and his will. "They should have blown off your fat ass, too."

He hasn't gone far before he realizes that the wolf is following him. "Go! Scat!" he says, but he doesn't mean it. He's grateful for the company.

A *s on an ocean liner* (or so he remembers being told by the combustible man, who, by habit, left nothing to chance and had studied the plan of the ship on which he was to sail after the season came to an end), there are three classes of accommodation at the Saint Gunther of Bohemia Home for Deteriorating Individuals. First class is reserved for the wealthy insane, the wives and daughters of landed nobility driven mad by purposeless days and a surfeit of embroidery projects, and mother-coddled, milksop sons incited to patricide by demeaning fathers. Danilo has never seen these quarters, but the chattering nurses, who speak freely among rank-and-file lunatics as if madness makes them only capable of infantile comprehension, have described rooms fitted out with gilt mirrors and pastoral watercolors imported from ancestral estates. These comforting details are meant to hasten convalescence or—and this is often the families' truest desire—convince the patients to choose a lifetime at the asylum over returning home. The rooms also come with maid's or butler's quarters so that the wealthy will be properly bathed and shaved and serviced with afternoon tea. Danilo can well imagine how a perfectly sane lady's maid must feel, trapped inside the labyrinthine building, once a monastery, where the screams of the mad resound against the thick stone walls of the corridors or gather at the upper reaches of the vaulted wards. He often wonders whether some of the shrieks emerging from the upper floor that houses these upscale quarters come not from insane barons and baronesses but from their entrapped and helpless help. The second class is reserved for merchants who have no staff or family heirlooms to keep them company but who, as bereft of sense as they might be, still maintain enough pride to refuse to be housed with the impoverished and the vagrant and the criminally insane. This third-class ward is where men like Danilo are housed, and he shares his quarters with two rapists, a sodomite, and a man who could not have accomplished either crime having cut off his penis. At his trial, the judge told Danilo he was lucky that progressive-minded lady reformers had made it their mission to protect brain-addled felons from the state prison. Danilo was relieved. Like every child he ever knew, he had grown up under the threat of being sent to that penitentiary of horrors for any number of childhood infractions. His mother routinely warned him that a stolen cookie would result in him joining the ranks of convicted thieves who had their wayward fingers crushed by thumbscrews.

Still, he cannot imagine that there is a place on earth more terrifying than the one in which he now finds himself, where on any given night he might wake to find a glowering cannibal standing above his bed regarding him with disturbing consideration, or where showers are places where men examine and exhort their bodies with the uninhibited abandon he can only remember exercising as a child, when he and his brother hid in the bushes and measured their respective lengths and trajectories. The unnerving freedom of the asylum, where the mad roam the halls and cloistered gardens at will, makes him wish for the confinement of a murderer's cell where the only visitor comes in the form of a tray of inedible slops passed through a slot by monstrously disfigured guards two times a day, *if you are so lucky*! All these years later he can hear his mother's voice. Gnarled and scrofulous hands still invade his dreams.

It would all be easier to bear if he were actually mad. There are times when he envies the man in the bed next to his who is content to hold dramatic and voluble conversations with himself all day long in a language no one can identify. Whatever he is saying makes him alternately laugh and frown or expound as though he were a philosopher playfully toying with the trickiness of his own logic. Or the man who lies so inert in the bed across the ward that Danilo has passed many sleepless nights trying to figure out if he is, in fact, dead. There are times when the behavior of the patients seems not that different from the carnival performers, and he sometimes thinks of his fellow inmates as attractions: the Frozen Man, the Giant Baby, the Drooler, the Twitcher. And what would he be called? The Wolf Lover? But try as he might, and he does try—going over the statements he made at the trial that aroused such derision from the crowd, anger from the prosecutor, and pity from the judge—to take their point of view and convince himself of the unreasonableness of his position, he can't. He has seen a beating heart in a jar, a man who can tie his limbs into knots, a woman who can clothe herself in her own fat. So why not a girl who transforms into a wolf? Why not a man who loves her?

EACH DAY UNFOLDS exactly the same as the one before. If he has managed to sleep, he is awoken by a nurse who stands at the head of the ward ringing a hand bell with more exuberance than is necessary. Along with the twenty other men, he visits the toilets where he must do his business in front of anyone who cares to watch, and there are a few. Next, the men are marched through long, dim hallways to the third-class refectory. That the nurses insist on using the old monastery designations only highlights the difference between what Danilo imagines was once a place where monks earnestly and silently ate their daily bread and the chaotic, sometimes violent place it is now. The dining room resounds with the voices of the patients, the clatter of dishware, and the occasional warning bark from one of the burly guards. Even though it is summer, the stone walls still harbor winter cold, and Danilo has to blow on his fingers before he can wrap them around a spoon. A serving girl who looks as furtive and tortured as the patients serves morning porridge that always smells sweet and stale, as if it has been predigested. A few of the inmates who have proved themselves unpredictable with tableware sit with their hands tied behind their backs and are fed by orderlies.

When Danilo first arrived at the asylum, he was brought to see the warden, a blunt but not unkind man whose hair, perhaps in deference to the building's history, naturally took the form of a monk's tonsure. Danilo expected to be questioned about the murder, but the man treated the meeting like an interview for a job. He asked Danilo to name his skills.

"I have none," Danilo said.

"Every man has something that he secretly feels he can do better than anyone else. I, for instance, can tie my shoes one-handed."

"What use is that?" Danilo asked.

"It dazzles my nieces and nephews. They think I'm an old fool, but it gets a smile out of them."

Put at ease, Danilo admitted that he could build torture devices, perform in pantomimes with half-human creatures, and shoot men in the back at close range, but not wolves. He could also, he said, make shoes, but not very well, as his apprenticeship was cut short.

The warden did not flinch during Danilo's recitation, having heard far more disturbing information from far more troubled men. His expression brightened, however, at the mention of shoemaking, and Danilo was assigned to the sewing detail.

Danilo understands that this "work therapy," as the man called it, not bothering to hide his skepticism, is a new program, although only the more stable of the patients participate. The delusional, the babblers, the ones who claim they are the

Emperor of Ethiopia spend their days wandering the unkempt gardens, staring, smoking their allotment of cigarettes, and getting into fistfights over cast-off butts. Danilo is grateful for the work. It passes the hours and gives him some idea of what is happening outside the asylum where talk of worldly events is forbidden. It is not considered palliative to suggest to the patients that there is a life beyond the walls that they can hope to rejoin. In the few months of his imprisonment, Danilo's work in the converted sacristy has changed from sewing priestly cassocks and surplices to making uniforms for soldiers. In this way, he has learned that the war still rages.

ONCE A WEEK, he sees his doctor, an excitable man named Mašek who always greets his patient with wide-eyed surprise even though they meet regularly on Thursday afternoons. At each meeting, the doctor is unkempt in some new way. One week his jacket is wrongly buttoned, one side lolling down his thigh as if it were trying to lick something off the ground. His hair is a mass of curls that corkscrew in different directions, giving him the look of a boy whose mother has not performed the customary spit and smooth before Sunday Mass. Sometimes, when Mašek speaks, his enthusiasm is such that bubbles of spit gather at the corners of his mouth. Occasionally, when his chin becomes slick with drool, Danilo tries to draw the man's attention to the problem with a pointed throat clearing, but this only prompts the doctor to ask him about his persistent tic. Mašek speaks at such a rapid clip that his inhalations often come as great, desperate gasps, leading Danilo to wonder if a person can be asphyxiated by speech. The doctor's office desk is piled with papers and files, and sometimes, when he is trying to explain something to Danilo, he will paw through the disorganization, knocking his hand against the bell that sits there, claiming that a certain article will make his point perfectly clear. More often than not, he gives up the search or simply forgets that he is looking, or the conversation has leapfrogged with such dizzying nonlinearity that the article in question is no longer germane.

During his time at the asylum, Danilo has observed the therapies that have been applied to other patients. Some are dosed so heavily that if they don't sleep all day and night, they look vacant, as if their souls have been sucked out through their eyes. Others have suppurating blisters on their wrists and ankles from restraints. A course of purgatives administered to a patient is so intense that the man dies after twenty-four hours of constant heaving. Danilo is terrified of these treatments, which is why, in his first session with Mašek months earlier, he was determined to convince the man of his sanity.

"You may speak freely," Mašek said during that encounter. "Do not judge your words. Say whatever you wish."

"You want me to talk?" Danilo said.

"Yes. Certainly."

"But you're the doctor."

"Freely, then," Mašek repeated hopefully. He sat across the desk from Danilo, his pen poised over a notebook, ready to take down whatever free words Danilo might offer him.

"What should I talk about?"

"Whatever comes to mind."

"What comes to mind is wondering what I should talk about."

"Good. Good," the man said, nodding his head rapidly, scribbling on the page.

"And now what comes to mind is wondering why what I just said is good."

"Yes," the man said.

"Yes, what?"

"Yes!"

"I'm not sure I belong here," Danilo said. "I'm not mad. In fact, I think I'm very sane."

Mašek made a hurried note, then looked up again expectantly. Danilo waited for a follow-up question but none came.

"I'm confused," Danilo said.

"Yes, you are," the man said sympathetically. "Terribly."

"I mean I'm confused here. Now. With you."

"Exactly."

The doctors had been injecting the Twitcher with something that calmed his nerves but created such craving for the drug that the man had begun to scratch his skin off during the time between waking from his calm stupor and the next dose of the narcotic. His bedsheets were streaked with blood. Danilo hoped his new and zealous doctor would not prescribe such a treatment.

Mašek put down his pen. "We've made great progress," he said gravely. "I will see you in one week." When he stood, he somehow managed to upset his desktop so that papers and books spilled off the edges. He looked as distressed as a boy who has woken to a wet bed. When Danilo helped collect everything, he saw the doctor's open notebook where he had written the words *Self-aggrandizing. Delusional. Roast of pork?*

All these months later, during each weekly meeting, Danilo feels obligated to speak but incapable of saying anything to prove his sanity that the doctor does not interpret as evidence of his mental incompetence. This problem makes him wonder if the difference between the sane and the demented is only a matter of language. He spends the long days at his sewing machine, pumping the treadle until his ankle hurts, trying to solve this latest problem of his life: people are only determined to be sane by virtue of not being considered insane, and so, having been proven mad in a court of law, it is now impossible for him to prove the opposite. He tries to behave normally. He sits and smiles and offers polite nods at appropriate times in conversations. He asks after the nurses' health and makes pleasant remarks about the weather. He lets the staff know that he understands just how disturbed the others around him are, aligning himself with the official side of things. But none of this seems to help his case. Each Thursday afternoon, Mašek sits silently, smiles obliquely, holds his pen above his paper, and waits for Danilo to further his doom. All the while, Danilo's attention is snagged by a bit of the day's lunch that is trapped in the doctor's mustache, and there he is again, clearing his throat, and there is the doctor, once more asking him what is making him so terribly anxious.

The doctor is a master of prolonged and miserably uncomfortable silence and, one day, when Danilo can't think of anything to say, he seizes on the list the doctor made at their first meeting. "Do you like pork roast?" he says.

"Mmm," the doctor says. Neither affirming nor denying.

"Do you like cabbage?" Danilo says.

"Do you?"

"Yes! Both red and white!" Danilo says enthusiastically. You see? he means to say. I am a normal person who has no strange preference for one sort of cabbage over another. I am not like the patient who must cut his meal into a hundred tiny bites and eat each one separately, or the one who sobs like a baby when he does not feel he is given as large a dumpling as his tablemates. "My mother makes a good pork roast, although I haven't had it for many years now."

Mašek straightens up, leans forward. "Go on," he says.

Danilo is wary. Has his interest in pork or cabbage or both signaled his craziness?

"And . . . ?" the doctor urges.

"She cooks it for eight hours," Danilo says, feeling himself falling deeper into a hole of his own making. "It is very . . . tender?" he adds.

"Tender." The man scribbles on the pad.

"Yes," Danilo says, deflated. He wonders if the doctor will prescribe the medication they give to the Twitcher. He looks at the skin on his arms fondly, thinks maybe it will be best to bite his fingernails down to the quick before he has the opportunity to scratch himself.

"Go on," Mašek says.

"It tastes very much like . . ."

"Like . . . ?"

"Like . . ." and here, Danilo knows he is walking straight into a trap but he is too exhausted to stop himself, "like someone is holding me in her arms."

DANILO'S SESSIONS go on this way for months. It is undeniably pleasant to spend an hour a week in Mašek's office away from the chaos of the ward. Try as he might, he cannot inure himself to the nighttime weeping of grown men, or their incomprehensible muttering, their catatonia, or incessant rocking. But as the doctor seems intent on turning his patient's every word into proof of his derangement, Danilo becomes increasingly worried that he will never be released and that he will never see her again. He begins to pull out his hair. Each morning he wakes to find a fistful of the stuff on his pillow. With a seam ripper he steals from the sewing room, he opens up stitches on the side of his mattress and adds his hair to the stuffing so that no one will notice. But the problem becomes difficult to hide. During one of his weekly showers, he is horrified to feel bald patches on his scalp. Mašek will see the state of his hair and count it as one more mark against his claims of mental health.

Then, something wonderful happens: a patient is cured. In fact, it is the Frozen Man who suddenly begins to move and talk and act otherwise completely normal. No longer does he lie in his bed like a corpse or sit at attention in the refectory, his hands on his knees, opening and closing his mouth like a nutcracker when one of the orderlies brings a spoon to his lips.

"It is a miracle," a nurse says, when Danilo asks why he has not seen the former catatonic for days. He wonders if the man has been transferred to another ward where his cure is being studied just as assiduously as his illness. She whispers because religious talk is not tolerated at the asylum, especially one where a patient carries a bundle of dirty clothes at all times and prefers to be addressed as Our Lady of Sorrows. "One day he stands up and starts walking. The next, he practically runs out of here!" she says excitedly.

"He escaped?"

"He was released! We nurses gave him quite a send-off party! But we were sad to see him go. He was such a charming man."

"He never spoke," Danilo says.

"Yes. Lovely manners."

While the nurse reminisces fondly about the virtues of catatonia, it occurs to Danilo that he has been trying to solve his problem the wrong way. Hoping to win his release, he's worked for months to convince Mašek of a mental clarity that could be ascribed to any sane man. But what can the doctor do with that? How can he make his professional reputation with a patient who is incurable because he is already cured? What Danilo needs to do is prove himself utterly and very specifically crazy and then allow the doctor to cure his disease. At the same time that he forms his plan, he begins to understand the doctor's particular interest in his mother's famous pork and his childhood fear of snakes, and especially the man's fixation on the dream Danilo related to him where he was being led down a narrow street by a strange woman whose face he could not see toward the locked door of a small house. The woman pushed open the door and Danilo slipped into a corridor that tilted slightly upward.

"You *slipped* in?" Mašek had asked.

"Yes," Danilo said, recalling the dream fondly. "Glided. As if I were greased for the purpose."

The man wrote so quickly his pen flew across the room, narrowly missing Danilo's head.

"I want to make love to a wolf," Danilo declares at the next session, speaking before the doctor, whose shirttail is sticking out of his trouser fly like a small white flag, has even taken his seat. "Well, she was a wolf girl before she was a wolf, but not really, and before that she was a dwarf, and I built a machine that stretched her and she grew, but that's another story."

"Why don't you start from the beginning," the doctor says.

IT TAKES DANILO a month of sessions to relate the entire history. He tries to rush through so that the doctor can begin to work on whatever cure he has in store, but Mašek gets stuck on details. For instance, they spend an entire session talking about, of all people, Danilo's long-dead brother.

"Your twin," Mašek says.

"Yes."

"Identical or fraternal?"

Danilo doesn't know the difference, but in his determination to be utterly and undeniably mad, he answers, "Both."

"Was he exactly like you?" Mašek says patiently.

"They said he was smarter," Danilo admits, although the insult, buried for all these years, stings. "I was never very clever in school."

"Exactly like you in his looks, is what I'm getting at."

"Oh. Well, I guess so. We both had dark hair and were about the same height, if that's what you mean."

The doctor appears momentarily uninterested.

"But we didn't look the same when we . . . undressed," Danilo says, testing out a theory he is developing.

"Go on."

"He was . . . bigger."

The doctor nods his head slowly. "And this was something you knew by—"

"Looking?" Danilo says. From the doctor's satisfied reaction, he can tell that his theory is correct, and that snakes and a dream of slipping into a narrow corridor are all of a piece.

"And your brother, he died how?"

"He got sick."

"But you didn't get sick."

"No."

"And after he died, your parents sent you away to live with Doctor . . . Doctor—"

"Smetanka."

"When they sent you away, how did you feel?" Mašek says.

"Sad?"

"Can you remember other times when your parents made you feel sad?"

Danilo thinks for a while. "One time, when I cut the leather for a pair of ladies' boots all wrong and my father took his belt to me."

"As a punishment."

"Yes."

"Because he blamed you for ruining the boots."

"But it was my brother's fault. He ruined the boots. I took the blame because he was more . . . was more . . ."

"Go on."

"Endowed?"

The doctor's enthusiastic nod tells Danilo he's given the correct answer. When Mašek is finished making his notes, he looks up, an expectant smile on his face. It dawns on Danilo what the doctor wants to hear.

"So, they punished me by sending me to Doctor Smetanka's because they blamed me for my brother's death?"

"Precisely!" Mašek says excitedly.

Danilo leaves the session feeling utterly confused. Without knowing exactly how, he has admitted to killing his beloved brother because . . . because his brother had a bigger penis than he did.

But his misgivings are no match for the doctor's enthusiasm for his patient, and Danilo soon learns that the digressions that seem to make his ultimate cure and release that much further off are exactly what convince Mašek of the precise nature of his patient's illness. So Danilo learns not to rush things during the session when Mašek wants him to describe what Smetanka looked like and to agree that, yes, even though the man was fair where Danilo's father is dark, and even though Smetanka was no doctor while Danilo's father is scrupulous and has a reputation for making boots that last a lifetime and wedding shoes that assure a fruitful marriage, the anger and passion Danilo feels toward them both have somehow transformed into his desire to make love to an animal that he can only, reasonably, enter from behind.

TWO MONTHS HAVE PASSED during which Danilo has admitted to many unseemly thoughts and sometimes deeds but has not received any treatment. In the wards, patients swallow pills that put them to sleep for days and others that wake them from their torpors. They receive injections that make them pleasantly happy, their loopy smiles permanently affixed, and injections that make the overly giddy controllably dour.

"Can I ask a question?" Danilo says during a session.

"Questions are as meaningful as answers," Mašek says.

"When will I receive my medicine?"

"Your medicine?"

"My treatment. So that I can be cured."

Mašek looks confused. "But this is the treatment."

"What is?"

"Our meetings."

"But where are the pills?" Danilo says, incredulous. "Or injections? I don't mind needles."

Mašek laughs, not unkindly. "Oh, I don't believe in any of that rubbish."

"Rubbish?" Danilo says, disheartened.

"What we are doing together is modern! It is the only true medicine."

"But all we do is talk."

"Exactly."

"But . . . but how will I get better?" Danilo says. "How will I be cured?"

"These things take a long time," Mašek says. "Sometimes years. My teacher in Vienna, why, he's worked with one patient for ten years! And he has yet to break through! You are a terribly sick young man. We have to have patience."

"But I don't have patience!" Danilo cries out. He stands and paces the room furiously. His mind reels from his horrible miscalculation. "I don't have ten years. I need to see her now!"

"Who?"

"Pavla."

"The wolf?"

"What kind of a doctor are you?" Danilo says. He's so distressed he doesn't know what to do with himself. He starts to pull books off Mašek's shelves. "Why don't you find me a cure in here?" he says, tossing a book to the ground. "Or here." Another falls, splaying open when it lands. "See this?" he says, crouching over the split spine. "To me it looks like a woman's parts. You see? I'm sick. I want to make love to this book! Why don't you cure me?"

Suddenly, he understands. He looks at Mašek, who is standing behind his desk now, frantically ringing the little bell there. "You haven't read them, have you?" Danilo says. He grabs one of the framed certificates off the wall and throws it to the floor, where it shatters. "You're like Smetanka, or those Chinese twins. You're a fraud!"

The door of the office swings open. Danilo does not put up a fight when two guards grab him and push him to the ground. When shards of glass bite into his cheeks, he doesn't even feel pain. He gives up. He will never see her again. It's over.

The smell isn't strong to begin with, just the smallest alteration prickling her nostrils that lets her know. Still, Ivan keeps walking with the other man on his back, and she follows. The sun is high, and the air is full of dust. It is only when Ivan is overcome with a fit of coughing and stops to rest that he realizes his friend is dead.

"Ah, Jiři," he says sadly, laying his hand on the man's cheek. "You kept me laughing through the worst of it. Well, get your best jokes ready. It won't be long for me. I'll see you soon." He takes off his bandolier and his heavy jacket. She settles down on her haunches not far away.

"Go. Shoo." He waves his hand at her. When she doesn't move, he turns out his trouser pockets. "See? I've got nothing for you."

She watches as he tries to dig a grave using the stock of his gun and then, when that doesn't work, his hands. Giving up, he places his jacket over the dead man's face, then sits down next to the body and stares at the wolf.

"Fine," he says. "If you want to watch me die, be my guest. I hope I taste good."

He sleeps. After the sun falls, she pads over to him and puts her muzzle in his face.

"No," he whispers. "No more. Please."

She butts him with her nose.

"Get away from me," he says, swatting her.

She starts to walk away.

"Wait!" he says, sitting up. "Where are you going? Don't leave me alone."

She begins to trot.

"You goddamn animal!" he says as he struggles to his feet. "Wait for me!"

SHE TRAVELS AT NIGHT and sleeps during the day. Ivan is slow and sometimes delirious from exhaustion and hunger. Sometimes he wanders off the road, and she doubles back, comes up behind him, and pushes him in the direction she wants him to go. She seems to be heading somewhere. But where? Where could a wolf go that would help him? Sometimes, overcome, he stops and weeps. At other times, he sings in a thin, wavering voice: *"Good night, my dear, good night."* The same line again and again. Sometimes he adds to it: *"May God Himself watch over you. Good night, sleep well. Dream a little dream, oh dream it. When you wake up, trust the dream."*

The words come out of him like ghosts rising from graves, unbidden and insubstantial. He doesn't recognize his voice. He is not certain he is alive. He wonders what being alive means.

She does not understand him, but his song enters her as surely as a bullet and lodges in her just as deeply. The tune compels her, and even though the territory is not one she and the others roamed, and she doesn't recognize any trees or outcroppings of rock, the man's song maps a pathway for her and she follows it. She deviates from her course only when she smells water. Then she will veer off the road and through dry meadows. Cursing, he follows. Although her coat protects her, his skin is so brittle that the sharp-edged grasses slice into his arms. He does nothing to stanch the blood. That smell is rich and alive and makes her want to run, but she keeps to a slow pace so that he won't fall too far behind. They drink from small streams where, owing to the blazing sun, the water runs low. Both soldier and wolf plant their faces into whatever puddle they find and they each emerge masked with silt. One night, he falls sick, and they have to stop while he writhes and moans. He curls himself against her side. His body shakes, and he clutches her fur when he convulses. *"Dream a little dream, oh dream it. Hmmm, hmmmm."* His voice is as light as the breeze. *"That I love you. That . . . I'm going to give . . . you my . . . heart."*

He sleeps through the night, and so does she. When day breaks, a smell wakes her. She stands up, suddenly alert. The fur on her back rises. She pushes at him with her nose, her paw.

"Go away. Let me sleep." He flings out an arm and manages to hit her with some force.

She yelps, steps back. Whimpers. Then she turns and heads toward the smell.

"Oh, fuck!" he says.

She hears him stumbling behind her.

"Wait," he says. "Or don't wait. Leave me. It's fine." He drops to his knees.

She circles back. She growls, bares her teeth.

"You don't scare me," he says, but he's getting up, using her back to steady himself. He sniffs the air. "Hold on," he says, suddenly alert. "What's that? What's there?" He points to a plume of smoke in the distance. He starts to run. "Hurry up!" he shouts. "What are you waiting for?"

The old man gasps when he opens the door and sees the armed stranger. "Please don't hurt us," he cries. He is frail and bent. He grips the side of the jamb to hold himself upright. Ivan tries explain himself but the effort is too much and he keels over, falling halfway into the cottage. The man tries to push him out of the doorway with his boot.

"Old man, what are you doing?" A woman appears. Like the man, she is withered and brittle. Her cheeks are sunken. A maroon scarf covering her head makes her mouth and eyes appear outsized on her pinched and wrinkled face. "My God, Václav. Is he dead?"

"I don't think so," Václav says. "He's only fainted."

"Then bring him inside!"

"Are you crazy? We don't know him, Agáta. He could be anybody."

"He's a soldier!"

"A soldier come to rob us, I'm sure."

"He's welcome to all our nothing."

Václav crouches down, begins to look through Ivan's pockets.

"What are you doing?"

"It goes both ways," he says.

"Have you lost your mind? Bring him inside."

The two drag Ivan into the house and hoist him onto the bed. Agáta slaps his cheeks. "He's as cold as a corpse. Better put a blanket over him."

Václav covers him with the comforter.

"Water," she says.

While Agáta holds Ivan's head, Václav puts a glass to his lips. Water spills over the soldier's chin and chest.

"Come on, boy," Agáta says, jostling him gently. "Wake up now."

"Let him sleep."

"If he sleeps now, he'll sleep forever," she says.

"Maybe that's for the best. The war takes men one way or another. Did you see that Petr Matejcek has come home? The boy's stark raving now. He'll be useless to Gita and that baby."

"I never liked him to begin with," she says. "He got our darling into trouble with that shameful picture, remember?"

Václav laughs softly. "I think our girl was smart enough to get herself into mischief without anyone's help. Anyway, that was a long time ago."

They are quiet for a few moments. Václav lifts the glass to the soldier's lips again. Ivan suddenly jerks and sputters, and the glass flies out of Václav's hand and shatters on the floor.

"Well, he's not dead," Agáta says.

"Good. Because he owes us a glass."

Ivan sits up. He's delirious and flails his arms so that the old people have to duck.

"Don't worry, son," Václav says. "We won't hold you to it."

"Where is she?" Ivan whispers hoarsely.

"Is there someone else with you?" Agáta says. She turns to her husband accusingly. "Did you leave someone out there? A woman, no less?"

"He's the only one I saw," Václav says.

"What have you done with her?" Ivan says as he tries to get off the bed.

"You need to rest," Agáta says.

"You've killed her!" Ivan says.

"We've killed no one," Václav says. "Who sent you here? We've paid the price for our sin. We've been shamed enough. We did not kill her. We loved her!"

"*Shhh, shhh,*" Agáta says, laying a hand on her husband's arm. "He's not from here. He doesn't know." She goes to the stove and fills a bowl with stew. "Eat," she says, bringing the food back to the bed. "Eat first. Tell us about who we killed later."

Ivan lets her feed him the first few bites, but then takes the bowl and slurps down the contents. She hands him a piece of bread and he swallows it whole. "Water," he says. After guzzling two glasses, he closes his eyes. Soon, he breathes evenly. Agáta inadvertently fingers hair from his eyes. Catching herself, she stands up, pats down her skirt, wrings her hands.

"It's alright, my dear," Václav says.

"I just—"

"I know."

"I can't—"

"I know."

She walks to the open window, breathes in the morning air, and screams. "Václav! Get the gun!"

"No!" Ivan says, waking up.

"There's a wolf out there!" she says.

Václav goes for the shotgun that hangs on the wall.

Ivan scrambles out of the bed. "Don't shoot her. Please!"

But Václav has already flung open the door.

She sees the man and gun. She runs.

"It's going for the chickens!" Agáta cries. "Shoot it, you fool!"

"She won't hurt you!" Ivan says.

"Without those chickens, we will starve to death," she says.

Ivan pushes past the couple and hurries into the yard just as the wolf disappears behind the coop. "Come here, girl," he says softly. "It's alright."

Behind him, the old man cocks the gun.

"No! Don't!" Ivan says, spinning around and putting himself between the gun and the wolf. "I promise you. She won't attack."

"Better move out of the way, son," Václav says as he starts toward the coop. "I'm not the shot I once was."

"Please," Ivan begs. "Let me show you." He turns around and makes his clicking sounds with his tongue. He holds out his hand. Slowly she edges out from behind the coop and comes toward him. She sniffs his palm. He strokes her head and massages her ears.

"You see?" he says. "She's not dangerous."

"She's hungry, though," Agáta says, standing behind her husband. "A hungry wolf is not a wolf I want at my door."

"If she hasn't eaten me," Ivan says. "I don't think she'll want you."

"Now you insult my wife?" Václav says.

"He's only telling the truth," Agáta says. "Between the two of us, there's not enough meat on our bones to satisfy a crow."

The wolf pants heavily. She settles down on her haunches.

"Skinny," Agáta says appraisingly.

"She hasn't had anything to eat in days," Ivan says.

After a moment of consideration, Agáta disappears into the house and returns with a bowl. No sooner is it on the ground than the wolf is at it.

"The two of you need a lesson in table manners," Agáta says.

"Tell me," Václav says, finally lowering his gun. "Do you regularly go around with wild animals?"

IVAN TELLS THEM the story. The old man interrupts at the more improbable parts. The wolf kept the soldier's dying friend warm? Even though Ivan had given up hope and was prepared to die, she pushed him on? It was she who first noticed the couple's house? *"Acch,"* Václav says dismissively at each turn of the tale, *"Pfft."* But Agáta tells him to keep quiet, to let the soldier speak.

"Well," Ivan says when he finishes, embarrassed to have commandeered so much attention. "It'll be a good story to tell your grandchildren, I suppose."

"What grandchildren?" Agáta says.

"The crib. I thought—"

All three look at the child's crib that stands against the wall. It is missing a set of bars at one end.

"You see?" Agáta mutters to her husband. "I told you to get rid of that thing."

Václav drops his head. "Agáta needs to forget. I need to remember."

The silence that follows is broken by the sound of scratching at the front door.

Agáta resists letting the wolf into the house. "I won't be able to sleep. And that wretched stink. And by the way, you don't smell much better," she says to Ivan.

"Could you let us rest here for a day?" he says. He kneels at the open door, petting her. "We'll sleep outside. We'll leave first thing in the morning. We'll be gone before you wake."

"Where will you go?" Václav says.

Ivan has no answer.

"They kill deserters, you know," Václav says.

"And the people who harbor them," Agáta adds.

"I can't go back there," Ivan says, suddenly overwhelmed. "Everyone I know has died. It's just—I can't fight anymore. I can't. I'm sorry."

The couple is quiet for a long time.

"Come back inside," Agáta says finally. "And you might as

well bring your smelly savior with you. If the neighbors see a wolf in our yard, things will be worse for us than they already are."

That evening, she lays a blanket on the floor for Ivan, then insists he tie up the wolf. "I'd prefer not to wake up with my head inside her mouth," she says, handing him a rope. He fixes one end securely to the leg of the kitchen table and the other around the thick ruff of fur on her neck.

Agáta watches the wolf submit willingly. "Strange," she says.

THE WOLF AND THE SOLDIER stay with the old couple for many days. She is not allowed to roam the yard, both because Václav doesn't trust her around the chickens and because he and Agáta do not want the neighbors to find out that they are housing both a deserter and a wild beast. Twice a day, after the wolf has been fed a mouse or, if she is lucky, a shrew, Agáta or Václav check to make sure no one is about. If the way is clear, then Ivan, using the rope as a lead, takes her behind a tool shed. She doesn't understand what she is meant to do or why the man keeps telling her to go. "Go!" he says, frustrated when she simply sits and stares up at him. But after the woman catches her crouching in the house and throws a pot lid at her, she begins to have some idea.

Ivan makes himself useful, helping Václav with the repairs he needs to make to the roof, which has weakened in places because of the heavy spring rains. After that, the soldier hoes the decrepit garden while Agáta reminisces about when it was an Eden of lettuces and carrots and tomatoes and cucumbers. She pulls a paltry turnip out of the ground.

"You know the story of the enormous turnip," she says.

"My mother used to tell it to us."

"It's a very good story," she says and sighs.

The couple's house is small and immaculate, but that doesn't stop Agáta from giving it a thorough cleaning every day.

"Let me do that," Ivan says, one morning, as she struggles to carry a full pail of water and a mop. "Let me do it all," he says. "You sleep a little."

"I'll have all my death to sleep," she says.

"My grandmother used to tell me that she had to rest up for her death. That it was going to be a lot of work in heaven having to talk to all the relatives she hated."

Outside, Václav is singing to the chickens.

"He thinks they lay better if he serenades them," Agáta says.

"He must be right. Those eggs are good."

"I'm not going to heaven," she says, frowning.

"How do you know?"

"I know what I've done."

"Let me help you anyway."

He sets up a chair next to the open door and, after much resistance, she sits and allows herself to enjoy the sun and the slight breeze. In a matter of moments, she is snoring deeply and peacefully. The wolf wanders over and sniffs her, then settles by her side. Agáta's hand slides lazily off her lap so that her fingers graze the animal's fur. The wolf's eyes shutter, and soon she sleeps, too.

Once he has finished mopping the floor that needed no mopping in the first place, Ivan finds Agáta's feather duster and rags and cleans the already spotless table and shelves. He straightens the bedclothes just as his mother did, giving them a yank and a smack, as if the sheets were just more of her unruly children. His mother. How will he face her? How will she be able to hold her head up with a deserter for a son? He can't think about her or about what he's done, so he concentrates on cleaning, running his brush over the small portrait on the mantel, hanging up a sweater. A long mirror is mounted inside the wardrobe door. He hasn't seen his face in a while. He looks too old to be himself. His eyes are more hooded than he remembers, as if the experience of war has made them less eager to open up and see things as they are. He looks older than his father will probably look in ten years' time, when the man will finally close his disappointed eyes for good. The war that killed Jiři in his prime has made Ivan already older than his father will ever be. It's a confusing world he's been spared for. He remembers now: he held a dismembered arm. The fingers looked like they were just about to close down on something. What? A gun? A comrade's hand? He closes the wardrobe door, dusts a shelf that holds a worn bible and a school notebook that is filled with immaculately laid out mathematical equations. Many of them are marked with a red X, sometimes an exclamation point, suggesting the teacher's frustration with a dim student. Once—it seems so long ago now—Ivan was top of his class in arithmetic. He tests himself to see if he can still work the numbers and arrive at the correct answer, but his and the student's conclusions are the same. The teacher must have been stupider than the pupil. Well, Ivan thinks, the people in charge are not always right. Look at this war. He puts the ledger back where he found it, goes into the small water closet, and relieves himself. When he reaches up to pull the chain, he notices a blue glass bottle sitting on top of the water tank. He takes it down, uncorks it. The smell of ammonia shoots up his nostrils and knocks his head back.

"Oh ho, wife. What have we here?"

The old man is back from the coop. Agáta, likely embarrassed to have been caught sleeping, barks orders at her husband. Ivan puts the bottle where he found it.

"Take off your boots, old man! I just finished cleaning," he says as he comes out of the water closet.

"A recent addition," Václav says, indicating the toilet. "It works nicely, doesn't it?"

"As well as any other, I suppose."

"Spoken like a man who knows nothing about plumbing! You should see the toilets that scoundrel Palček is putting in these days. And charging double what they're worth. Which is nothing. They are complete shit."

"Shit for shit," Ivan says.

"This is not an original joke," Václav says. "Here, I'll show you."

He leads Ivan back into the water closet and flushes the toilet again, explaining the smooth operation of the mechanism, then describing the pipes that take the water underground, their length and trajectory, how those from different homes meet and how the waste from them flows into a single artery. He tells a few stories of his more challenging jobs and his proud successes.

"Well," he says sadly, when he has finished, "a man cannot rest on his laurels. The world moves on, and you are forgotten. Which is as it should be, I suppose. But sometimes you can spend a lot of sorrow trying to change things for the better when what was first was best. It's only that you were too foolish to realize it."

ON MARKET DAYS and Sunday mornings, when the neighbors are away from their homes, the couple agrees that it is safe for Ivan to take the wolf on longer walks. They swim in a stream beneath a narrow bridge. They wander beyond the small farms and into a meadow where the wolf hunts weasels and rabbits. While she eats, Ivan lies on the soft grass. Sometimes he sleeps. When he wakes, she is always there. Why doesn't she run away? He supposes she's become used to human comforts. The old woman is not a bad cook, after all, and although her husband disapproves, she hands the wolf bits of bread and chicken bones under the table during meals. The house is warm and safe. Frankly, Ivan could easily imagine staying here forever. When the sun passes overhead, they make their way home in order to be indoors before the neighbors return laden with marketing baskets and churchy guilt.

"She knows this land," Ivan tells the couple one evening. They have finished their meal and sit quietly around the table. Agáta has washed Ivan's uniform, but because she is too nervous to hang it outside where it will dry more quickly, she has lent him Václav's trousers, which are both too wide and too short for him, and one of the man's better shirts. "No matter how far we go, she finds her way back here."

"She uses her nose," Václav says.

"Maybe," Ivan says uncertainly.

"She smells Mother's cooking."

"Don't be an idiot," Agáta says, unable to hide her grin.

"That must be it," Ivan says.

They are quiet again.

"After the explosion, while we were walking—she knew where she was going then, too."

Agáta frowns. "We make up the sense of things after they happen," she says. "We tell stories. This happened because of that. We string things together one by one so that it seems like there's a reason to it all. But there is no reason. The most unbelievable things can happen and you have no idea why." Her eyes become glassy.

"Why don't your neighbors come to visit? You are old. They should be taking care of you, bringing you food, helping you," Ivan says.

"We have no need for their help," Václav says. "We have our garden and our coop. We're fine."

"What about your child?" Ivan says gently, glancing at the crib. "You have one? Maybe more than one?"

"We have a daughter."

"Where is she?"

"Wherever she is, she is better off without us."

"She owes you her care. You gave her life."

"You've been in war," Václav says. "You see how little life accounts for."

"And you?" Agáta says. "You must want to see your family."

"I don't think I'd be welcome. My father would turn me in himself if he had the chance."

"So you know what monsters parents can be," she says.

THE NEXT MARKET DAY, once the neighbors have left their homes with fattened pigs and wheelbarrows full of vegetables, the wolf and her soldier walk through a meadow. The sun is warm on her fur. The smells of the earth are rich and she rolls in the grass. She traps a hamster. The soldier lies down in the shade and tries to sleep, but the wolf is restless, distracted by every bird and insect, by the shifts in the breeze.

"Calm down," Ivan says, his eyes closed. "It's a beautiful afternoon. What are you so nervous about?"

Soon, he has his answer. Two men lumber across the meadow, hoes slung over their shoulders. Ivan picks up a rock, gets to his feet. When the farmers come close enough to see the wolf, they stop. Slowly, they take their tools and grip them like weapons. She bares her teeth, growls, and is about to charge when Ivan throws the rock. She shrieks. He throws another and then another, hitting her on the back and the sides until she runs away.

———

"WE'VE BEEN SEEN," Ivan says, when he returns to the house, breathless.

"By who?"

"Farmers."

"Brothers?"

"Maybe. I don't know."

"One tall. One short. Both ugly as mud?"

"I guess."

"Kaminský," Agáta says definitively.

"And the wolf?"

"I threw rocks at her. She ran away."

"Did they ask questions?" Agáta says.

"I told them I was just passing through. I thanked them for saving me from being eaten by a wolf."

Agáta looks at him. He is wearing his uniform. "They may be ugly, but they are not stupid," she says. "And they won't turn their backs on a reward."

"I didn't mention your names. They didn't see me come back here. I'm sure of it," Ivan says.

Václav and Agáta glance at each other nervously.

"I'll leave," Ivan says. "Right away."

"Wait until the sun goes down," Václav says. "You'll have better luck in the dark when they're drunk."

"She must hate me now," Ivan says softly. "After all that she did for me. And I threw stones at her. She'll never come back."

"Those Kaminskýs are barbarians. They nail live hedgehogs

to trees and shoot them," Václav says. "You saved her life. Now you're even."

For the remaining hours of the day, while Agáta prepares food for his journey, Ivan and Václav take turns with the gun, watching out the window. As soon as the last of the light slips from the sky, the old woman hands Ivan a bundle filled with bread and potatoes and hard-cooked eggs. She embraces him. Václav tries to give him his box of bullets.

"You keep them," Ivan says. "Otherwise you won't be able to defend yourselves."

"We don't need to protect ourselves anymore," Václav says, pressing the box into Ivan's hands.

"If they come for you, tell them I forced you," Ivan says. "Tell them I held a knife to your throats. That you had no other choice than to take me in."

"Don't worry about us," Agáta says. "We know what to do."

"You're old," Ivan says hopefully. "They will forgive you."

"We will not need forgiveness," Václav says.

"I'm sorry I brought trouble into your home," he says.

"It will be a story to tell," Agáta says.

"A soldier who thinks he was saved by a wolf," Ivan says.

She smiles. "No one will ever believe it."

SHE FINDS A VACANT DEN and hides inside it. Her soldier has not traveled far when they surround him. He tries to run. They shoot him, and he falls. They tie him behind a horse and drag him through the woods. She stays in the den for days, but finally, she is too hungry. During the night, she crawls out and finds her way back to the house. All is quiet. The window is open. Rising onto her hind legs, she climbs through. The room is half lit by a full moon. They lie on the bed. She knocks a paw against a glass bottle on the floor and sets it lazily spinning. She sniffs it, backs away. She noses the faces of the old man and woman. They smell of the same stuff. She whimpers and moves to one side of the bed, then the other. Again, she nudges them, but they are dead. Agitated, she prances backward, circles around herself. She is starving. She paces the room, sniffing every corner and crevice, hoping to find something to eat. There is nothing, not even a crumb. An insect darts away from her nose. She lets it scurry halfway up a wall, then with a swipe of her paw, she brings it down to the ground and laps it up. It moves inside her mouth for a moment before she swallows it. She knocks her tail against the wardrobe and the door opens. She buries her snout in the clothes there. Then she bites down on the material and drags it onto the floor. She shakes her head violently, just as she would were she holding a small animal between her teeth. The clothes smell of their bodies. Her saliva softens the material so that she can suck out the dirt and bits of food and the taste of skin encrusted in the fibers. Unsatisfied, she returns to the wardrobe and bites into a shoe, tearing at the leather, chewing, swallowing, then flinging the carcass of wooden heel and sole across the room. Her tail whips against the wardrobe door and sets it swinging. A scabbard of light ricochets around the room. She jumps back. Something is alive in there. She moves closer and sees—she stops. Her ears pull back. Her tail lowers. She lets out a low growl. The animal growls in return. Its ears are flat against its head. She makes another warning sound, shifts forward slightly without moving her feet. The animal does the same. She flares her nostrils. She is ready. But the animal does not move. It does not have a smell. She inches closer until its body disappears and all she can see are eyes.

There are voices outside. She hears the familiar ratchet of guns. She leaps onto the bed and drapes herself over the bodies.

T here are children living at the asylum now. They arrive weekly, deposited at the front gate of the old monastery. Danilo watches from his window as the children jump off the backs of canvas-covered trucks into the arms of soldiers who carefully place them on the ground as if they were made of glass. But of course they are made of much sturdier stuff than those soldiers, who, if they survive battle, will return to the safety of family homes and mothers' arms. Not so these children. There are no mothers and fathers waiting for them. There is no invisible thread that, no matter how far they stray, will connect them to a familiar place. They are orphans of the war, and someone has decided that the safest place for them to live out the uncertainty of their childhoods is alongside the lunatics in the asylum.

The children are housed across the courtyard from Danilo's ward. He hears them at night through the barred windows that are left open to let in the evening air and the bugs that bite so that the men scratch their necks and behind their knees while they sleep. He hears the howls of the children's nightmares and also a softer descant of weeping. He knows they cry because they are lonely and scared, but he finds the sound comforting, and it helps him sleep.

During the day, their noise is a much harsher aberration. When was the last time he heard the excited cries of children at play? Their laughter? Their gleeful shouts as they insist on rules and regulations for games that have been made up on the spot? During the periods when the orphans are in the cloister garden, the lunatics are kept inside. If Danilo is working in the sacristy, stitching rough wool trousers and sewing brass buttons onto jackets, he is not aware of their activities, but if he is in the ward, he watches them. He is mesmerized by the constantly shifting choreography of their play. They run this way and that. They cluster in small groups for a moment then split apart and form others. One will walk from here to there and, in the middle of his journey, begin to skip. Why skip? Danilo wonders. Did this child suddenly say to himself, *I must skip now*? Or is this just some spontaneous urge of the body, some small explosion of internal exuberance, present circumstance be damned? Was there ever a time when Danilo skipped?

He is not the only one affected by the arrival of the orphans. The patients react in various ways. Some, like Danilo, find their presence calming, and he even catches those with normally vacant expressions responding to the children's voices with nostalgic smiles, as they remember their own childhoods when things were easier for them than they are now. Others become agitated, even enraged, and their doses are increased to keep them in line. One man stands by a window watching the children while his hand works inside the front of his trousers. He cannily keeps his activity to the times when the nurses are not in the room or are busy with more demanding patients, but once he is discovered, he is taken away. When it comes to these especially offensive cases, the guards do nothing to hide their work, and the man returns to the ward with a bruised and bloodied face. After that, he is chained to his bed.

Following Danilo's outburst in Dr. Mašek's office, he was taken to a room that was entirely bare save for a drain in the center of the floor and two metal handholds welded to a wall. He was ordered to strip, face the wall, and spread his legs. Fearing the worst, and beginning to imagine the girth of what dangled between the guards' thighs, he stood with his own pasted together and clenched his buttocks. But the assault was not what he expected. First, he heard the screech of ungreased metal, and then, before he realized what was happening, he was thrown against the wall by a torrent of ice cold water shooting onto his back. It felt like a thousand splinters had found their way into every pore of his skin. Grabbing the handholds, he managed to look behind him to see the men holding a hose that writhed in their grip as if it were alive. It was impossible to know the best way to endure the attack. He tried to angle himself to the side in order to take the brunt on the smallest area of his body, but letting go of one of the handholds was a mistake. He slipped and fell, slamming his hip onto the slick concrete. All he could do was curl up like a pill bug and wait until the torment was over.

As a treatment for agitation, the cure was successful. He was so exhausted, and his muscles so wrecked, that he had to be carried back to the ward on a stretcher. After this, he developed a paralyzing fear of the shower. Even the sound of a sink faucet turning on sent him into a panic. These new symptoms were determined to be the effects of a buildup of toxins, so he was prescribed a treatment of cathartic medication that had him visiting the toilet five times a day, putting him in more frequent proximity to the plumbing that terrified him, and effecting no amelioration of his nervous condition. Finally, it was determined that the only hope for him was the sleeping cure that had turned so many of the patients into droopy-headed slobberers. Now, a single dose of Veronal keeps him knocked out for twelve hour stretches of a deep, mindless sleep he has never experienced in all his life. He wakes feeling as if he is absent from himself, that his body is currently unoccupied, and that he is no more animate than a line drawn on a blank sheet of paper. For a long time, his thoughts loiter out of range of his perception, and when they do edge closer, they are nothing more than the shadows that float across his vision when he stares too long into the sun. No thoughts. No worries. Nothing. It's incredibly pleasant. Once the medication begins to wear off, though, his nerves feel inflamed so that even touching the pads of his finger to his thumb sends spikes of pain shooting through his body. He clamps his jaw to try to withstand it and cracks two teeth. All he can think about is when he will get his next white pill. The only consciousness that he savors comes right after he swallows that small lozenge. Just as he loses awareness of the sheets on his bed, the humid air, the close, bodily smell of the ward, he begins to sense the buoyant expansiveness of the drugged world he is about to enter, the lightness and possibility of its delirious vacancy.

The hours of insentience have, unfortunately, come to an end. The war continues. According to the nurses' whispers, fighting is intensifying in the east. The need for uniforms grows daily, and the asylum cannot afford to keep one of its best workers in a semipermanent coma. Owing to the sudden and total stoppage of the medication, his skills are compromised. His hands tremble, and a physical restlessness makes it seem like rodents are scurrying up and down the hollow corridors of his bones, nipping at him from the inside with their sharp teeth. Sometimes he thinks he can hear them scratching and scrabbling, and even if he stops up his ears with cotton, the sound only becomes louder. Added to this, as if to make up for all the time he has recently spent happily numb, he cannot sleep. He passes the nights in a state of half-crazed distress. That the lunatics around him sleep soundly, dulled by the drugs he craves, feels like a rebuke. In his worst moments, he imagines sticking a finger down a man's throat so that he will vomit up some trace of the medication, then swallowing the spew. Better to be truly insane, he thinks, than have to endure the life that awaits him. He does not believe he will ever be released. He will have to live out his days tormented by the curse of being just sane enough to know he is not mad. His only hope is that, over time, his mind will become so warped by his surroundings that he will surrender to the diagnosis and accept this confinement. Then, perhaps, he will be thankful for the boundaries of the thick monastery walls and locked gates, for the occasional straitjacket, and for a life that requires him to do nothing more than sew an inseam and listen to the laughter of children.

Lying in bed one night, trying to quell his insomniac jitters with these thoughts, he hears an altercation break out in the orphan's ward: the shrill sound of high voices hurling insults and complaints and the grunting exertions of weak wrestlers. He goes to the window and tries to make out what is happening across the courtyard, but it is too dark. Finally, a door opens into that room, letting in light along with two nurses whose angry voices cut through the commotion. A child screams. Then another. He hears "Quiet down!" "Get off him!" and "Stop that! Stop that or else!" And then, rising above it all, he hears a wail that begins as an anguished stutter but develops into a wretched howl that carries across the courtyard. It's a powerful noise, mournful but also as beautiful as music. Danilo grips the windowsill so fiercely that his fingernails carve half-moons into the soft wooden frame.

He is still standing at the window the following morning when the children are let out for their exercises. The orphans play at their games and enter and exit their small, constantly shifting dramas as if nothing unusual or upsetting happened the night before. But just as Danilo is about to leave for the sacristy to begin his day's work, a nurse arrives in the garden, holding a young boy by the hand. The boy has the familiar lethargy of so many of the men who hug the corridors of the asylum. When the nurse drops the boy's hand, it falls lifelessly to his side. Danilo knows this boy is the one. He is certain of it. This is the child who made that unearthly, intoxicating sound. Even after the nurses put an end to the fighting, and after the rattled children were finally asleep, he could still hear that long, aching note echoing inside him.

THE BOY USUALLY SITS ALONE when the children play in the courtyard. Occasionally, if they need an extra body to even out the sides, someone will pull him onto the field of play. He follows willingly, or rather, without any will at all. He stands wherever he is told to go. He stares at his shoes or gazes vaguely at the sky. He is oblivious as the other children rush back and forth screaming. Once, his arms rise almost of their own volition and, without even seeming to look, he picks a ball out of the air. When he has it in his hands, he stares at it as if he doesn't know what comes next. He only reacts when the biggest of the orphan boys, a thick hulk who looks more adult than child, starts to barrel toward him. Then he runs incredibly fast, nimbly dodging the obstacles of the other orphans. The game dissolves into a chase as the children try and fail to trap him. His speed and agility are noted, and in later games, when sides are chosen, he becomes the object of competition between team captains. But once selected, as often as not, he will stand in the midst of play in his dull way, frustrating those same children who vied so fiercely to have him on their team. Sometimes, if the nurses are not watching, someone will kick him. It is all Danilo can do not to shout out the window to warn off the bully and get the nurses to protect the boy, but if he does, he'll expose his interest in the children and he will be forbidden from watching them any longer. Who knows? The orderlies could take him away for a beating or chain him to his bed. He can't let this happen for he has come to believe that if he is not there to stand guard, the boy will suffer something more dire than drug therapy and a black-and-blue shin. On the days when he is kept late in the sacristy or when it rains, as it did solidly for one ten-day period, Danilo works himself into such a state that the nurses give him a pill. He has learned how to swallow it in such a way that, when the nurses leave, he can hock it back up. He fears what will happen to the boy if he sleeps.

One day, the boy finally reacts to his tormentors. Instead of fighting the big bully, though, he goes after a punier sycophant. The otherwise tractable, listless child has his victim on the ground in no time and pummels him with all the power of his small fists. Danilo is startled by the violence of a boy whom he thought utterly defenseless and he is astounded by the precision of the beating. Unlike the other orphans who fight with uncontrolled effort, their arms swinging and missing, the boy seems to summon skill and strategy from a place inside him that circumvents his drugged torpor.

Watching the boy deliver his blows makes Danilo realize how far he has fallen into reticence and dumb agreeableness. He has stopped thinking about when he will be released from the asylum. He looks forward to the daily meals of boiled vegetables and hard bread. He is upset by change, whether it is the sudden appearance of meat on the menu, or the fact that his Saturday shower, which he no longer fears, has been inexplicably shifted to Tuesday. He is no longer bothered by the madness around him but finds it somehow comforting to see the Twitcher's spasms or to listen to Our Lady of Sorrows minister to her baby Jesus. He can barely recall a time when he resisted like the boy is doing now.

Having been summoned by the hysterical nurses, orderlies enter the yard and separate the children. The next day, when Danilo sees him, the boy is once again lethargic. He slumps against the cloister wall beside, but not within, a rectangle of shade. Either he doesn't realize he could be cooler or he doesn't care. Maybe, Danilo thinks sadly, he is too lost in a hallucinatory muddle to feel the day's heat. The other children ignore him.

THE BOMB STRIKES during the midday meal. One minute, the servers are filling bowls, the next, hot soup is spraying in every direction. Danilo, who was sitting on a refectory bench between two catatonic men is now on the other side of the room, sprawled on the floor. Or is it the ceiling? A rafter beam lies beside him. When he tries to move, he has the feeling his bones have disintegrated. He can't lift himself up. He can't breathe. Dust clots his nose and throat and his eyes sting. He can't hear anything. Not the screams of the man lying next to him whose head lies at a very wrong angle from his neck, not the words of the orderly whose mouth is so close to his face that Danilo can see into the back of the man's throat. Despite the evident hysteria, Danilo feels calm and purposeful. He manages to get to his knees and then his feet. He moves automatically, his mind giving his body a set of instructions. *Climb over that, push this aside, shake off the hand that has grabbed onto your trouser leg, nod and agree to anything anyone seems to be telling you.* One entire wall of the dining hall has crumbled. The destruction looks venerable, as if it has been there for hundreds of years and is a place people visit to remember that something important once happened here. For a moment, Danilo becomes disoriented. Perhaps he is the visitor learning about the history of a war and about a bomb that destroyed a building that once housed believers and then the insane, who, perhaps, had even more faith in the unseen. He nearly trips over a leg that sticks out from between two fallen stones. He knows there are probably bodies buried underneath the rubble, patients who were sitting nearest that wall, the unlucky serving girls who were attending to them, but he can't think about that. He climbs through, or out of the room. His thoughts confuse him. Is a room still a room when it has no wall? Is the outside really inside, or is it the other way around? Making his way down a corridor, he passes a constant stream of doctors and nurses who guide bleeding patients. One of them is crying. "Help us! We're dying!" He can hear her. He is no longer deaf.

Sunlight pours through the broken walls of the orphans' refectory. The air is filled with dust and floating debris. The room is so quiet and still that for a moment Danilo thinks the children must have been somewhere else at the time of the blast. But then he hears whimpering and realizes they are huddled together in a far corner, barricaded by overturned tables and chairs. When he comes close, they shrink back in a mass as if he were the embodiment of the terror they just experienced. None of them speaks or even cries loudly. He wonders if they have been told to keep quiet on pain of an even more terrible punishment. The only adult among them, and barely one at that, is a serving girl.

"Are we going to die?" she says, and bursts into loud sobs.

The boy crouches next to a wall. He appears sharp and alert to the possibility of a further attack. Danilo climbs over the furniture and the other children and kneels down beside him. He lifts his hand, and the boy rears back. Danilo turns his palm over. He has no weapon, no pill. "Come with me," he says.

"But they told us to stay where we are!" the serving girl shrieks. "I'll get into trouble!"

"There's nothing for either of us here," Danilo says to the boy. "Do you understand? It's time for us to go."

N*o matter how kind or solicitous he tries to be,* the boy doesn't trust him. And the more Danilo asks him how he is doing or if he needs to rest, he realizes he sounds no different from the doctors and nurses who pretended to care but were only hoping for an excuse to dose the boy and give themselves one less problem for the day. Or maybe he reminds the boy of those friendly soldiers who probably fed him sweets and said they were taking all the children to safety only to deposit them at an orphanage that turned out to be a madhouse. Maybe the boy doesn't trust Danilo precisely because he is kind.

"What's your name?" he asks, as they walk down a deserted road.

"I don't know," the boy mumbles.

"You don't know your own name?"

"Fuck you."

"What did they call you at the asylum?"

"Number twenty-three."

"I never heard the children being called by numbers," Danilo says.

"Why were you listening?"

"The windows were open. It was impossible not to hear."

"They called me nothing," the boy says.

"I don't believe you."

"Believe whatever you want. I don't care."

"You can call me Danilo."

"I don't have to call you anything."

"That's true. It's just the two of us."

"I don't owe you anything."

"I didn't say you did."

They walk for a while in silence. They lost sight of the bombed asylum hours earlier, and the peppery scent of ash is only a bare trace in the air. The day is hot, the sky cloudless. Danilo is grateful for the occasional breeze that cools the sweat on his neck and back. When a covey of rooks flies off a tree, it looks like the leaves have sprouted wings. He watches the billowing shape the birds make as they head in one direction and then turn the opposite way. How do they know to do that? What signal do they hear that tells them the right way to go?

"How old are you?" he asks.

"Fifteen."

Danilo checks his laughter. "You're a bit small for your age."

"Fuck you."

"I'd put you at about eight. Maybe nine."

"I'd put you at about a hundred or a thousand."

"I feel like I'm a thousand."

"Are you stupid? No one lives to be a thousand. Why do you keep walking next to me?"

"We're traveling together."

"I'm not traveling with you." He trots ahead a few steps, checking behind him to make sure Danilo isn't trying to catch up. Danilo hangs back to give the boy some privacy. There is no risk of losing him here. They have been walking half a day and have not seen a soul. On either side of the narrow road lie potato fields in full flower. Danilo is thirsty and hungry and imagines the boy is, too. The potatoes are a taunt. To eat them, they'd have to build a fire, but the smoke would be a flag of surrender. As it is, he looks back over his shoulder every few minutes, waiting for their inevitable capture. He and the boy walk in single file for a while. The boy's legs are too short to stay ahead without his having to run every so often. His mind seems clear; the explosion took care of that, snapping him out of his medicated dullness in an instant. But he runs sloppily, as if the drug still lingers in his muscles. Finally, he seems to give up and lets Danilo walk by his side.

"What village are you from?" Danilo asks.

"I don't know."

"What is your family name?"

"I don't know."

"What was your father's business?"

"His business was shit!"

Danilo feels badly for reminding the boy of his dead parents. "Well, like I said, my name is Danilo."

"How do you know?"

"How do I know? It's the name my parents gave me. It's what people call me. It's how anyone knows his name."

"It's stupid to take someone else's word for it."

Danilo laughs. "I suppose you're right. I guess that's been my problem all along. I take everyone's word for it."

"Is that why you were in there?"

"The asylum?" Danilo is about to tell him that taking people at their word is not a proof of lunacy, but then he thinks that perhaps it is. "You're very smart."

"Smarter than you."

"I've never been very smart. I've made a lot of stupid mistakes."

"Like what?"

"Like I lost the girl I loved."

"Where did you lose her?"

"If I knew where I lost her, I'd know where to find her."

"Ha, ha," the boy says drily. "I already know that joke." Suddenly, he takes off running into the field, leaping over the neat rows and landing in a furrow. He stops, listens, then launches headlong and lands on his belly. When he stands up, he's holding the hairless tail of a vole. He slams the animal against the ground. Once, twice, a third time. He waves his catch over his head in circles, then lets go and cheers as he watches it sail toward the road, where Danilo stands. His aim is perfect. The vole lands right at Danilo's feet. The boy bounds over the plants, making one final, elegant leap onto the road, then snatches up his catch. "You can't have it. It's mine," he says.

"Why did you do that?" Danilo says, horrified.

"I'm hungry." He stares at Danilo for a long moment. Then he snaps the vole's neck, rips off the head, and tears into the hide with his teeth. He chews and swallows and wipes the blood from his mouth. Then his face goes white, and he vomits.

Danilo kneels down and cleans the sick off the boy's shoes with dirt and leaves. He wonders how long the boy had to fend for himself before he was brought to the asylum, how many rodents he had to eat to stay alive.

"You have a stupid face," the boy says, looking down at him. "Your lashes are too curly, like a girl. And you have eyes like a cow."

"And you have the eyes of . . ." Danilo says, staring into the boy's, which are the palest chestnut color flecked with bits of gold and green. "The eyes of—"

The sound of a motor in the distance distracts them both.

"Hey!" the boy yells. He jumps up and down. He waves his hands over his head. "Over here! Help! Help me. I'm being stolen!"

Danilo clamps a hand over the boy's mouth and holds onto him. The truck appears from behind a scrim of dust, lumbering over the road, its engine stuttering as the gears shift. A plume of exhaust dirties the sky. The boy manages to free himself but before he can run, Danilo pulls him off the side of the road. He pins the boy facedown, and his protests are buried in dirt. The rumble of the truck swells and then subsides and finally disappears. As soon as Danilo climbs off him, the boy jumps up and runs back to the road, chasing the dust left in the truck's wake, screaming and waving his hands over his head. Finally, winded, he stops and stares down the empty road. His narrow shoulders rise up by his ears, and he starts to shake.

"They wouldn't have helped us," Danilo says, as he approaches the boy. He tries to touch him, but the boy wheels around and puts up his fists.

"Fuck you! Get away from me. You're one of the crazy ones. They told us to stay away from all of you."

"I'm not crazy."

"I saw through the windows. I saw a man hit his head against the wall a hundred times. I counted. His whole face was bloody but he didn't care. And I saw the one who always watched us. I know what he was doing. He showed it to us once. It was big and purple. Once he squirted on us in the courtyard. I saw you, too. You were always looking at me. Maybe you were doing the same thing." He puts his hand in front of his crotch and mimes rubbing.

"I wasn't doing that."

"Why were you watching?"

"I don't know."

"Because you're crazy."

"I wasn't there because I was crazy. I was there because I killed someone."

The boy studies Danilo carefully. "You're just trying to scare me," he says. Suddenly, his eyes grow wide. "You're going to kill me." He starts to run away. "Help! Help! He's going to kill me!" he calls out to no one but the potatoes and a lark pecking in the dirt.

"What do you think will happen if they find us?" Danilo calls out.

"They'll throw you in jail," the boy shouts. "That's where killers go. And perverts. Pervert killers."

"And what will they do with you? They'll take you to a place just like the one you were in. They'll give you drugs to keep you quiet. Is that what you want?"

The boy mumbles something, but the breeze snatches it up.

"I didn't hear you," Danilo says.

"Fuck you!" he yells.

"So you keep saying."

THEY EAT RAW POTATOES that taste terrible and give them bellyaches but at least have the advantage of containing moisture. They fall asleep in a ditch. In his dream, Danilo feels secure and warm. When he wakes up, he realizes that sometime during the night, the boy nestled up against him. Danilo doesn't move, tries not to breathe deeply. But then the boy stirs and is on his feet in seconds.

"Get off me, you sick pervert!" he says.

"Calm down," Danilo says, picking dirt out of his eyes and slowly getting to his feet.

"If you try anything, I'll kill you."

"I believe you. And now I have to take a piss."

"I knew it! You're going to take it out!" the boy says, staring in horror at Danilo's trousers.

"Unless you know another way, then yes, I'm going to take it out." Danilo walks down the furrow and, with his back to the boy, does his business. Despite how little he has had to drink, his stream lasts for a long time.

"What are you, a horse?" the boy says.

"I once knew a giant who could piss for fifteen minutes straight."

"I don't believe you."

Danilo finishes, does up his fly, and walks off the field and onto the road. The boy catches up to him. "How tall was he?"

"Over two meters."

The boy looks up, slack-jawed with wonder, as if the giant were standing before him.

"I knew someone who was born with fins on his back," Danilo says.

The boy narrows his eyes suspiciously.

"I knew a dwarf who was stretched to the size of a normal person."

"How?"

"On a machine."

"Did it hurt?"

"Yes," Danilo says.

The boy thinks about this for a while. "That's not true. You're just making up stories."

"Maybe."

They walk on. The haze of the morning gives way and heat settles in so heavily that, after a while, neither has the energy to talk. The only sound comes from their shoes scraping the dirt and the unmusical buzz of flies that becomes so loud that the boy walks with his hands covering his ears. At times, he sits down and refuses to move. But Danilo reminds him that if he stops, he will be no closer to water or food or a bed. "And you'll be stuck with me forever," he adds.

The boy spits at him and his logic but he cannot even summon a worthwhile gob.

Legless men, men missing arms, sightless men who hug the buildings as they walk, and when the buildings are not there, paw the air. The wounds of others are less obvious. The old woman selling plums from a street cart appears perfectly healthy, robust even, as she calls out her prices, but when the boy stares hard and longingly at the fruit, she snarls at him and calls him a son of a whore.

"I am no one's son," the boy says.

They flatten themselves against a wall in order to let a phalanx of soldiers pass. Danilo watches the men banter and joke, bragging about getting drunk and lying about things they've done with girls, wearing uniforms Danilo might have sewn. If it weren't for the fact that he murdered someone, he'd be one of them. Maybe this would have been a better fate for him. He would have joined up and perhaps even killed people but he wouldn't have been punished for it. He would have been called a hero. His parents would have taken him back into their home and paraded him boastfully past the neighbors. He would have finally exonerated himself of the sin of outliving his brother.

The town has suffered in the war, but the destruction is haphazard and irrational. A perfectly intact bookshop stands next to what was once a ladies' dress shop but which is now the site of a massacre of mannequins, some armless or headless, all of them naked, having been stripped of the latest fashion by looters. The church is sheared in half. Like the apoplectic Smetanka once pretended to cure, the left side of the building stands, its rose-colored glass windows reflecting the late afternoon light, while the right side is only a mound of bricks and splintered wood. On the preserved side of the building pews are still set in their close, orderly rows. Danilo wonders if people continue to pray there, huddled like those in a capsizing ship who must move continually to the highest elevation to avoid sliding into the sea.

Evidence of deprivation is everywhere. Danilo realizes just how well the asylum staff kept news from the lunatics. But he must also blame his own incuriosity. It's as if somehow, without knowing it, he gave into the isolation of that place, surrendered to the relief of his ignorance and the way it kept his worries for her at bay. If nothing in the world was changed, then he could believe she might still be alive, her beautiful coat shining, her wild, amber eyes flashing, and maybe some part of her thinking—well, not thinking exactly, he does not know what goes on in the mind of a wild animal, but perhaps sensing—that he is somewhere, that he is looking for her, will always look for her, that this will be the preoccupation of his life. When he hears his own thoughts, his conviction falters. Maybe Dr. Mašek was right, and she is nothing but an illusion brought on by—what did the man say—abandonment by the mother? Mašek never said *your mother*, it was always *The Mother*, implying that there was one gigantic, hugely bosomed, enormously lapped, all-powerful matriarch for everyone in the world, a feminine deity who might turn her back on one or another of her millions of children on a whim, relegating them to a life of insane imaginings. Mašek told him that Pavla was his symbolic creation and that he needed her to be a dwarf and then a deformed person and then an animal because he was terrified by The Female Genitalia. As he listened to the excited doctor form his conclusions, Danilo imagined an enormous vagina soaring overhead like an extravagant bird. The only vagina he'd ever seen—well, he hadn't really seen it, had he? Lidmila had been fully clothed when she let him lie on top of her behind the schoolhouse. And then—he is not even sure how it happened—his prick was inside something warm, which he didn't immediately identify as being part of her body, and then, a minute later, it wasn't, and the school bell rang, and she was skipping toward the door with the rest of the students as blithely as she would had she spent her recess gossiping with her girlfriends and eating roasted peanuts. She never bothered with him after that, and when he tried to get her to meet him again, she looked like she had no idea what he was talking about. Was he hurt by her casual cruelty? Yes. Was he embarrassed that all her friends laughed knowingly? Shamefully so. There were many days when he chose a beating from his mother over subjecting himself to the humiliating gauntlet that school had become. But did he hate the place where his penis had been? No. He craved it, made facsimiles with his pillow at night, or his spit-coated hand, or the jar of softened grease his mother kept by the kitchen stove, trying, mostly unsuccessfully, to manufacture that warm, moist—yes, the doctor was right—corridor. Dr. Mašek had asked him what images came to mind while he touched himself. And when Danilo, ashamed to be talking about such things, admitted that he sometimes thought about food, specifically the spiced sausage his mother made at the end of Lent, the doctor grew very excited. "You think of sausages?" he said, practically laughing with joy. What incredible luck that his patient exhibited so exactly the textbook description of, as he explained it, Sexual Mania in Extremis, a term Danilo could only remember by humming to himself the doxology he'd chanted each Sunday when he was a boy. Sexual Mania *in Excelsis Deo*!

As he and the boy round a corner, they nearly collide with a woman and her children on their way out of a shop. A loaf of bread rises from her marketing bag like a warm, yeasty beacon. The boy's gaze latches onto the bread as they follow the family. His expression is furious, as if he bears malice toward that loaf, the embodiment of everything he does not have: food and comfort, a mother, a home. Two police officers pass by, and Danilo instinctively shrinks within himself and stares at the ground. How long will it take for word to get out that a madman convicted of murder has kidnapped an orphan and escaped the asylum? Surely someone has alerted the constables in the nearby towns. When will an officer pull him aside, or even just a nosy patriot, curious about a fit young man who is not in uniform and an urchin who is about to—

"Thief! Thief! Stop him!"

The boy has snatched the loaf out of the woman's bag and is already halfway down the street. She screams, clutching her children to her as if she is at risk of losing them as well. Her cries draw the officers who, along with a few other men who have nothing better to do, chase the boy. Danilo follows, trying both to keep up and avoid particular notice, all the while cursing the foolish boy who will be caught and put right back into another orphanage. If he continues to plead ignorance, claiming not to know his name, his age, the village where he was born, he will surely be scrutinized and experimented upon by some eager doctor with a head full of preposterous theories about the ravages of war, a zealot like Mašek who will be fascinated by the boy's blend of intelligence and determined ignorance.

The chase comes to an abrupt halt when the men lose sight of the boy. The valiant pursuers of justice become a group of deflated, befuddled, somewhat embarrassed citizens who, seized with a momentary purpose, are cast back once more into their aimlessness. The police, eager to look authoritative, begin questioning everyone in the vicinity, their frustration turning their interrogations into near accusations. Before they turn their attention to him, Danilo slips away.

By nightfall, he is exhausted. He's walked up and down streets, searching alleyways and behind and inside garbage cans. The more tired he becomes, the more he wonders why he is trying so hard to find a boy who does not want to be found, who feels no more attachment to Danilo than he does any single stranger on the street. Less so, probably, because Danilo has so little to offer. The boy is right: he owes Danilo nothing. It is vain to think he saved the boy when all he really did was steal him from a place where, destroyed as it was, there might have been someone to look after him, at least that. If Danilo were honest with himself, he would have to admit that he has only harmed people—his mother and father, Pavla, certainly Klima, although he killed him in an effort to save her, so a relative harm. He tries to imagine himself walking away without the boy, being free of his cunning petulance, leaving him behind in this village so that Danilo can—do what? For a moment he stops walking, stunned by the plain truth: He has nothing. He has no home, no relatives to take him in, no work, not her. He has no idea what on earth he is meant to do.

"Fuck you!"

The voice is as unmistakable as the vocabulary. He rounds a corner, and there is the boy, being held between the same two policemen who were chasing him earlier. The offended woman stands in her doorway. Her children crowd around her, thrilled that their mother and their home should be the focus of such excitement.

"I'm sorry for stealing your bread," the boy says unconvincingly. "There. I said it. Now put me down!"

"How will you punish the little bastard?" the woman says.

"Don't worry about that, madam. We know what to do with him."

"Markus!" Danilo says, hurrying up. "There you are. I've been looking for you!"

Everyone turns to face this surprise. The boy gives Danilo a savage look.

"My God, boy," Danilo says. "What trouble have you gotten yourself into now?"

"Who are you?" one of the police says.

"I'm his father. I've been looking for him all day. What has he done?"

"Your son is a thief."

"Markus!" Danilo says. "Is this true?"

"I don't know him," the boy says. "He's crazy. He's a lunatic. A real one!"

"Of course you'd say that," Danilo says. "When you know my punishment will be far worse than what these officers will do to you." He turns to the policemen. "You understand, I'm not cruel," he says solicitously. "But ever since the rest of my family was killed, I've had to use a strong hand with him. I'm sure it's grief that makes him do these things, but right is right, and wrong is wrong. Isn't that what I always tell you, Markus?"

The boy lets out a furious snarl. The woman gasps and pushes her children behind her. "You better hide from me," he says. "I might catch you and eat you up!"

Danilo lets out a suffering sigh. "He was such a good boy . . . the light of my wife's short life. But after—"

"After what?" the woman whispers, fascinated.

"Ah, I don't like to talk about it, much less think about it."

"Of course," she says.

"Who would want to think about enemy soldiers storming into your home, throwing your beloved wife to the ground and, well, you know, taking her, right in front of you while you are being held back, just as you are holding my son now," he says to the officers. "She was dead before they were through with her," he adds, he thinks, affectingly.

"You're awfully young to be his father," one of the policemen says.

"In the countryside our motto is 'early and often.'"

The man nods his head admiringly.

"You poor man," the woman exclaims, wanting to claim her part in this affecting drama. "This terrible war! To lose your wife, his mother. What tragedy." She sniffles and even manifests a tear just as one of her daughters wriggles out from behind her. She grabs the girl by her hair and yanks her back. "Don't punish the boy," she begs the policemen, her voice trembling selflessly. "What is a loaf of bread compared to what he has lost?"

The policemen confer over the boy's head, then let him go. He stumbles and Danilo deftly steps toward him so that it seems like the boy is falling willingly into his arms. "That's right, son," Danilo says. "I'm here now." The boy bites Danilo's nipple beneath his shirt, but Danilo manages not to react. "My apologies, madam," he says. "It won't happen again."

With a hand firmly gripping the back of the boy's neck, Danilo pushes him down the street. When they are far enough away from the police, the boy shoves his elbow hard into Danilo's ribs.

Danilo lets go of the boy and massages his side. Suddenly, it all seems pointless. "Just go," he says.

The boy doesn't move.

"I'm not your jailer. You're free. Go wherever you want. Do whatever you want. I've had enough." He walks away. As he nears the corner, he thinks to himself, *I will turn left and it will be over. The boy will go his way, I will go mine. He will be better off without me and I without him.* But his resolve is weak, and he glances over his shoulder. The boy is still there.

"I hope you got to eat the bread at least," Danilo says.

"I dropped it."

"What?"

"When they were chasing me."

Danilo starts to laugh.

"Stop making fun of me!"

"No, no. I'm not," Danilo says, sighing. "It's only that . . . sometimes this life is hard to believe." He walks back to where the boy stands.

"I don't like it here," the boy says.

"I don't like it much either."

"We should go somewhere else."

We. Danilo tries not to react. In the distance, a train horn blows. The boy lifts his chin to the sky as if to hear the message more clearly.

T *he train is the first revelation.* When he traveled with Smetanka and the carnival, the old mare dragging the caravan behind her, the distance from one village to the next was never great. Each new town was just like the one they'd left, and the landscape between stops was unchanging. When he traveled with the wolf tracker, he had no sense of distance at all. The forest with its obscured sight lines and unfamiliar markings made him feel lost, and he relied entirely on the man to tell him where he was and where they were going. His ignorance made him powerless. Now, standing next to the dirt-streaked window of the speeding train, pressed on all sides by refugees from bombed villages and wounded soldiers making their way back to their homes, he watches the land pass in a blur of metamorphosis. Forests become fields become villages that disappear back into fields that are, in turn, overtaken by woods.

The scenes that slide from right to left across the train window seem no more permanent than the backdrops of the carnival sideshows that created the illusion that the fat lady sat in a crimson-colored bordello and the boy with fins lived among the creatures of the sea. He imagines that in these quickly appearing and disappearing towns, performances are unfolding. Mothers hold their sons or chase them away from a freshly baked pie, fathers teach them, or hit them or, worst of all, ignore them. Children make do with whatever bounty or meagerness of affection they are born to because they know nothing else. Parents die, and homes are sold or sundered, and villages dissolve into one another, and war comes and war goes, and no one can remember why it was fought. On and on, mile after mile. He will never know the people who live inside the homes the train passes, and they will never have the slightest idea of him. Hardly anyone on earth exists for any other person, and everything is change.

It is possible, he thinks, that he and the boy will not be discovered, that this train will take them to a place where no one will have heard of an escaped lunatic criminal and a stolen child. And if they do hear about it they will not care because they will be busy loving or berating their children and praying in a half-demolished church, or they will be running alongside the train, finding a handhold or even a generous outstretched arm, swinging themselves and their bundles onto the platform between two cars and into a new life, just as men and women and children are doing now as the train slows through a village too small to merit a full stop. People risk death for the chance to be swept away from everything they once were. The sheer numbers of human souls stepping out of one life and into the hope of another. He feels the same thing he did when he fit the puzzle of a shotgun together. All the misery of his life disappeared in that moment of transcendent focus.

As the train hurtles into the future, he realizes that, until this moment, he never thought of one for himself. He never thought beyond what was expected of him by any of his employers. Completing a given task, no matter how egregious—that was as far as he could imagine. His destiny did not extend beyond whatever someone told him to do or wherever someone told him to go. And so the world was small. Infinitesimal. Even the fortune-teller offered him no future. But now, that life feels like a story that happened long ago and very far away and to someone else.

He realizes that it is possible to become new.

The boy sleeps at his feet, his head resting on bags stuffed with sausages and spice jars and old wedding dresses and christening gowns and carving knives and cuckoo clocks and whatever else these travelers have decided will be enough to start their lives afresh. Danilo turns away from the window. He studies the scene unfolding in a private berth where a well-dressed mother wearing her traveling hat gives chocolates to her children who sit across from her. The boy is dressed like a sailor, bold white stripes decorating his shawl collar and his sleeves. The girl wears petticoats, and her hair is done up in ringlets. Next to the mother sits a man who, Danilo imagines, is the head of the family. He dozes, still holding his newspaper up to his face as if his arms were not aware that the rest of him has fallen asleep. The train takes a curve. The boy falls against the girl. She hits him. He starts to cry. The father opens an eye then shuts it quickly before he is drafted into service. Meanwhile, just outside their berth, a man balances precariously on top of his suitcase in order to relieve himself out an open window.

At Danilo's feet, the boy stirs and then stands up. He rubs his face and looks outside. "Where are we?"

"I don't know."

"Where are we going?"

"I don't know."

The boy remembers the joke, but is too sleepy to smile. "Why did you call me Markus?"

"It just came to me. In the moment."

"I hate it," the boy says.

"I can call you whatever name you like. I can call you Orphan Number Twenty-three if that suits you."

The boy is quiet for a long time. "Markus," he says finally.

"I haven't called anyone that for a long time," Danilo says.

"Is it a good name?"

"Very good."

THE SECOND REVELATION is that he is not a philosopher but a fool. The train stalls once, owing to a dead cow on the tracks, and then again, when the engineer, having pulled into his home village at the end of his shift, simply abandons the train, leaving it unmanned for three hours during which time the passengers have to wait for the next driver to emerge from his inebriated sleep and take his place at the gears. It is two in the morning when the train finally arrives in the city. Dazed and cold, Danilo and Markus stand on the platform and watch other passengers meet the people who have waited for them through the night. There is laughter and chatter and the confusions of baggage. Everyone seems to know where to go. Danilo realizes that while it may be possible to become new, it will definitely not be easy. He and Markus follow the crowd into the station, a building so enormous it makes him even more aware of his naive belief that he could step off the train and into a wide-open future. Electric lights reveal a rich interior decorated with coats of arms, statues tucked into niches, and a floor polished by a thousand footsteps.

"Is this heaven?" Markus says, craning his neck to look up at the domed ceiling. A drunken man stumbles across the floor of the station, stops directly in front of them, and vomits.

"I hope not," Danilo says, leading the boy through the arched doors and into the city.

The silence of a country night is filled with noises—hooting owls, wind shaking the trees, a dog barking at nothing or something, which is followed, in turn, by a door opening, a sleepy man's curses, then the high, pathetic whimper of that noisy dog as he's kicked out into the cold. Quiet dramas of man and nature that make a wakeful boy feel alone and not alone at the same time. But the quiet of the city feels tense and sinister, and the sounds that do interrupt—a glass breaking on cobblestone, and the susurration of a lone car as it glides down a street and slips around a corner—make Danilo ill at ease, as if each of these noises forecasts some greater danger that nothing in his life has prepared him for. A high-pitched scream comes from somewhere. Or maybe it's laughter.

And the smell! The city in late summer is awash in odors, but not the fresh, grassy scent of manure or the oversweet, decaying smell of flowers past their prime, a perfume that always reminded Danilo of his grandmother, who would spritz herself with an atomizer to cover the scent of impending death. These urban odors are—he does not have the language for them yet. Petrol from cars. A clot of horseshit below the curb that smells putrid and not at all like the rich hay a country animal eats.

A light rain begins to fall. With no money, Danilo and Markus have to find some moderately dry and safe place to wait until daylight when Danilo can begin to figure out how they will live. The broad avenue that fronts the station feels too exposed, and there is the matter of the night watchman who patrols the area. Danilo leads the boy across the avenue, stepping over the trolley tracks and trying to avoid the pools of light cast by electrified lamps. They turn down a crooked street and thread their way into a neighborhood of derelict buildings. There is no one on the streets at this hour. A deflated ball in the gutter, a single shoe dangling by its laces from a fence, a mangled bicycle frame that seems menacing, having suffered some kind of violence. Danilo picks up a half-eaten apple that tops a pile of garbage, wipes the skin on his pant leg, and hands it to the boy who devours it in four swift bites, gnawing at the core for every last bit of pith.

"If you eat the seeds, an apple tree will grow in your stomach," Danilo says. "My mother used to tell me that."

"She's a liar."

The rain falls harder. Danilo and Markus shelter against the side of a building underneath a line of laundry someone has forgotten to pull in. Danilo takes off his jacket and covers the boy. Markus lies closest to the building, Danilo behind him, protecting him from the street. He will take the brunt if they are bothered by a drunk or a thief.

"Don't try anything funny," Markus says, but before Danilo can answer, the boy is asleep.

Danilo *wakes to the clatter and scrape of metal.* It sounds like a fearsome animal is trying to break free of its chains. Where is Klima? Where is his shotgun? He sits up in a panic and tries to remember where he is. The mist is thick, but when his mind breaks through the web of dreams, he sees there is no beast, only dark figures that seem to be rising out of the earth, one after the other. As if hell has released its denizens, they emerge and then disappear into the fog. All but one, that is, who lumbers toward Danilo and the boy. Danilo hears the unmistakable sound of a belt unlatching and, before he realizes what is happening, warm piss splatters his trouser leg. "Hey!" he says, grabbing Markus and dragging him to his feet. "Can't you see there are people here?"

"I don't see any people," the man says. His voice gurgles with phlegm that he promptly spits.

"Fuck you," Markus says sleepily.

"Why don't you tell your father here to get a job so you don't have to live in the gutter," the man says as he continues to pee.

"It's the pissing giant!" Markus whispers.

"Ahh, fuck me," the man says contentedly. After a few final spurts, he groans, buckles his belt, and hitches his trousers. "What did your boy call me? A pissing giant?"

"It's only a story I've told him," Danilo says. "Nothing to be offended by."

"I'll admit to a prodigious bladder," the man says. "But they don't hire giants to do the work I do." He takes a final assessing look at Danilo and Markus, then turns and walks away.

"What work is that?" Danilo asks, catching up to him.

"Nothing you want to know about."

"I'm in need of work in the worst way."

"Well, it is the worst work. I'll give you that."

Danilo reaches for the man's shoulder. "Please, sir," he says. "Tell me what you are."

"I'm no sir, that's first," the man says. "And second: never touch a man from behind if you don't want a knife planted in your gut. And third: I'm a waterman."

"Hurry it up, old man!" someone yells.

A horse and wagon is loaded down with chunks of rock and rubble. On top of this pile sits a group of dark-faced men.

"You can't hurry Mother Nature," the man says. "She comes when she comes."

"He's too good to piss and shit down there along with the rest of us," someone else says.

"If God intended me to do my business like a rat, he would have given me a tail," the man says. He climbs onto the bench and takes hold of the reins. The horse reacts unhappily, shaking its head and snorting. "Calm down, you nasty old hag," the man says.

"Give me a job," Danilo says.

"Give you a job?" the man says, looking down from his perch. "Is that how it works, then? I just hand out a job to every beggar who asks for one?"

"I can do whatever you need. And I can hold my piss for hours."

The man gives the reins a shake. The horse startles and snorts and after some coaxing, begins to pull. "You're out of luck today. I have a full crew."

"I was out of luck yesterday," Danilo says, trotting alongside the wagon as it gains speed. "It'll cost you nothing. Just enough for me to get some food into my boy's stomach. He can work, too. He's small but you'd be surprised by his strength. Both of us for the price of one!"

"Your boy's got the right idea. He doesn't ask, he takes!" the driver says, laughing.

As the wagon pulls ahead, Danilo sees that Markus is riding with the other men on top of the mound of rocks. Danilo chases the wagon and, just before it is out of reach, pulls himself onto it. Once he's settled, he looks around at the men. The whites of their eyes gleam against their dirt-smeared faces, their every wrinkle etched in black dust. Danilo waits for one of them to throw him and Markus off, but the men only stare impassively.

"They're very clean," one of them says finally.

"Not for long," says another.

The wagon makes its way through the streets of the waking city. The horse is stubborn, and the driver frequently snaps the loose end of the reins across her rump and lets loose a string of insults to keep her moving at a trot. Shopkeepers roll out their awnings and sweep the sidewalks clear of nighttime debris. Children race out of doorways with half-eaten buns between their teeth, satchels banging against their sides, dodging the garbage being thrown out of windows that lands with varying degrees of accuracy near the cans that hug the sides of buildings. Men wearing rumpled suit jackets and carrying worn leather cases tucked under their arms head toward the avenues to join other rumpled men who dodge trolleys and automobiles. Well-dressed women step around piles of manure as they head importantly into the day. Danilo is transfixed by the activity, which seems smooth and purposeful, every citizen part of a machine. He imagines that there is someone, somewhere, who has figured out how all these thousands of separate parts will move without catching on one another and jamming the whole works. As the horse pulls the wagon down one street, then the next, the watermen jump off and head toward their homes, until only Danilo and Markus are left. Finally, the horse comes to a full stop by the banks of a river. The driver lumbers down from the bench. He picks up a shovel wedged beneath the pile of rubble and tosses it to Danilo.

"Make yourself useful, then," he says.

By the time the three of them have transferred the dirt and

rocks into the river, Danilo and Markus are as black as the waterman, who throws his shovel into the empty wagon, climbs back up onto the bench, and shakes the reins. "Come if you're coming," he says. Danilo and Markus jump onto the back of the wagon without questioning where the man is taking them, grateful only for this possible bit of fortune.

A quarter of an hour later, the wagon stops outside a freestanding building fronted by a set of wide, arched wooden doors latched shut with a crossbar.

"Door!" the driver commands.

Danilo jumps down from the wagon and lifts the plank, then opens the doors, releasing the unmistakable hide and hay smell of a stable.

The man gives the horse the gentlest of whips. "Anuska, my love," he says, "we're home."

The waterman tells the boy to feed the horse, and to Danilo's surprise, Markus doesn't put up a fight. He even seems happy as he carries armloads of hay from the cropper to the stall, whispering enticements to the horse as she noses her fresh feed, then returning to ask what he should do next. The man hands him a curry comb and then turns to Danilo.

"And you, sir, can draw my bath."

Danilo looks around for a tub.

The man laughs and fills a rusted bucket with water from a spigot. "The last time I had a proper bath was—well, I'm too damn old to remember." He takes off his hat and jacket and hangs them on a hook outside the horse stall, then peels off his dirty shirt. As he scrubs the filth off his face and arms, Danilo gets a look at his new employer. The waterman's body is thickly muscled, and even though his skin sags with age, his strength is evident. His hair is thick and so silver it seems nearly made of the substance itself. Energy that belies his age seems to pulse just below his pale, luminous skin. He picks up his discarded shirt and hands it to Danilo.

"It could use a wash," he says.

"How much will you pay me?" Danilo says.

"You filch a ride on my wagon and come into my home and now you want me to pay you?"

"Honest pay for honest work," Danilo says, trying to hide his desperation.

"And what do you think honest pay would be for an honest laundryman?"

Danilo thinks about what Smetanka paid him each night at the carnival, then quotes double the amount.

"You're either a terrible worker or you don't think much of yourself," the man says.

Realizing his mistake, Danilo asks for more.

"No, no, no," the man says, wagging a finger. "Now that you've told me what you think you're worth, you won't convince me you're more valuable."

Feeling both stupid and duped, Danilo takes the shirt and plunges it into the bucket of dirty water.

"Now I know why I'm paying you so little," the waterman says. He dumps the dirty water into the horse trough and, with a glance at the spigot, hands the empty bucket to Danilo. "You're a lousy laundryman."

———

HIS NAME IS BORIS HOMULKA and he has been a waterman for as long as he can remember. "And my father before me and his father before him," he says. "Although in my grandfather's time, the work of a waterman ran to digging wells and carting sewage. If you wanted running water in those days, you just"— he claps his hands twice—"and the water came running. That would have been your job," he says, turning to Markus, who stands next to Anuska, stroking her neck as she calmly chews her hay. "We'd have given you a yoke and a couple of buckets and you'd be racing here and there from morning to night."

"I could do that," Markus says eagerly.

Boris laughs. "I'm sure you could, boy. But we live in modern times and we've got water running every which way and up into your kitchen sink, and all you have to do is think to yourself, my, wouldn't it be nice to have a cool glass of water right now, and then up it comes with a mere twist of your wrist, and all thanks to the likes of me working all my life down in Hades, digging tunnels and laying pipes."

"I could do that," Danilo says.

"I clock you better for my personal valet."

"Watermen have personal valets?"

"They do if said valet and his supposed son are hopeful of a place to sleep where a man won't wake them up with a golden shower."

Danilo is about to defend his paternity but stops himself. That the man is on to him comes as an enormous relief. Perhaps now he can stop ferreting around, hiding himself and the boy, living in fear of being discovered. He has been discovered! It is a marvelous thing, he thinks, to be known.

Danilo and Markus adapt to the nocturnal schedule of their patron. Each evening, as church bells across the city chime the six o'clock hour, Danilo wakes from his straw bed, lights the fire in a squat brazier, and prepares coffee. While the water boils, he runs to the nearby baker and buys a loaf of bread at end-of-the-day half price, then to the cheese monger for a slab of sweating olomoucké tvarůžky that smells like feet. Finally, he picks up a blood sausage and heads back to the stable. By this time, Markus will be feeding and watering Anuska, who follows the boy's directions without protest. The smell of brewed coffee will wake Boris who can be heard before he is seen, grunting in the hayloft where he sleeps and from which he descends by way of a ladder, fully naked, displaying the two full and hairy moons of his buttocks. Still naked, his penis, depending on his ultimate dream, either curving up like the spoke of a coat stand or dangling between his legs, all unrealized potential, he commences his setting-up exercises. He touches his toes five times, leans to the left and to the right, his ample belly jiggling with the effort. He ends the routine by pounding on his chest and heaving up a clot of mucus, which he carries in his cheeks across the room like a secret he can't wait to share, and spits into Anuska's feed bucket. It is not until these rituals are concluded that he looks around him, seeming to register where he is and who is with him.

"A man and a boy," he says appraisingly, as if Danilo and Markus were characters in a dream he is only just remembering.

Once Boris is dressed, it's time to hitch the horse to the wagon. The waterman gives Markus the important task of bridling her. Markus shows no fear of the giant dray even when she protests and stomps her petrified hooves, big as dinner plates. He puts his face into Anuska's neck, and whether he is whispering encouragement or curses, Danilo can't tell, but the horse seems to pay better attention to Markus than she does to her master. As a reward, Boris lets Markus ride beside him and handle the reins as they make their rounds to pick up the watermen for the night's shift. Danilo doesn't mind sitting in the back. He is interested in these men. One by one, they climb into the wagon, all of them sozzled, the smell of fermentation oozing from their pores. Not one of them appears capable of doing the dangerous work of dynamiting tunnels and laying pipes that will funnel water into otherwise unplumbed parts of the city. The men pick their teeth and belch and talk about boxing matches and bets they've lost or won. They groan about their bodies, all of which seem to be wrecked in one way or another. When Danilo shows interest, they happily display their scars and missing fingers and single blind eyes, and he realizes their complaints are a form of pride. Their stories have been told so often that a single name elicits the same emotions as would the entire account if someone took the time to tell it and well. Someone has only to say "Emil" and every man crosses himself. "Stepan" draws a laugh and a shake of the head at the expense of this apparently beloved but feckless man. "July seventeenth" and the watermen fall silent. Expressions are somber as the men contemplate whatever terrible event happened on that day and how it separated who they were on July sixteenth from who they later became. As Markus leads Anuska through the streets, and the wagon takes on more workers, and as it draws closer to the place where they will descend into the earth for the night, the men undergo a change. They become utterly sober, their eyes sparkling and clear. Those same maimed and aching bodies now appear strong and ready. Even their liquor-soaked breath seems to dissipate. When the wagon stops, the men gather their tool belts and jump to the ground like the most capable fighting battalion, their movements methodical and compact. Boris pulls aside the manhole with an iron hook and counts the men one by one as they descend to be sure that, come next morning, the same number climb out. The men offer him jaunty salutes but there is no mistaking that they are about serious business. Boris is the last to go down the hole and before he does, he turns and offers his own salute. Markus returns the gesture gravely, then shakes the reins, and the boy and the valet head home.

Most days, she doesn't speak. She doesn't know what to say. She has only questions: How did she get here? When will she be allowed to leave? The last question is the most pressing but she senses that it would be the most foolish to ask, that it would betray a naïveté that would be used against her. For as long as she's been here—has it been months? Longer?—she's been observing the women and she knows there are some who make it their sole purpose to ferret out weakness in others and use it to their own advantage. The one called Iveta is like that. Scrawny, with sharp, covetous movements like a mouse darting here and there, never stopping long enough in one spot to be easily trapped, the woman is clever. She knows who is hoarding food beneath her mattress or collecting napkins for her monthly bleeding even though stockpiles are against regulations. If Iveta senses advantage in betrayal—an extra slice of bread, say, or being the first to visit the latrine after cleaning day—she will think nothing of it.

No, it is better not to speak. And if she has to, she is careful to make whatever she says as free of innuendo as possible. In this place, language must be flat and uninflected, impossible to decipher for hidden codes and intentions.

She lies awake on her pallet but none of the others around her stir. She doesn't know if it is morning yet. There are small windows built at the very top of one wall of the barracks, windows not made for looking into or out of but to provide cheap illumination. The glass is so dirty, though, that it is impossible to know whether the occluded light that enters is natural or only the oblique spill from the powerful tower lanterns that scrape across the prison all night long. She tries to figure out how many hours have passed since the women were told to go to bed and the door was locked. Four? Five? Time is her constant preoccupation. For a while, she kept track of the days, making marks on the bottom of the bunk above hers with whatever she could find—a sharpened stick, a wafer-thin stone, her fingernails until they became too brittle. But the accrual of those four straight lines crossed by a fifth became disheartening. Each neat bundle was meant to organize time and bolster the belief that it was finite and that when some was used up, there would be less of it to come. As if time could be ticked off and then a specific future would be reached, at which point those little packets could be put away into a drawer marked "the past" and she would walk outside the high stone walls that encircle her life and be—well, what would she be? What lies beyond those walls? What is her place there? The calculations were only delusions, and she stopped making them. Others cling to the practice, and she has to keep herself from glancing at their marks because another woman's time is not hers. Time is personal and particular. A woman will talk about the time when she was a little girl and picnicked at a lake with her family, or the time it took for her husband to get his nightly job done (the shorter amount of time the better, according to the other women's reactions). Someone might tell the story of the time it took to give birth, two days of hard labor ending in nothing but a blue baby, a result that made what might have been a heroic effort into a waste of time. "I remember a time when . . ." the women are always saying to one another as they untangle the matted nests from their hair with their fingers because they are not allowed to have combs. They tell stories to pass the time. But can time can be passed? Can you run ahead of it and win a race against it? Isn't time, with its high, impassable walls, its dull, plodding, endless trajectory forward a prison itself?

She is fascinated by these stories and listens carefully while trying to appear disinterested. She has none of her own to add but hopes to recognize her history in the details of other lives. Has she ever had a man fall asleep with his face between her legs? Did she have a mother who knocked her senseless when she first began to bleed or an uncle who lay down on top of her at night? What about a husband who deserved what he got? She has a sense of a before but only as a vague shape that shadows her; when she turns around to sneak a look, it disappears. She knows the women mistrust her because she does not offer her version of the family outing or the way her man sounds when he lets go. She cannot even explain the scar on her thigh, its purple-red heart surrounded by damaged flesh. She runs her finger over the lumpy tissue. The skin is numb and when she is particularly anxious, she finds some comfort in touching it. She tells herself that she has proof of her past because once upon a time, *this* happened to her.

The door opens and light spills across the floor. So it is morning, she thinks without pleasure.

"Showers!" a guard shouts.

In no time, the women scramble out of their beds. The prison is housed in a century-old armory too far from the center of town to have yet received the benefits of underground plumbing. Showers are infrequent, and when they do happen, water from the cistern is rationed. No one wants to be last in line and miss her chance to get clean. The guard—they call this one the Tongue because of the way he can't keep his inside his mouth while he watches the women strip and wash themselves—marches the prisoners across the yard. In groups of four, they shower in a curtainless stall that is barely big enough for two. When it is her turn, she steps underneath the spigot just as a limp drizzle of water is released. The water is so cold that she doesn't experience pain, only a kind of panic of the skin. The four women, and unhappily Iveta is among them, wash quickly, trying to ignore the fact that the most intimate parts of their bodies press against one another as they reach and bend and turn, breast against breast, buttock to crotch. They pass around a bar of gritty soap, the same abrasive they are given to wash their clothes, that leaves them smelling like beef fat. As she rubs away the layers of dirt on her arms and neck, passes the soap, then waits for it to make its round back to her, she considers how these showers are just another form of punishment along with bedbugs and the incessant crotch rot that plagues them all so that at night the rustling of sheets is not a sign of private pleasure but of incessant, blood-raising itch.

"Look at this!" the woman named Monika says, slapping the skin on her belly that has gone flaccid from weight loss. Her laugh is as coarse as the soap. "There was a time when I was as round as a peach, and now look at me."

"My tits were out to here," the one named Barbora says, holding her hands in front of her withered breasts. "Nipples like bullets!"

They look at her, waiting for her to chime in. Her own concave belly sinks between her hipbones. At her underarms and around her groin, striations discolor her skin. She wonders if she, too, is a shrunken version of herself, if her skin was once plump enough to hide her skeleton. Was there a time when there were no sores lining her gums that make it painful for her to eat and drink and perversely grateful for the tasteless gruel and thin, lukewarm soup that are the staple meals? Were the welts along her spine that make it impossible to sleep on her back always there? The other women tilt their faces up, their eyes closed against the spray so that, if you didn't know better, you might think they were luxuriating. Even perpetually sneering Iveta looks serene. She wonders what her own face looks like. As if self-reflection were a freedom, the women are not allowed to have photographs or mirrors. The ones who have been incarcerated for the longest complain that they have forgotten what they look like. The only opportunity for them to see their faces comes following a night of rain. The women have surreptitiously placed a bucket below a gutter on the backside of the kitchen building, where garbage waits to be removed along with the week's dead, a place so rank the guards refuse to go there. They use the collected water to wash more often than these infrequent showers permit, and those who get to it first thing after a downpour have the best chance to study their reflections. But she has never been first and has only seen herself as an opaque blur in water flecked with bits of dead skin and oil. It is nothing like peering into the surface of a clear lake, waiting for the exact moment to catch a trout. She was always more patient than the others. They would punch the water whenever they spied movement, creating a whiplash of froth and disturbance but no catch. Soon, they'd give up and wander off to look for other adventures in the woods or rest in the sun, but she would stay behind. Slowing her breath until it ran in rhythm with the desultory late afternoon tide, she would wait for the fish to forget their recent brush with death and swim up to the surface to gobble the insects floating there. She would see herself then, but she cannot remember that face. And she can't be sure this happened, this idyll by a lakeside. And who were those others? And why would she be catching fish in her mouth? And then the whole scene, too fragile to withstand the weight of examination, disintegrates and becomes just part of that amorphous dark shape she drags behind her.

The other three women stare at her scornfully.

"Are you deaf as well as dumb?" Iveta says. "Answer the question."

"Yes, tell us. How many monsters have you popped out?" Monika says.

"Monsters?" she says.

"Brats," Iveta says. "Those teats of yours looked sucked dry. Or maybe your man got hungry and confused you with his mother." The women laugh.

"I don't know."

The women look at her curiously, especially Iveta, who, she can tell, is already considering how this odd response might benefit her.

"It's not something you're likely to forget," Barbora says. "It's like shitting a pumpkin."

The shower turns off abruptly. They curse and brush soap scum off their bodies while they file out of the stall. They dress themselves quickly, yanking clothes over their wet skin. The Tongue turns on the shower again. Four new bathers let out a collective gasp.

THE DAY SPREADS before her as empty as all the others. To combat the monotony, the women tell stories about notorious escapes. One woman, it is said, flew up and over the wall on a particularly windy day, tethered to the strings of a homemade kite. Another managed to play dead and was loaded into the back of a garbage truck and driven to freedom. The details change— there was one kite or three. The woman who faked her death was a champion swimmer and could hold her breath for prodigious amounts of time, or she had once worked as an artist's model and knew how to hold a pose. These stories are volatile things. If there is not enough outlandish embellishment to keep them a safe distance from reality, or if the emotion of the telling hints at hope, the women become testy. Someone will accuse another of breathing too loudly or of smelling too foul. Insults will be hurled. There will be fistfights.

She keeps herself at a distance from the others and their trumped-up arguments and dramas. Instead, she focuses on solving the central problem of her life. Who is she? Usually, the question results only in a frustrating blankness, as if she's come to the end of her mind's capacity for thought. But sometimes she senses an answer flickering at the outskirts of her consciousness, some image or sound or smell. She reaches for it, thinking that if she can just grab hold of a solid detail with her mind, she can pull her life toward her.

"TELL ME," she says to Němec, the pock-faced guard who keeps a toothpick lodged in the side of his mouth at all times, even when he eats, even now, behind the barracks, while she holds his cock in her hand. *If I did my husband by hand once a day, I got whatever I wanted.* One of the women in the barracks once said this and the others agreed, although they all had variations—in the mouth, up the backside. One woman provoked cackles of laughter when she claimed she had only to let her husband suckle her big toe. Němec exhales his stinking breath in her face and stares at her with dead, unblinking eyes. When he doesn't answer, she releases the pressure. "Tell me," she repeats, as she watches his expression contort in agony.

"I will. I will," he says, "Just . . ."

He reaches down and presses her hand tighter around him until he gives a short, mirthless grunt. And then, because he has not held up his end of the bargain, she squeezes in a way she has learned will cause pain.

"Murder!" he says.

She lets go of him, stunned.

"Old people," he adds contemptuously. And then, to make the crime all the more abhorrent, he says, as he buttons his trousers, this extra detail offered as a tip for a job sufficiently done, she was discovered sleeping on the very bed where she killed them. "That's really quite sick," he adds. He peers around the corner to make sure no one is near, then leaves her alone to clean herself.

All that she remembers is that she woke up one morning on a plank bed in a chilly, cavernous barracks surrounded by women who seemed unimpressed by her appearance. Day and night, she tries to re-create the scene of her crime, hoping that some part of her imagination will unlock her memory and she will be able to say, like the other women, "I remember the time when . . ." But she can't remember, doesn't even know how to. The only way she can manufacture the sensation of sadness and loss (for this must be what memory feels like because the women retreat into morose silence or weep after sharing their stories) is when she smells certain things. The mossy, moldering odor of damp trees. The smell of urine, dense and pungent and alive.

The sweet-sour curdle of the rancid milk they are given to drink that is also, maybe, the smell of skin. Her monthly blood smells like shower water when it is first released—all pipe and hollow and stone. This particular smell is so precise that she can feel it tickling the hairs in her nose. She can taste it on her tongue, and it makes her inexplicably hungry. But what does it all mean?

The only time she has a hope of locating her past is during Sunday visiting hour. The women stand on one side of a chicken-wire fence across from their families, who wave and shout messages. Guards patrol the fence on both sides, making sure that no one tries to poke a finger through the diamond-shaped openings in order to touch a prisoner's hand or stroke a baby's cheek. Each Sunday she waits, expecting nothing but still hoping, but there is never anyone who calls out to her, and she recognizes no one. She is compelled most by the children. Whether they stand near their adults or are small enough to be carried in arms, they are attentive to the cacophony surrounding them, the names urgently shouted, the prisoners elbowing one another to get closer to the fence, guards shouting warnings, frantic conversations as people exchange as much information as they can in the little time available. Despite this emotional tumult the children seem unperturbed. If their lives have been upended by the circumstance of having a mother or a sister in prison, they offer no clue. Occasionally, one of them notices that she is staring and he might smile or stick out his tongue or, if he is a little older, offer up a crude gesture. They frighten her, these children, as if they might do her harm, or she them.

After visiting hour is over, the women return to the barracks.

No one speaks. It might seem an obvious time for stories about *a time when*, the excitement having stirred memories, but the proximity of what is lost makes this kind of talk too dangerous. Even Iveta seems dull and uninspired after a visiting day that serves only to remind her that all her schemes are meaningless because not one of them will land her on the other side of that fence.

But unlike Iveta and the others, and even though no one has come to claim her, she feels a weird, restless energy and she paces up and down the narrow aisle between bunks until someone yells at her to stop. The children possess her thoughts. She is agitated by their ruthless ability to adapt to their circumstances. She feels—yes, this is what memory must be made of—a yearning.

*A*nd *where would you like to go tonight?"* Danilo says to Markus one evening after they have dropped off the watermen and returned to the stable. The dark hours are their daytime and they have many to fill before they have to hitch the horse back to the wagon and collect the workers. The question doesn't need answering; he knows exactly where the boy wants to go.

At night, the chaos of the city subsides. Variously electrified, the streets become landscapes of light and shadow. Markus and Danilo's nightly strolls feel private and somehow secret, and Danilo senses he is on the brink of discovering something. He can't say what, only that to be walking so fearlessly on these streets is to feel every breath, to glory in the swing of his legs and arms, to hear his footfalls echo, and to know in a way that is less certain during the day that he is alive and that to be alive is something besides working and eating and sleeping. It is to move through a city and not hide the sound you make. He'd like to shout. He touches Markus's back as they turn a corner. The boy is part of this feeling. He is not alone. The two of them together are a foundation.

They walk easily through the cramped neighborhoods they have come to know well from their wagon rides. But when they turn onto a broad street lined with elegant homes decorated with flowering window boxes, where the cobbles, cleaned daily of garbage and manure, glitter in the abundant lamplight, they feel like apostates inhaling sanctified air. Still, they must pass through this fine neighborhood each night to get to the clock tower.

The street lamps that stand in the town hall square cast a glow over the face of the clock so that its discs shimmer. At the hour, two doors slide open and the twelve apostles appear and disappear in slow procession. Below them, tucked into niches, other figures are set into stuttering motion—a man holding a mirror, one clutching a moneybag, another wearing a turban. A skeleton figure holds an hourglass and rings a bell every time the clock strikes, death reminding everyone that the final hour draws ever closer. Although he's seen this performance unfold many times now, Markus's face always registers wonder. The fact that the figures move hour after hour, night after night, is a kind of miracle of continuity. That the boy doesn't trust the clock to delight him from one week to the next seems to Danilo a sad testament to Markus's past, but there is another part, this continual willingness to be freshly delighted, that he envies. When the hour is struck, and the little cock at the very top of the tower crows, Markus always laughs, waking the three-legged piebald dog that sleeps at the foot of the building. The dog lifts its head, regards Markus and Danilo for a few moments, remembers that they offer nothing in the way of food and, sighing heavily, settles back to sleep. Some nights, Markus will beg to wait a full hour for the chimes to play again, sometimes twice more. Danilo always agrees although he puts up a little resistance so that the boy can feel his victory is hard and well won. But the truth is that Danilo is as captivated by the clockworks as the boy. The rotation of the figurines, the way they imitate life but are not life. With their stiff poses and mechanical movements, the figures suggest something about destiny. He wonders about his own fate and whether he has no more control over it than these wooden characters. Perhaps Pavla was right and his future is already written for him. But what if that future does not include her? The thought frightens him. He's comforted by the fact that each time he and the boy watch the clock, the performance is exactly the same. The figures live in an ever-repeating present where time past is not really past and the future—the next hour, or the one after that—is only a return to a familiar place in a never-ending loop. Will she and he circle back to each other again? Or could he somehow return to a place he's been—the forest, maybe? The carnival? Even back to Smetanka's doctor's office? Would she be there? A wolf, a wolf girl, a dwarf, all of the ways she has ever appeared to him existing at once?

"What does it mean?" the boy asks. "What's the story?"

And each time, they tell a different one. The man with the mirror is staring at himself because he thinks he's handsome. But he's so busy admiring himself that he doesn't notice the other man steal all his money. Death wants to take the turbaned fellow to heaven or hell, but the man runs away. He's not ready to die.

"And what about him?" Markus asks, pointing to a figure that doesn't move.

"The one with the book," Danilo says. "He's telling the story."

"What story?"

"It's been two hours, Markus. I'm exhausted!"

But Markus begs to stay for one more hour, and Danilo gives in.

Danilo wonders what the story was for the person who built the clock hundreds of years earlier. Only that man knows the true tale. Perhaps, Danilo thinks, he and Markus are characters in the clockmaker's story. They are the young man and the boy who come each night to stand in the amber-lit square, faces upturned, waiting for the inevitable and yet surprised by it all the same. They are the ones who take such pleasure when the doors open, who grow quiet and somehow a little bereft when the little scene comes to an end, the apostles disappear, the doors shutter, and the story ends all over again. The lame dog might be a character, too. Danilo puts his hand on Markus's shoulder but takes it off quickly, suddenly self-conscious, as if he were only acting out the will of this long-ago narrator.

"What time is it now?" Markus asks.

"You tell me." The boy can neither read nor write. Danilo is trying to teach him to tell time.

"What will you give me if I do?"

"Admiration."

"Not worth it," Markus says. But then he gives in to the challenge. "Ten minutes past . . . te—eleven."

"You have my admiration."

"Ha, ha," Markus says.

Night after night Danilo tries to decipher the symbols on the clock. The golden numerals in the center ring represent the twenty-four hours of the day; that much he knows. The hands of the clock are a sun and moon. He thinks another of the disks shows the astrological signs. He recognizes the one for the twins. His mother showed it to him and his brother when they were little but warned them not to tell anyone, especially the priest. But what do the stars have to do with time? And what about the strange markings on the third disk? Are there three kinds of time occurring simultaneously? The idea that the moment he occupies right now might be another moment entirely—well, if that is possible, than what isn't? Is there anything that cannot be believed?

Markus finally turns from the clock and, as has become his habit, heads toward the bridge that spans the river. They pass the ghostly statues of the saints and heroes that line either side. Some of them hold books or crosses; others have their hands firmly around the hilts of their swords. A statue of a lion captures the beast just as it rears up on its hind legs to battle a many-headed dragon. Danilo smiles to himself as Markus charts a wide arc around that one as he always does, careful not to catch Danilo's eye and admit his fear. Once they reach the opposite shore, they begin the steep climb toward the castle whose turrets and crenellated walls are etched against the night sky.

Here the city becomes one of steep pitches and switchbacks, rooftops climbing one on top of another. The cobblestone streets are so narrow that it is easy to imagine a busy cook could stretch a flour-dusted arm out her kitchen window to take a bowl of sugar from her neighbor. Danilo thinks of lovers whispering to one another and although he tries not to, he thinks of her. The higher they climb, the more the city below becomes a frozen painting, a darkly tranquil landscape of copper-green cupolas and needle-thin spires. The bells of the city's many churches strike the hour unevenly so that the contrapuntal notes wash the air. Once Danilo and Markus reach the top of the hill, the street empties out onto a flat esplanade that precedes the ornate castle gates. Two armed sentries stand at their posts, as frozen as the statues on the bridge. Danilo becomes nervous around officials of any kind, even these ceremonial ones who seem no more dangerous than tin soldiers. But Markus insists on waiting in the shadows, hoping to see if one of the men will scratch or sneeze and give himself away as human. That they never do is both a frustration and a satisfaction to the boy who would be disappointed were the scene ruined by something so ordinary as an itch.

Well past midnight, Danilo and Markus sit on a grassy verge overlooking the river. The lights from the bridge throw oscillating reflections onto the tide. Boats roped to pilings nudge one another apathetically.

"Did you really kill someone?" Markus asks.

"Yes," Danilo says.

"Who?"

"A hunter."

"Was he trying to kill you and you killed him first?"

"No, that wasn't it." Danilo imagines what would have happened if that scenario were true. Perhaps he would not have been put in the asylum. He might have had the chance to find her. "He was going to kill a wolf."

"That's what hunters are for."

"I know that. But I didn't want him to kill this particular wolf."

"Why not?"

"Because."

"That's not a reason."

"Sometimes I think it's the only explanation for anything that happens," Danilo says.

For once, Markus does not question his logic. The boy lies back and stares up at the sky, and Danilo does, too. The stars are out. He recognizes the constellations Klima pointed out to him.

"What was he like?" Markus says.

"Who? The hunter?"

"The wolf. Was he fierce?"

"He was a she," he says. "And yes. She was fierce. And also kind."

"A kind wolf?" the boy says incredulously.

"Maybe that isn't the word. Maybe she just . . . accepted her fate."

"What was her fate?"

"To be a wolf."

"Did you save her?"

"I don't know."

"Where is she?"

"I'm not sure if she was ever there to begin with. She might have been, I don't know, just a dream I had."

"So you killed someone because you had a bad dream?"

Danilo laughs lightly. "I never thought about it that way."

"That's because I'm smarter than you."

Danilo sits up and looks at boy. "I had a brother once," he says. "His name was Markus."

"The same name as me," the boy says, understanding coming slowly. Something shifts in him as he recognizes that his name has meaning and that it connects him to Danilo in a particular way. He sits up. "What happened to him?"

"He got sick and died."

"I'm not sick."

"No."

"I'm fierce." He makes claws out of his hands, bares his small teeth. "I'm as fierce as a wolf!"

The two have fallen asleep by the side of the river. Danilo wakes first. Dawn has broken. The ground is wet and cold and his bones ache. The previous night, he and Markus were somehow contained in a warm, safe membrane, but now that protection has disappeared. The boy sleeps curled in on himself, his hands tucked between his thighs.

A truck rattles across the bridge. A garbage scow carries its load down the river.

"We'll be late," Danilo says, nudging the boy. Markus whines and resists until Danilo offers to carry him on his back, and like that, they cross over the bridge, past the statues, which seem smaller and less forbidding in the daylight. Still, Danilo puts distance between himself and the lion, if only to honor his burden.

Back at the livery, Markus harnesses Anuska. These days, the horse walks the route without any provocation. Danilo holds the reins idly, and the boy dozes against his arm, waking when they arrive at the work site. Sooty and tired, the watermen fill the wagon with the collected rubble of the night's work, then climb on top and settle in for their uncomfortable ride home. Boris takes Danilo's place on the bench, and Danilo joins the men in the back of the wagon. He listens as they grumble about the time lost carrying the heavy pails out of the tunnel. They are paid by every meter they excavate and their progress of late has been slow.

"What we need is a mule down there," a man says.

"We have Borek," someone says to general chuckling and the half-hearted objections from the broad-backed man.

"Be serious," someone says. "I barely make enough to feed my family."

"Pulleys," Danilo says under his breath.

"A man should open his mouth only if he has something worthwhile to say," Boris calls back over his shoulder.

Danilo is about to demur; he doesn't want to appear naive in front of these men. But his mind has already latched onto an idea, and in no time at all he conceives a plan in its entirety. A system of ropes and pulleys and levers. Perhaps a flywheel. He explains his idea in a rough way. "You'll be able to take out twice the amount. Maybe more," he says, trying to moderate his excitement.

He spends the following week making drawings and calculations. He shows the final layout to Boris, who, having just awoken, surveys it stark-naked and sporting a proud erection. Finally, he looks up, inhales and exhales deeply. "I have no more use for you as my valet," he says.

Discouraged, Danilo looks at his sketches, trying to figure out what has displeased the man. "At least keep the boy on," he says quietly. "He's good with the horse. Turn me out, but not him."

"Tonight," Boris says, "you become a waterman."

ONCE IMPLEMENTED, the new system is a complete success. Full buckets of rubble move from the deepest part of the tunnel to the mouth just as empty ones return to be filled. The true engineering triumph, however, is the system that Danilo devises to lift the heavy buckets out of the manhole. Instead of the diggers wasting time and energy hoisting the awkward loads up a ladder, one man stationed aboveground need only push down on a lever. The flywheel spins, a weight drops, and the bucket flies out of the hole as if borne aloft on a rush of air. When this is demonstrated for the first time, the watermen applaud.

Danilo stays underground to work the new contraption. Markus, after complaining richly, is allowed to help, although he is sent out of the tunnel whenever it is time to set off dynamite. Even without those explosions, the noise in the tunnel is thick with shovels and picks and buckets clanging and men shouting warnings about falling schist. Half the men dig and carry, the others follow behind, shoring up the sides of the trench with square frames of timber and support joists. Dust particles are illuminated by ventilation shafts and by torches that hang intermittently from the provisional stanchions that shoulder the roof of unstable rock. When the men take their meal break, sitting against the sides of a recently blasted section, chewing on rinds of sausage and bread and smoking, Danilo and Markus take a torch and explore the network of finished tunnels. Ovoid in shape, the brick-lined passageways are tall enough for a man to stand and wide enough for workers to walk alongside the massive pipe that runs down the center. Markus likes to put his ear to it and listen to the sound of the water rushing through. The pipe is made of bolted sections of heavy iron, and Danilo doubts the boy hears anything but he humors him. Is Mrs. Pigface having her bath? he says. No, Markus says. It's Mr. Snotnose flushing his toilet. They marvel at these roadways, a secret map of the underside of the city known only to this special group of men of which they are now a part.

During one such meal break, Danilo takes an apple out of his pocket, splits it in two, and hands half to the boy. The olfactory announcement goes out swiftly, and in no time, they hear the scrabble of claws. A rat appears out of the darkness, its eyes shining. It stops, stares at them, its long tail drawing an S shape on the tunnel floor. Markus chews his apple slowly. He puts the last bite into his mouth then spits it out and holds it between his fingertips. The rat's nose twitches. It stands, frozen. And then, in less time than a blink, it darts forward, snatches the apple from Markus's fingers, and disappears down the tunnel.

"I had a dream," Markus says, as they walk back to the work area. He balances on the pipe, his arms akimbo.

"Tell me," Danilo says.

"I was on a journey. I walked for a long time. Sometimes I was running very fast. But I never got tired."

"Where were you going?"

"I don't know where I'm going," the boy says, back inside the present tense of his dream. "But I'm not scared."

"That's good."

"Finally, I get on a boat. When the boat docks, I look for her but she is not there to meet me."

"Who?"

"But then I pass a café and she is inside, sitting at a table by herself."

"She must be lonely."

"She's not. The waiter is there. He's smoking a cigarette."

Danilo smiles to himself, content that the boy does not yet know about that most hopeless kind of loneliness that you can experience in a crowd. "And does she see you?" he says.

The boy doesn't answer.

Danilo thinks about Dr. Mašek and his talking cure. Maybe it would be good for the boy to speak of his dead mother, to admit to his sadness. "Markus, what happens next?"

"I don't know," the boy says. "The dream ended. I woke up."

His tone is not convincing, but Danilo doesn't press him. "I once knew a woman who claimed to be able to tell the past of complete strangers," he says.

"Is this a story?" Markus says.

"Yes, but it's also true. She called herself 'Fortunate Františka.'"

"Was she pretty?"

"Ha! Listen to you!" Danilo says. "Already you have your eye on the girls."

"I don't!" Markus says, grinning.

"In fact, she was terrible looking. A face like a rotten grape." He remembers the woman's suspicious gaze, how cold her hand was when she took his and, flipping it over, traced his palm with her yellowed fingernail. Pavla said the woman reminded her of a gypsy she once knew. That gypsy was the reason she was born, she told him, although he didn't understand what she meant. "People lined up to have Františka read their fortune because she was always right. She could tell you the names of your parents and how many brothers and sisters you had. She could tell you things you thought but never dared to say."

"Why would you pay someone to tell you what you already know?"

Why, indeed. "Because," Danilo says, trying to figure out the answer as he goes. "I knew things had happened to me. But when she told me, I *believed* that they had happened." He recalls the strange sense of peace he felt when he left the soothsayer's tent the time she told him he had a dead brother. The miracle of a stranger knowing their past was what people paid for, but what they left with was the sensation that their lives had somehow been made true and maybe even eternal. He often watched customers as they walked away from a session with the fortune-teller into the bright sunlight, dazed as newborns. The world had just been revealed to them, and they were alive to its abundant mysteries.

"She could tell the future, too," he says. "Things that were going to happen to you."

"How did you know she was right?"

"You didn't. You just had to hope you'd live long enough to find out."

"Was she right about your future?"

Danilo remembers: *One of you will be brave. One of you will be a coward. One of you will believe. One of you will doubt.* "I don't know," he says. "I haven't lived long enough, I guess."

He doesn't think Markus is any kind of seer only that, like the water pipe he now jumps down from, he's a conduit. Something rushes through him. Something as pure as water from a faraway mountainside that has made its way over dams and through aqueducts into these underground pipes, heading exactly where it needs to go. But where is that place? Where will the two of them end up?

I *veta is called from the barracks for special question-ing.* When the guard appears to summon her, the other women look at the floor or, if they are lying down, turn their faces to the wall as if they don't want him to make a mistake and choose them instead. Usually, a woman is called for special questioning if a guard or a lieutenant has a need. When the chosen woman returns, sometimes with visible marks around her neck or unable to sit without crying out in pain, the others ignore her. She has become an object of suspicion. The prisoners sense that after becoming intimate with an officer, her natural inclination will be to side with the man who, despite or because of his violence, has kindled in her the memory of a kind of intimacy that once went hand in hand with loyalty. No matter how battered she is upon her return, how tenderly she must undress, they ignore her. There is also the matter of jealousy, for to be chosen is to be lifted above the others who must then consider whether they have lost the last shreds of their allure and whether the stories they tell of the time when men chased after them are only preposterous delusions. "The Rhino would fuck a rabid dog," someone might say, as the chosen woman is escorted away by the guard so named because of the protruding mole that sits in the center of his forehead. The rest will offer their assessments of the various guards' deviant sexual proclivities, and through the exaggeration of these debasements, justify their exclusion.

A day earlier the women were made to line up in the yard for a head count. They waited for nearly half an hour until the door of the building that houses the prison commander's office swung open and the man appeared. She had only seen him once, and then quickly, when he was passing through the yard in his open car. He was a small man, his body so inconsequential that it hardly troubled the material of his smart uniform. His cap sat low over his brow as if it were a size too large. He never addressed the prisoners directly but spoke quietly to his subordinates, who then shouted his orders, as if their continued employment depended on volume. On the whole, he looked unthreatening as he surveyed the ranks of the women. When each prisoner's number was announced, that woman took a step forward, repeated the designation, then returned to her place in line. When Iveta was called, she was made to stand for a longer time while a lieutenant leaned over and spoke quietly to the commander. Everyone knew. Her ostracism had already begun.

When Iveta returns to the barracks after her first summons, she is uncharacteristically quiet. She keeps her eyes down as she walks to her bed and presses a bloody cloth to her forearm. Over the next weeks, she is ordered to the commander's office again and again, and each time she returns with a new wound. On her cheek. On her shin. Since she is the particular victim of the man who controls their lives, the others are even more careful not to engage with her.

When she returns one day with blood on the back of her dress, she is surprised that the prisoner she hates most, that nearly mute one who can't even remember if she's borne a child, comes over to her holding a ribbon of torn sheet. Destroying prison property is one of the worst offenses, and from Iveta's expression, it's clear that she is deciding how she can use this to her advantage. But then she seems to lose heart. She unbuttons her dress, lets it slide off her shoulders, and allows the woman to tend her.

She cleans and dresses Iveta's cuts as gently as she can. "Why does he do it?" she says.

"What do you care?" Iveta says.

She does not dare admit that while the other women look at Iveta's scars and see them as something outside of themselves, someone else's problem that causes them only the same kind of cosmetic reaction as a story of a stranger's death, she experiences the wounds differently. Her skin throbs and aches at the places on her body where Iveta bleeds as if she were the one enduring the torture. She does not know why, but she understands what Iveta feels when she looks at her lacerations, unable to make a reasonable connection between whatever it is that happens to her in the commander's office and these defacements. More than understands—Iveta's dissociation is her own.

"He doesn't even fuck me," Iveta says, laughing bitterly. "And if I make any noise at all, he rages. That little piece of shit."

As she tends to Iveta's cuts, her mind travels elsewhere. She is in a room. Where, she doesn't know. But it is a familiar place. She is lying down. She has to lie perfectly still and make no noise. In order to do this, she makes the pain into something else. A flower. Opening. She sees it first as a closed pod, and then, as something pulls at her flesh, she watches as the petals slowly unfold, pushing up all together and finally spreading so that each petal separates from the ones to its side, revealing the delicate filaments hidden within, each topped with the tiny sac the bees rest on. She watches until the petals are fully splayed. She studies the colors, the way the black center gives way to deep purple which fades by degrees so that the delicate edges of the petals are a pale, nearly translucent violet. Or sometimes the flower is red. "Picture a flower," she says.

"What the fuck are you talking about?" Iveta says.

"You should picture a flower," she says, trying to cover for her distraction. "To think about something besides the pain."

"A flower!" Iveta says, sneering. She turns to the room of women. "The murderer says it will all be better if we think of flowers!"

The *Brotherhood of Municipal Watermen is,* depend-ing on one's idea of family, either aptly named or an ironic misnomer. The crews, working in every part of the city, are highly competitive with one another when it comes to how long it takes to mine a tunnel and the amount of rock and dirt that can be scraped from the bowels of the earth. Every waterman in the central district knows that Ladislav Franek's crew on the north side has recently struck gold in the form of soft rock, which is the easiest to blast through and which allows the crew to move at a pace that others can only envy. Watermen are covetous of their tunnel sites but they also take possession of entire neighbor-hoods. If a man from the eastern district drinks a glass of beer at a tavern claimed by the men who work on the south side, it will take nothing but a misplaced glance for a fight to start. Still, when news of the doubled earnings of Boris Homulka's crew spreads as though through the network of tunnels themselves, curiosity leads to all manner of territorial incursion. The first to arrive is grizzled, tarry-skinned Rudolf Karlik, whose southside crew has, of late, been bedeviled by rock so impermeable that he's had to spend his daylight hours petitioning the Municipal Water Directorate for more than his share of dynamite so that his crew can make headway. When Karlik shows up at Boris's site at the end of a night's work, the crew makes a grand show of grunting and groaning as they climb the gigantic pile of rubble in the wagon, complaining loudly as if their bounty were a hardship. When Boris finally emerges from the hole, last as always, he is enraged to see the competing crew boss and orders his men to pelt him with rocks. Andrej Dudak from the far side of the river is sneakier, sending one of his newest and youngest crewmen to loiter about the worksite during the night, a man so fresh to his job that his skin is still pale and his hands soft. Nervously, he watches the top man work the levering mechanism as bucket after bucket is pulled from the tunnel at a breathtaking rate. Pretending to be nothing but an interested passerby, the spy manages to engage the top man in conversation. But before he can glean any hard information about the doings belowground, Boris climbs out of the manhole to relieve himself and terrifies the youth with threats to various parts of his nether regions.

Slavomir Blodek's territory is the most prestigious as it includes the castle and the entire hillside neighborhood it stands on. However, as the castle was the first to receive an up-to-date water and sewage system, there is not much new tunneling for his crew to do, and so they are relegated to the unheroic and less remunerative work of patching cracked pipes. It is Blodek who decides that the reason Boris's crew is suddenly and unreasonably productive is because of the boy.

Watermen are, by nature, men torn between two opposing beliefs. Although they lack formal education, experience has made them learned scientists in the subjects of geology and, to some degree, physics as they know, from terrible experience, the grave consequences of unbalanced air pressure. But raised as they have all been by mothers who don't think twice about throwing a shoe behind them for luck or inspecting the core of a sliced apple and shivering with dread if the five seeds assume the shape of a star, it comes naturally for these men to vacillate between reason and superstition. More often than not, superstition wins the day as it lifts the burden of responsibility off human shoulders and places it squarely on the much stronger ones of magic. Each man on Boris's crew has his own set of rituals, which, performed properly, will ensure his safety during a shift. One will not descend into the manhole without first snapping his fingers three times. Another spits twice, once in each palm, then uses the gunk as a pomade to smooth his hair. A year earlier, when a supporting beam snapped in two, Mikoláš Dudik, a thirty-year veteran of the underground, died. It was generally agreed that no one had heard him recite the names of his wife, three children, and dead parents before climbing down into the hole as was his custom, and this, more than a poorly secured strut, was determined to be the reason for his tragedy. Children are no part of the watermen's lives. Their days are spent sleeping and their nights working, so they are virtual strangers to their offspring. In fact, a prevailing belief holds that to draw too close to a child is to tempt death. The men will avoid boasting of a son's wrestling prowess or that their infant has been selected to stand in for baby Jesus in the holiday crèche. If they speak of their children at all they are careful to dismiss them as ingrates or mouths to feed so as not to tempt fate. So the presence of the boy, Markus, the respectful way the others on the Homulka crew treat him, his effortless way with the famously oppositional horse, the fact that even with the child around there have been no accidents—all this convinces Blodek and the others that Markus is not an actual child but a talisman, and that his presence is somehow responsible for Boris and his crew's good fortune.

The Homulka Miracle, as it is now known, galvanizes not only rival watermen but Boris's crew itself. The men are excited not only by their increased wages but by their local fame. Their dedication to increasing both their weekly pay and their renown motivates Danilo, their unofficial engineer, who spends his days thinking of ways to improve his invention. Although he admires the pulley system for its elegant simplicity, he realizes that the deeper the men bore the tunnel, the more of them it will take to pull the lengthier and heavier rope. One day, as Markus and Boris and Anuska sleep, a trio of snores and snorts and sighs punctuating the quiet of the stable, he lies on his straw bed and lazily recalls the train ride that brought him and Markus to the city. An image comes to mind: a small handcar he saw in one of the train yards. He'd pointed it out to the boy and they had both laughed at the sight of a yardman seesawing the walking beam to propel the car.

Danilo sits up in bed with a shout.

The handcar, once built and implemented, is a huge success, but a complication remains: what to do with the loaded skip when it reaches the mouth of the tunnel. His elevating contraption is only fit for a bucket, and it takes too many men and far too much time to transfer the rocks into pails. The problem is glorious. Danilo thinks of nothing else for weeks. No matter if he is working in the tunnels or walking the city streets in the early mornings with Markus, he is working out the problem of how to lift an entire load of rocks out of the manhole in one go.

"What happens if the clock breaks?" Markus says one early Sunday morning as they stand in the square waiting for the hour to strike. Since they have been working underground they are only able to visit the clock tower once a week. As soon as they stabled the horse that morning, Markus ran through the streets, fearing that, in his absence, the clock had disappeared.

"A clock maker fixes it."

"How does he get up there?"

"Stairs," Danilo says. He isn't really listening to the boy. He's too consumed by his latest challenge.

"The stairs are inside the tower?"

"I suppose."

"Do they build the stairs first and the tower after or the other way around?"

"*Shhh*, Markus. I'm thinking."

"So am I," the boy says.

"Think more quietly, please."

"If I think more quietly then I can't hear myself think. And if I can't hear myself think, I won't know what I'm thinking."

"Markus, you're talking in circles."

Suddenly, the boy takes off running across the square and into the town hall. By the time Danilo catches up to him, Markus has already found the door that leads to the clock and has climbed halfway up the stairwell, which, as Danilo rounds one corner and then the next, feels like it will go on forever. At the top, on a narrow landing crammed with the inner workings of the clock, there are two lateral turnstiles holding six apostles each. Before Danilo can figure out how all the parts function, the hour sounds and the machinery moves.

To be so close to the noise of the ringing bell is terrifying. The din is so loud, so huge and total, that it becomes a space that Danilo and Markus are inside of and that they can't escape. Danilo feels it in his ears, behind his eyes, in his gut. It is a weight pressing down on his chest. But the sense of obliteration is exhilarating. He feels like he has jumped off the edge of a cliff and is flying. He screams. Markus screams. They can't hear each other and that makes them both laugh. The works are moving. The chain that connects and synchronizes the two turnstiles passes over the rollers. The apostles are carried forward up to and then past the open doors. Finally, they complete their solemn circular procession, returning to where they started—

"Markus!" Danilo shouts. The boy can't hear him, but it doesn't matter. He's figured it out.

IT TAKES SOME CONVINCING, but Boris finally agrees. He doesn't like the idea that the new apparatus will be aboveground for his competitors to see, but he orders the men to widen the manhole. He cannot argue with the fact that, by means of a drum mounted on an axle that works as a verticle winch, an entire skip full of earth can be lifted out of the hole, and production will double.

"Triple, even," Boris says. "We won't be able to dig fast enough for you. The men will curse you for the extra work." But he is unable to hide his enthusiasm.

It takes four watermen to work the turnstile, which is three more than either Danilo or Boris would like, so Anuska is pressed into service. She is initially resistant, whinnying and arcing her neck angrily, but Markus leads her around for the first few nights, encouraging her with praise and carrots, and soon enough she allows herself be harnessed to one of the spindles.

As for the men, far from cursing Danilo, they work faster than ever. The tunnel grows steadily deeper. Each night it takes longer to reach the place where they must drill new blasting holes and set explosives. Danilo has the feeling that they are walking the length of the entire city. The watermen congratulate themselves; they will reach their goal ahead of schedule and their wallets will grow fat.

ONE SUNDAY MORNING, Danilo and Markus decide that instead of visiting the clock and the castle, they will follow the river north. After a time, they find themselves at the fringes of the city where civic zeal seems to have lost heart. Unfinished roads are lined with half-built or half-demolished buildings as if optimism and resignation were pitted against each other in a long-winded battle that neither cares to win. Where trees have been cut down, their stunted trunks remain. Weeds spring up in unfinished doorways. Wheelbarrows have been left upended as though the workers who would normally push them ran off in a hurry, heeding some ominous warning. A few wild dogs sniff around in hope.

"Let's turn back," Danilo says. Now that he works below-ground, he does not have as much energy for these daytime adventures. "There's nothing interesting here. I need to sleep."

A few paces ahead, Markus stops and stands as rigid as those castle guards he so admires. When Danilo catches up to him, he sees why.

Like some contrapositive version of the magical castle on the other side of the river, this edifice is just as enormous and prepossessing. But where the castle is all lightness and whimsy with its exuberant buttresses and its cake-like crenellations inciting the tongue to imagine what they might taste like if they were made of sugary batter, this massive complex appears as dense and unforgiving as the word of God. That it is a prison is obvious not only because of the high spiked wall that surrounds it but because

the sight of it produces in Danilo the vertiginous terror of a repeated nightmare.

Seemingly out of nowhere, people appear, all of them heading toward the prison. The elderly steady themselves with canes
or are pushed in wheeled chairs, mothers cradle babies, fathers
carry baskets and bundles. For the most part, the people walk in
silence as though they are on a religious pilgrimage and their
every footfall is an opportunity for holy contemplation. When
they reach the wall, they form into a line that snakes around
the perimeter.

"We're not safe here," Danilo says. It has been a long time
since he's thought of himself as an escaped criminal but now
he feels that at any moment he will be caught. He tries to pull the
boy away, but Markus shakes him off.

The day began sunny but clouds move in quickly and a cold
drizzle begins to fall, flirtingly at first. No one appears impatient
or inconvenienced: they have come to wait. Danilo puts his arm
around Markus's shoulder, a feeble attempt at keeping the boy
dry, and although he knows they ought to try to find some shelter, maybe under the frame of one of the abandoned structures,
he is as mesmerized as the boy is by this strange scene. After a
short while, the rain stops and sun pokes through the clouds.
People lay coats down on the wet ground, open their baskets and
bundles, and lay out small picnic lunches.

"I don't have any food," Danilo says.

"I'm not hungry."

"You are always hungry."

Just as the boy starts to defend himself, the people scramble to their feet, hastily pack up their belongings, and call their children back from wherever they have wandered off to. The leisure of only minutes earlier is replaced by a collective anxiety. The gates of the monstrous building open, and uniformed guards file out, shouting a litany of orders at the crowd. *Stay in line! Keep moving! If you slow down, you will be ordered to leave. If you attempt physical contact with a prisoner, you will lose your privileges!*

A guard notices Markus and Danilo standing apart and approaches them. "Get in line," he says.

"We were just out for a morning stroll," Danilo says, trying to appear composed despite his racing heart. The guard looks skeptical and Danilo regrets his excuse. In a city of churches and palaces, who would choose to spend his leisure in a place like this?

"Either line up or move on," the guard says.

"Come on," Markus says, pulling Danilo toward the prison. "You promised."

"I didn't."

"You're a liar!" the boy says, tears forming in his eyes.

Danilo doesn't know what Markus's game is, but he can't believe that the boy is creating a commotion. Has he forgotten the asylum? Does he not care that Danilo, who has protected him and kept him safe all this time, is just one curious guard away from being arrested? Finally, he manages to put Markus in a lock the boy can't wriggle out of and, making excuses for his unmanageable son, drags him away.

The boy's fascination with the prison grows by the day. He no longer wants to walk to the clock tower or observe the guards at the palace. Nor is he interested in visiting the street of cobblers, where the smell of leather hangs in the air and where Danilo has patiently explained to him how a shoe is made first to last, or in visiting the street of fishmongers and wandering among the bins of slick, wide-eyed, iridescent pike and flounder. He can't even be tempted by the baker's alley where the boy once stood so long outside a shop watching a man transform butter into sculptures of swans and delicate sprays of flowers that he was given a broken cookie from a warm batch. He wants to go to the prison.

After an argument one Sunday morning that begins as soon as the men finish their shift and lasts until Markus, Danilo, and Boris have offloaded the last of the rubble, Danilo succeeds in forcing Markus to stay at the stable. Thankfully, the boy has exhausted himself with his incessant pestering and he falls asleep quickly. But when Danilo's eyes flutter open a few hours later, Markus is gone. It's not hard to find him. He's at the prison, standing at the end of the line of visitors.

"You have to come away from here," Danilo whispers, but it is too late. The gates swing open, the guards emerge, shouting their orders. Danilo knows he can't risk drawing attention to himself, so when the line moves, he follows Markus through the entrance. The moment the gates close behind him, he starts to shake and can't stop. A guard runs his hands up and down Danilo's body, checking for hidden weapons. The feeling of being trapped is so visceral that he can hardly catch his breath. The visitors form two lines, one for the men's side of the prison, the other for the women's. Markus is already falling in with the line headed to the women's side, and Danilo has no choice but to follow. After moving down a short tunnel, they come out into an open area with a fence running down the middle. The prison wall is at their back. On the other side of the fence is a dirt yard and beyond that, low, utilitarian structures. The visitors stop and wait. No one speaks. Finally, women emerge from the buildings. They all wear the same gray dresses. Some wear ill-fitting sweaters and ragged shawls. Others fold their arms around their chests to keep warm. The guards order the prisoners and visitors to stand back from the fence line, but neither group obeys. Danilo grips Markus's hand tightly. The boy is too transfixed by the scene to object. People shout back and forth across the divide. *Hello! There you are! You look well!* Some dispense with the preliminaries and immediately begin to share pressing information. *Your mother has gallstones! The mattresses are infested with bedbugs! The horse has gone lame! They won't let me see a dentist!* The banality of the conversations startles Danilo. Despite the obvious privations of the prisoners, all of whom look worn, some so weak they seem about to fall over, and despite the guards who pass back and forth making sure no one comes within two meters of the fence on either side, the scene reminds him of when he was a small boy and his mother took him and his brother to the market square where shopping was only an excuse to trade gossip. But when he looks more carefully, he sees that the exuberance on the visitors' side is not nearly matched on the prisoners'. The women seem overwhelmed, and their smiles look more like the rictus of the dead. One woman forgets herself and reaches toward the fence, but a guard moves swiftly to hit her arm with a painful crack of a baton. She falls back without reacting. Danilo remembers how men who entered the asylum with the glittering gazes of the anarchic mad quickly turned lackluster, their expressions so devoid of spirit that it became hard to distinguish one patient from another. Here, too, except for height, or hair color, or the occasional woman who is, against all odds, plump, the prisoners look unnervingly similar. Their skin shares the same pallid tone. Their eyes dart back and forth, attentive to oblique dangers. They listen to the information that is thrown at them about growing children and dying grandmothers and the escalating price of bread but they might as well be hearing words in a language they don't understand.

Markus stares across the chicken wire, fiercely attentive to everything. He lifts his chin, breathes quickly through his nose as if he were sniffing the air for signs of fire or food or a clue to something.

"Hey," he whispers, and then, excited, he says it louder and points. He pushes past the other visitors to get closer to the fence. A guard immediately shouts at him. Undeterred, he stands on his toes to try to see over the shoulders of people who block his view. "Here I am!" he cries. "Over here!" His excitement seems genuine. In fact, he looks fragile and guileless all of a sudden, a boy waiting for a promise to be kept.

"There's no one here for you," Danilo says gently.

But Markus has set his sights on a woman who stands far back in the crowd somewhat apart from the others. She wears no sweater but does not seem bothered by the cold.

"Here I am!" Markus repeats, but she doesn't notice him.

"I think you're confused," Danilo says, heartbroken for the motherless boy.

But Markus persists and, after a few moments, the woman notices at him. She appears startled at first, then wary.

"What's going on here?" a guard says.

"Nothing," Danilo says. "He is upset."

"Who are you here to see?"

Reluctantly, Danilo points out the woman who stands alone.

"She doesn't seem to know him," the guard says. He is young, and he holds his baton awkwardly, as if he's never used it. He seems nervous and unhappy to have stumbled upon a problem that might force him to make a decision on his own.

Danilo thinks quickly. "It's been a long time since he's seen her." He puts his arm around Markus's shoulder. "He was just a baby when she was taken away."

The woman pushes through the crowd until she is close to the fence. Her expression betrays neither recognition nor excitement, only curiosity. The guard stays where he is, looking from her back to Danilo and Markus, waiting to be convinced by this performance. She stops the prerequisite distance from her side of the fence.

"It's her," Markus whispers. And then, louder, "It's you."

The guard grips his baton so tightly his knuckles are white.

"There you are!" Danilo calls to her. "We thought we'd missed you! Look how he's grown. You probably don't even recognize him!"

The woman stares at the boy with such intensity that Markus falls silent. "Do you know me?" she says. Her voice is hoarse, unused.

"Of course he knows you!" Danilo says, glancing at the guard.

Now she turns her attention toward Danilo. She cocks her head, seems confused. He waits for her to say something that will expose him and the boy as imposters.

"Do you know me?" she says again, more urgently. "Can you tell me who I am?"

Danilo's heart is beating hard. He doesn't recognize her. And yet he feels that a seam has ripped open and he has stepped not just across to the other side of the fence but into another world where all the unruly and lost parts of himself are gathered up and shuffled into order. "I'm sorry it has taken so long for us to come," he hears himself say.

"Move along now!" the guard says. "Visiting is over."

Before Danilo realizes what has happened, Markus runs to the fence and pushes his hand through the chicken wire.

"Stand back!" the guard shouts, his voice alerting his counterpart on the prisoners' side who brings his club down on the woman's arm just as she reaches out to touch the boy's fingers. The rest of the guards take this moment of intransigence as a reason to shove and batter the prisoners back toward their barracks. Markus bangs his fist against the fence, crying, "Mama! Mama!"

At the sound of his high-pitched wail, some of the women turn back. Markus starts to climb the wire but the guard pulls him off and throws him to the ground. His cry is drowned out by the roar of the women who, seeing the violence done to the child, swarm back to the fence. Danilo falls on Markus to shield him, and the guard's club comes down on his back.

The following morning, when the women are marched to the latrines, she is ordered to wait behind for special questioning. *Think of flowers*, Iveta advises sarcastically. But the others are sympathetic. Everyone knows she is not being selected for her appeal or for the reputation of the work of her mouth, but because she incited the riot.

The boy's cry unleashed something in the women. No matter how the guards came down on them with their clubs, the prisoners ran toward the fence. And when the boy was finally carried away, the women continued to hurl themselves senselessly against the chicken wire. A siren flared but it served only as a rallying cry, and the women became more courageous. They threw themselves onto the guards, jumping on their backs to stop them from hitting other prisoners. A few women tried to climb the fence only to be pulled down before they had gotten beyond the guards' reach. One managed to make it to the top before she was shot. The other women watched her fall, her fingers catching in the crosshatched wire. When she landed, she stood for a brief moment before gently collapsing.

Up until that point, she had stayed on the periphery of the uprising. She was so disoriented by her encounter with the man and the boy, so tormented by feeling, that she was closed off from what was happening around her. But seeing the dead woman unlocked something in her. Rage started as a heat in her belly and then quickly spread through every part of her body until it had nowhere to go but out, and she attacked the nearest guard. She hit and kicked. She clawed at his eyes and bit into his arms. The other women, encouraged by her unexpected ferocity, redoubled their frenzy. A convict bit off one of the guard's fingers then ran around the yard with the bloody digit between her teeth. By the time the uprising was finally contained, two prisoners were dead, including the one who, rather than surrender her prize, swallowed the finger whole.

SHE CAN STILL HEAR the boy's cry. Not the exact sound of it— that is lost among the voices and noises of prison life. But she hears its recognition and the purity of its need. And the man. She can't remember his face exactly, only that he seemed undone when he looked into hers. That boy. That man. Can she join in the daily conversation now? I remember the time when . . . ? Still, there is no story. No walk in a park. No Christmas dinner. There is only the feeling of having mislaid something, the bewilderment of knowing that she cannot remember what she knows.

She is led from the barracks by the guard the women call Teardrop because of a condition that causes his left eye to weep constantly so that he is forever dabbing at it with a ratty handkerchief. She considers what lies in store for her. Perhaps he will be as sympathetic as his false tears make him appear. But it is more likely that he'll be crueler than all the guards in order to prove the opposite. She already feels an incipient pain between her legs, her body preparing itself to be torn apart by whatever he will do to her to slake his need. But he does not lead her behind the latrine or to the area behind the kitchen building where the two dead women and the week's garbage await removal. They walk toward the commander's building. Is she to be Iveta's replacement, then? Does the small man want to desecrate a fresh human canvas? But Teardrop leads her past that building. Now she knows where he is taking her.

The small structure that the women call the hole stands far enough from other prison buildings so that what goes on inside it cannot be heard. When they are nearby, the prisoners avert their eyes, believing that if they look at it directly, the hole will somehow be their destiny. She has seen women emerge from this place after their long, solitary confinements, has observed the feral quality of their movements, the dark mania in their gazes. They are reduced to a series of protective gestures. At meals, they eat swiftly, certain that, at any moment, a guard will come in and snatch away their food. They avoid physical contact of any kind and seem to lose a measure of personal awareness so that their hygiene becomes abhorrent, their stink part of their self-protection.

Once they are inside the building, Teardrop leads her down a set of stairs and into an underground bunker, past a desk where a lamp burns, and into a lightless room dug out of the ground. The floor and ceiling are made from hard-packed dirt. Roots and rocks protrude from cracks in a coat of plaster and paint that barely covers the walls. The uncirculated air smells of damp earth and mold and all the others who have been imprisoned here before her. Does anguish have a scent? Does hopelessness? Does a spirit decay and give off this odor of sour rot? A soiled mattress lies in one corner. Next to it, a small bucket where she supposes she is meant to relieve herself.

"Royal digs," Teardrop says. He wipes his eye, and she reminds herself that he is not moved by her predicament. "The paint'll kill you, by the way," he says as he leaves the room. He closes and locks the door behind him. She stands in absolute darkness, thinking about a woman so starved that she ate the walls.

The initial panic that surges through her is overwhelming. She is alone. She is trapped. There is no light. No air. She can't breathe. She paces. She hums. She will not survive this. Not even for an hour. There is no way out of this room, but worse, there is no way out of this unmanageable terror that is building up inside her. She screams.

In the quiet that follows, her head clears. And suddenly, she is calm and strangely reassured by something familiar:

Everything that is happening to her has happened before.

She has been trapped in a small, tight space. She has been inside this darkness and knows it as a condition of wakefulness and movement, a precursor not a finale. She recognizes the expansive silence that feels like fullness rather than a lack. She feels like she is floating. She cannot see the space she inhabits or herself within it but she can see colors: red, ocher, a deep, dark green, every color imaginable imbricated in the blackness.

TIME PASSES but it does not move forward. It surrounds her. She is at its center. Even though she has nowhere to go, she feels borne by time. She is not confined within this small space. She travels through something that is without boundary. She is the flow itself, shifting and roiling, changing but unchanged. She cannot tell day from night, only knows that occasionally the door is unlocked, a fog of ambient light from the guard's lamp spills into the cell. A bowl is placed on the floor, questions are asked, and then the door closes. She despises these interruptions. They seem not to mark the time but somehow wreck it. She begins to think that all the things humans do to define time only destroy its beautiful fluidity. They want to dam it, interrupt it, break it down into passable bits. Mostly, they want to define it. *The time when.* She understands: there is no "time when" because time circles and comes back so that time when becomes future time that has not yet been reached.

She does not despair. She imagines that other women in this place have felt the terror of being cut off and discarded. But she does not fear these things. She is not scared at all. She tests herself: three steps forward and, yes, as she suspected, there is the wall. Six steps backward, and there is the door. Holding her arms akimbo and rocking side to side, her fingertips graze the paint-washed dirt. Be careful not to put your hand in your mouth, she tells herself, remembering the warning, but she is not hungry. Each day, when her meal is delivered, Teardrop asks the same questions: *Who was the man? Who was the boy?* Her answer never varies. *The man was a man. The boy was a boy.* Sometimes he will even coax her: *They might let you out of here if you answer*, he says. *The man is a man*, she says. *The boy is a boy.* Teardrop closes the door. It takes her a few moments to return to her safe solitude, to rid herself of the need that the guard's visit encourages in her. How easy it is to fall into the trap of wanting, of believing she can't live without. The minute she hears the lock rattle, her mind falls into old habits of anticipation. The door will open, then the light, then the bowl, then the questions, and then, even though she works hard to rid herself of this, she experiences the desperation of his departure and the readjustment to isolation.

No, she does not like the interruptions. Even for the few moments of light that accompany them. Light is unnecessary. She does not need to look around her cell or at her hands or her legs, her belly or her breasts. Unlike the women in the showers, she does not need to think about what she looked like before, because before is nothing. The short conversation, that diffuse ambience, the presence of another human—these are distractions. She allows herself only the water, which she sips judiciously. She pours the soup onto the floor, where it is absorbed by the dirt. Food, like those twice-daily intrusions, makes her feel tethered to the world outside. It makes her craven and in thrall to whoever decides when and what she should eat. She wants no relationships, not to people, not to food. Not eating makes her stronger than need, stronger than hope. Wanting nothing gives her an exhilarating sense of being.

As usual, *Boris, Danilo, and Markus* drive the wagon to the work site each evening, past the shopkeepers closing up for the day, packing up their sidewalk displays to make room for the prostitutes and drunkards who will take up their nighttime posts. Danilo watches men file into taverns. Children, freed from the burden of lessons, play on the street until it grows too dark to see a ball fly through the air. Activities, once unremarkable, now seem uncanny to Danilo. These too-perfect renditions of the "life of a city at twilight" seem freighted with self-consciousness: Now we are walking home for our evening meal. Now we are going for our nightly drinks. Now we are smiling and coaxing a man toward us with a tantalizing wink. Now we are casting a disinterested eye on a boy and two men and their horse that pulls a wagon past us, dirtying the air and our party outfits with dust, damn them. How could anyone be other than a fabrication in a world where he has encountered her so changed, so other, yet so certainly, so undeniably herself?

Danilo's ribs have nearly mended. The bruises on his face have mellowed into mustard-colored stains. There was no way to explain what happened to Boris and the others. What could he say? That he was beaten up at the very same moment he finally found the woman he loves who was once a dwarf and then a wolf and is now a convict who he does not recognize but who he knows just as he knows his own heart? That Markus was once an untamed child who ate field animals and before that a wolf pup who was born from the very wolf who became the imprisoned stranger Danilo loves? Morning after morning, the boy insists on going back to the prison, where visiting days are now forbidden, if only to lean his forehead on the wall or fall asleep at its feet, finding maternal comfort in the hard stone. Danilo cannot refuse him. And he can't deny that he wants to be there, too, putting his hands on those stones as he so often fantasized laying them on her body. He can't deny that when he does, he feels that she can, that she must, know that he is there.

He's noticed lately that Markus's lips move as they walk toward the prison. Every so often the boy exhales a sound, and the sound is a number. One hundred. Eight hundred sixty-seven. Four thousand and five. Danilo doesn't stop him. He feels that he and the boy have entered an enchanted circle and he doesn't want to break the spell.

He tells Boris and the others that he was beaten by thugs. Immediately, the watermen imagine that Danilo's attackers are rival crews intent on undercutting the prodigious work of the

Homulka Miracle by destroying the mastermind of their success. Danilo doesn't correct the false assumption.

The boy becomes fanatical about his work in the tunnels. He shovels dirt into the skip with more determination than even the most diligent of the watermen. He is unhappy when it is time for a meal break, and rather than wander down the empty tunnels with Danilo to eat and talk, he stands over the men, pestering them to get back to work.

"Someone wants your job, Boris," one of them says.

"Well, I'll be dead one day," Boris jokes. "The boy has a knack."

"The boy's a pain in my ass," the man says genially.

"That, too," Boris says.

Markus refuses to go aboveground during detonations. He argues so insistently that Boris finally gives in. "You'll be deaf before you sprout hair on your cheeks."

"I have good ears," the boy says.

"It's true," Danilo agrees, remembering how Markus heard the smallest animal in those potato fields.

Often, after a detonation, when the men walk from the mouth of the tunnel back to the blast site, Danilo sees Markus's lips moving. He worries for the boy. He thinks about the men in the asylum who carried on fierce and passionate conversations all day long, their voices sometimes escalating into shrieks as they argued with themselves.

"Markus," he says one night. "What are you saying?"

"*Shhh*," Markus hisses, his lips still moving.

"Markus, tell me."

"Ugh!" the boy exclaims in frustration. "You made me lose count!"

"What are you counting?" But the answer comes to him immediately. "Are you sure?" he asks, but he knows the boy is not only certain but that he is right, and that his sense of direction is as impeccable as, well, a wolf's. Klima told him how, year after year, wolves follow the same route around their territory. No matter if months of snow and rain have washed away scent and signposts, no matter if there have been fires and the once bountiful trees are nothing more than singed trunks. "They always know where they need to go," he said.

Markus inhales so deeply that his whole body seems to levitate. Danilo wonders if he intends to count his way to her all in one breath.

A t first, *Teardrop,* whose duty it is to bring her food each day, food he knows she will not eat, was scornful of her hunger strike, certain that there would come a day when she would no longer be able to resist, when her body would take over from her enfeebled mind and demand to live. He nearly swaggered with the assurance that she would fail, and that when she did, he would be the triumphant one who broke her. But lately, his attitude has changed. For the longer she goes without, the stronger she seems. When he opens her cell door, rather than lying withered on her mattress unable to move or speak, he finds her pacing back and forth, counting. *One, two, three, four,* she says. And then the next day it is *thirty thousand and three, thirty thousand and four.* Each day, her voice grows stronger, as though the figures nourish her and keep her alive. She counts to numbers he has never thought about. When would he have occasion to consider one hundred thousand and thirteen? What use is three hundred thousand and twenty-seven to a man living on this earth whose life consists of four children and one wife and figuring out how to feed them all on twelve koruny a day? Even if he gambles, lying to his wife and telling her that his paycheck has been docked for the week due to government shenanigans, he is only thinking about sixty koruny or perhaps, if he is lucky, which he almost never is, one hundred and twenty koruny, double or nothing. The prisoner has become someone as incomprehensible to him as the numbers she chants in her low, affectless manner. Rather than demand that she eat, as he has been instructed, or ask her incessant questions, to which she has only the same opaque answers, he apologizes for interrupting her. He places the bowl on the floor as quietly as he can so as not to intrude on her work. He bows his head, ashamed to offer her something so banal and useless as bone broth.

But the strangest thing: when he is home at night, instead of slipping into a beery haze that helps him forget the dreary work of the day, he feels restless and eager for his next shift when he can be near her, when he can sit at his desk outside her cell and listen as she paces and counts. She disgusts him. Of course she does. Her ragged body, her eyes sunk deep in their purpled sockets, her matted hair, her rank smell. And yet, if he were to be honest with himself, he would choose all that over his wife's powdered skin and her plump cheeks, her body that, even after four children, is ripe and available to him each night. All the life in his house, the bickering and crying and laughing and the kisses and soft snores of his children seem nothing compared to the life inside that cell, where a woman blooms as she withers.

Within the walls of the prison a rumor spreads that something peculiar is happening in the hole. Other guards use their break time to come see the miracle of the dying but living woman. The door of her cell opens and closes, opens and closes all day long. She is aware of this, hears the men's whispers, can sometimes even smell their body odor or the shaving colognes that fail to mask it, but none of it bothers her. She has moved beyond their curiosity, beyond their need for her to explain what is happening. She inhales and swells with lightness. She exhales and floats. Inside her head is a vast emptiness that is filled to the brim just as the heavens are filled with stars. She no longer feels the boundaries of her skin. She is powerful beyond strength. She is beyond. She dances, holding an imaginary partner. *Two steps to the left, two steps to the right, circle around, join hands.*

"She's gone mad," one of the guards says as he observes her.

"Wouldn't you?" says another.

"But you know," the first says. "Something strange. She looks . . . she looks—no, it can't be true."

"Yes . . . you're right. She looks—"

"You know how sometimes you see something so normal. A bird. Or the way your wife runs a comb through her hair, or when I come home, my little one, he hides under the table and I have to find him. I can see him clear as day, but I have to make a show of looking."

"And each time—"

"I'm not ashamed to say it: I cry."

"It's just that—"

"She looks . . . is she . . . no, but . . . is she—"

"Beautiful?"

IN THE BARRACKS the prisoners talk of nothing else. Suddenly, the woman who rarely spoke and whose introversion made her seem practically invisible becomes an object of veneration. Even those who believed Iveta when she told them the woman had murdered her child ("Who doesn't know if she's given birth? A baby killer, that's who!"), a crime considered so depraved that even the prisoner who dismembered her own mother found it distasteful, are mesmerized by the stories that the guards tell about how she does not eat and yet grows strong.

"She's planning her escape," Barbora declares one night. The women debate how this might be accomplished. She will pretend to be dead, they agree, and once again, someone tells the story about the prisoner and the kites. "It was before your time," Barbora says, when one of the convicts is skeptical.

A hush falls over the room as the women contemplate this befuddling phrase: *before your time*. They can recall the time before, when they were mothers or lovers or stood for fifteen hours a day at weaving machines trying to keep their fingers clear of the pinch rolls. But that other thing, *before their time*. They cannot conceive of this and they are struck with wonder. Suddenly, the possible opens up to them. They are no longer hemmed in by their memories, dragged down by what was once but can be no more. Because no one can remember themselves before their time. And with this newfound sense of the infinite that stretches both forward and back comes a lightness. In the days that follow, the women no longer strike up petty arguments among themselves. Iveta, who by this time has lost the commander's interest, holds on to the old ways for longer than the others. She informs on the woman who allows another to take her place in the shower line out of kindness and on the one who gives her bread to someone who is ill. But the guards are no longer interested and offer her no privileges in return for the intelligence. Finally, she stops and then she experiences the buoyancy that fills the others and lifts the corners of their mouths. She cannot help but smile for no reason, too, and, yes, when the women hold hands in the yard, when they circle to the left five steps and then to the right for another five, when they break apart and spin around and then reach for one another again and lift their joined hands, Iveta dances with the most exuberance of them all.

"When did she come here?" they ask one another when they discuss the prisoner in the hole, whose name, they realize, they don't know, but who they think of fondly, with love, even. "Does anyone remember?"

"She was always here," another says. "She was always there." She points to the empty pallet. "It was she who made those marks."

The women study the underside of the bunk, which is scored by hundreds, by thousands of lines. Four lines crossed by a fifth, again and again. The bundles spill down the wall next to the bed and onto the floor and then across the floor and up the opposite wall. The women wander the barracks, studying what they took to be the grain of the wood but which they now realize are days. Weeks. Months. Years.

"She was so quiet, you wouldn't notice her," another says.

"She was always there. Alongside us."

The women smile. They are comforted.

"Is she still here?" a woman says. She is new to the barracks. Young. Her body still fresh and full, her eyes clear.

The others are not sure what to say. The guards tell them nothing when they ask after her. But the men's faces betray them. Their eyes shift warily, as if they are not sure it is safe to talk of what is going on in the hole. They mutter like boys who don't know the answer to the question the teacher has posed. Something has confused them. They become derelict in their duties. When the women dance, they watch with open-mouthed amazement, as if they were seeing water spring from stone.

"**WHY DON'T YOU EAT?**" the commander says to her, puffing his chest to make himself appear tall in his perfectly pressed uniform.

He is furious. His guards are lazy. There is laughter and dancing in the yard, and nothing is done to suppress it. He has even seen one of his lieutenants help a prisoner who has stumbled. When the minister of prisons comes for his twice-annual review, he will see the situation and the commander will certainly be censured. This is the first time he has actually been inside the solitary cell. The place is sickening and, he'd have to admit, frightening. It reminds him of his grandfather's cellar where he was forced to go as a child to retrieve the winter put-ups. He was certain that a vodnik lived there, and even though his grandmother assured him that those water creatures lived near ponds and could only survive for short amounts of time on land, he swears he saw a gilled, green man down there, saw his long, bony, algae-covered fingers, his mischievous grin. Not unlike the woman he faces now, who, if truth be told, or maybe it is just an effect of the light coming in the open door and casting shadows, has a green tint to her skin. Her flesh hugs her bones. Her eyes are a sickly yellow.

"If you believe we will be lenient because of your condition, you are mistaken," he says.

"I don't believe anything," she says.

"You think your death will provoke your compatriots, that they will rise up in your defense, and that we will have another riot on our hands, but you are wrong. You mean nothing to them. I've seen it all before. Prisoners are the most selfish people on God's earth. Believe me, when you die, they will not even remember you ever lived."

"I'm not dying."

"Look at you," he says, helpless to conceal his pity.

"How can I?"

Frustrated by her unnerving calm, he turns to the guard, that idiot who looks like he's crying all the time. "Get me a mirror!"

"We have none, sir."

"What do you mean?"

"Mirrors are forbidden," Teardrop says, nervously reminding the man of his own arbitrary rules.

The commander leaves the cell. She hears him climb the stairs. A window shatters. He returns holding a section of broken glass. He closes the cell door so that only a trace of light filters into the room. He holds the makeshift mirror up to her.

"Look at yourself. What do you see?" he says.

She stares into the glass. "Nothing."

"Look at yourself!"

"I'm not here," she says.

Barely suppressing his fury and suddenly aware that his hand is bleeding, the commander leaves, ordering Teardrop to follow and lock the door behind him. "And keep it locked," he adds. "Don't bother feeding her anymore. Let her rot."

When other guards come to observe her, Teardrop tells them that he cannot open the door, that he is under orders. But even though there is no longer any reason for him to stand at his post, he doesn't leave. He stays through the rest of the day and all that night. He's sure his wife is fretting over his absence, that his children miss him, but he can't abandon her. From time to time, he puts his ear to the door. He hears nothing. No dancing. No counting. Perhaps she is resting, he thinks. She needs her rest.

Past midnight, when he still does not hear her stir, he can't help it: He unlocks the door. The cell is empty. She is not lying down or crouching in a dark corner. She is simply not there. Stupidly, because he doesn't know what else to do, he looks under the mattress, even inside the pail, as if somehow she were able to curl up there to die. But if she is dead, where is her body?

His confusion overcomes him. He feels bereft, the way he does when he wakes from a perfect dream of happiness. He lifts his dirty handkerchief to his eye and as he sheds a tear, the ground begins to shake.

A*t that very moment, the final blast was ignited,* a blast so powerful that it not only bored laterally through the earth as was intended but ripped open a hole right in the center of the prison yard. Despite the enormous explosion, it took no time for the watermen to clear the debris using their handcar and turnstile. Their speed, it was said (and it was told and retold, down through the months and years and decades, passed on from grandmother to mother to child, until no one could say exactly when or where it had happened, only that it had happened because grandmothers and mothers for as long as anyone could remember said so), was due in no small part to the prodigious effort of the crew's young mascot who managed to clear more rubble than ten grown men, proving to all the envious watermen of the city that the boy was indeed the reason for Homulka's success. The watermen were paid a record sum for their effort, and at the christening ceremony of the new leg of the city's waterworks, attended by the mayor as well as an official representing the recently elected president, who was also celebrating the fact that the tiny and unimportant country had, against all odds, managed to declare its independence, Boris and his crew were recognized for their part in bringing free-flowing water to the prison.

"We are a modern and enlightened country," the official declared, "where even the lowest among us shall have the benefit of excellent plumbing!"

The crowd cheered.

But what of Markus and Danilo?

Even before the blast was cleared, Markus crawled through a gash in the earth, and Danilo followed. The boy ignored the prisoners and guards, who were stunned by the explosion, and ran toward a small building as if he knew all along who he would find there.

The door was open, the cell unguarded. When Danilo caught up, he found Markus alone.

"She is here!" Markus said. "I can smell her."

Danilo looked around the horrible room, at the bucket, the mattress, the bloodstained shard of glass on the ground.

"There's no one here, Markus. I'm so sorry."

"You're wrong!" Markus cried. "She is here!"

"You're the boy and the man," a voice behind them said. Teardrop stood in the doorway. "The boy and the man. Just like she said."

"Where is she?" Danilo said. "Is she—?"

"She was here. And then she was gone."

"But she can't be dead," Danilo said, suddenly overcome. "She doesn't die."

"Not dead. Just gone. She just . . ." Teardrop rubbed his thumb against his fingers, studying his gesture as if he were trying to understand what he meant by it. "She just—vanished."

MARKUS WAS REMARKABLY CALM. He and Danilo walked back through the prison yard, crawled through the blast area and back into the tunnel. The watermen were still working, but Boris didn't ask questions when Danilo and the boy walked all the long way to the mouth of the tunnel and then up and out of it, past Anuska as she worked the turnstile, past the wagon overflowing with rubble. They walked their familiar route. They watched the clock strike the hour, then crossed the bridge and climbed up to the castle where Markus didn't sneeze or cough or otherwise try to distract the sentries on duty. There were many hours until morning so, after walking back down the hill, they sat on the embankment by the river. They had not spoken since leaving the prison.

"Listen," Danilo said finally. "I'm going to tell you a story and you will not believe it. You will tell me I'm an idiot or a fucker or a fucking idiot and while you might be right about that, I swear that what I am going to tell you is true."

"I'm ready," Markus said.

"Picture a flower," Danilo said.

He told him everything he knew and everything she had ever

told him about her life before they met. He told him about a dwarf and a wolf girl and a wolf and about a pup who ran away. About stretching tables and jars filled with pygmy feet and beating hearts. About a man who could tie himself in knots and twins who were not really attached at the shoulder but whose parents glued them together each night to create the effect. He told him about murderers and madmen, the Twitcher and the Emperor of Ethiopia. Danilo told Markus about himself, too, about how he was brave and cowardly, a doubter and a believer, that he had love and also did not have love.

Markus was enraptured. His face registered wonder, disbelief, worry, fear, anticipation, delight, and pride, too, when he became a figure in the story, the one who finally had the courage to rescue her.

When Danilo finished, Markus was quiet for a long time.

"Am I real?" he said finally.

Danilo reached out to touch him, and then he gathered him to his chest. Surprisingly, the boy didn't resist. Danilo held Markus tight.

"You're suffocating me," Markus said.

Danilo released him. "Then you're real."

"Where is she now?"

"I don't know."

"Will she ever come back?"

"I don't know."

It was their same, dumb joke. Markus punched him lightly.

"What if I called to her?" the boy asked. "Do you think she would hear me?"

"You could try."

Markus stood up. He lifted his face to the stars, opened his mouth, and sent out his sound. *Ahh-oohhh!* he cried, his voice high and thin and yet impossibly strong. It was as piercing and gorgeous a sound as Danilo had ever heard. Possibly, he thought, it was just now being listened to by someone who wondered where that unearthly howl was coming from. Or maybe someone heard it but thought it was only the noise of the passing wind and paid it no mind. Or perhaps there was someone, or something—who knows what she'd become—who would know that this was the sound of longing.

Markus fell silent. Danilo looked at the sky and watched the sound disappear into the vast emptiness where nothing and everything exists and where all stories begin.

ACKNOWLEDGMENTS

My deepest thanks go to David Rosenthal and Sarah Hochman, who are wise, bighearted, and true. You have given me the best of homes at Blue Rider and I am grateful for that. My thanks also to Aileen Boyle and Brian Ulicky, who launched the book into the world with care and determination. Jason Booher and Rachel Willey: thank you for the beautiful artwork. Thanks to Sonia Sachs and Terezia Cicelova for assistance with translations. Sarah Shun-lien Bynum, Mona Simpson, Amy Wilentz, and Kate Manning generously shared the process. Amy and Kate: thanks for cracking the daily whip. Teo Alfero allowed me to observe his magnificent animals at Wolf Connection. My conversations with Rachel Kushner about writing and life are essential. Ken Kwapis never tires of sorting through a tangle of wrong ideas and half-right notions with me and I love him for many more reasons than that. I'm grateful for my sons, Henry and Oliver, who are becoming the kindest of men, and whose journeys I now stand back and watch with awe and pride.

A version of "The Giant Turnip" is based on the folktale as re-counted by Aleksei Tolstoy, and the excerpt from "The Elves" is a slight alteration of the version told by Philip Pullman in *Fairy Tales from the Brothers Grimm*.

This novel is dedicated to Henry Dunow, who understood what I was doing even before I did and who offered crucial suggestions and elucidations that helped make the book what it is. I couldn't have done it without you, Henry. I mean it.